The WISDOM of SHEPHERDS

RHETT ELLIS

The WISDOM of SHEPHERDS

RHETT ELLIS

SPARKLING BAY
BOOKS

For my Sister

ONE

The old man had a heavy, white beard, thick, white hair, bushy, white eyebrows, dark, squinty eyes, broad shoulders, and strong, calloused hands. He was a shepherd.

Sheep and goats must learn to love and stay near the voice of their shepherd so talk, talk, talk, yak, yak, yak, all day long the old man talked to his sheep and goats.

During the rouge-gray finale of a December sunset, the old man approached his *Christmas cottage*, a shelter to which he had laid claim for fifty or more years, every year, around the time of Christmas. The owners of the land upon which the crumbling little building sat had never minded the old man's annual assertion, for the shepherds were the custodians, the watchmen, the guardians of the region, and the landowners welcomed shepherds.

A candle glowed in a window of the cottage.

The old man spoke low to his flock, "What might this be? Bandits living in my Christmas cottage? Do you have an opinion, Lop Ear? No? How about you, Freckle? Not bandits, you say? No, of course not bandits. Could not be bandits. Since when would a

1

bandit post a candle in the window of his hideout? Who then? Any ideas Big Head? No, Big Head– would not be another shepherd, could not be another shepherd. The old ones know whose cottage this is for Christmas as well as they know which cottage or cave is theirs for Christmas, and there are no young ones anymore, no young shepherds these days. You don't think whoever it is might have found what I buried beneath the chimney, do you, Pretty Girl?"

Before Pretty Girl could answer, the old man heard a sound that stopped his walking. He whispered, "Is that singing, Dead Eye? Yes, Dead Eye, you are quite right, it is singing. Listen. Is that the voice of a little girl, Lop Ear? Yes, Lop Ear, the voice of a little girl singing a Christmas song. What is that song called, Swallowed Medicine? You don't know? I don't know either. Never heard those words, but they are Christmas words, would you not agree, Pretty Girl? Listen."

> *"Tender child, Prince of Peace*
> *Born this night to release*
> *Our souls from sin and death,*
> *With Mercy from above,*
> *To give new life and breath,*
> *And raise us up in love."*

"Did you hear that, Big Head? She's got a good voice." the old man said, but before he enjoyed the song very much, the realization that his Christmas cottage was occupied turned his face red.

"Christmas singing or no Christmas singing, this will not do, will it, Tobacco? As of December this is our cottage, always has been and always will be, will it not, Bow Legs? We will have a word with this child. And besides, why should a child be camping three miles outside of town? Her mother must be told of this. The sheriff of Merrydale must be told of this. A run-away or a school skipper, yes, Pretty Girl, that is what she is, a run-away or a school skipper, and I'll be cursed if a lawless little loafer steals my Christmas cottage."

2

The old man stormed down the hill to the door of the cottage and pounded it three times with his fist, and to his great surprise, a female voice older than the singing child's voice asked, "Who's there?"

Startled, the old man stepped back, drew a long breath, and answered feebly, "Caleb's my name. Caleb the Shepherd." He felt embarrassed about the hard blows to the door now.

"Old Caleb?" the voice asked.

"How does she know I am called Old Caleb, *Swallowed Medicine?* Yes, Old Caleb, here."

The door creaked open, and a young, red-haired woman stood before the old man.

"You're just like he said you would be," she said.

"Like *who* said I would be?" the old man asked.

"The other shepherd, what's his name, I can't remember, skinny fellow, bald head, talked kind of funny."

"Jerubabel?"

"Yes, Jerubabel. Jerubabel said you would be coming in December. Said this is your cottage for Christmas. And of course it is. We won't get in your way. We'll steer clear. In fact, we'll leave if you don't feel right about us being here."

"Who is *we?*" the old man asked.

"My daughter and me, just us, that's we."

"And your husband?"

"My husband is out to sea, but he'll be back soon. We won't bother you, Mr. Caleb. Just let us pack our things. We'll be leaving. This is your cottage. We have no right."

The old man could not understand why a mother and daughter would take up residence in a cottage that was old before he was young, a cottage without much of a roof over three of its five rooms, and he wanted to know more but could not muster the nerve to ask. They were poor, that had to be it, just poor people, a seaman's wife and his destitute child– probably had not come by any money of him in a year, probably had not heard from him in a year.

"No, no" he said. "I sleep under the stars every night. If Jerubabel said this was my cottage, he meant it loosely, you understand. The cottage is just a temporary place– I stop by some years, not every year of course. I don't own it any more than the crows do. I'll sleep out tonight, and you and the little girl sleep in."

"You're sure? Jerubabel said, well, Jerubabel, said… well, sure then, we'll sleep in, but if you need anything, you'll holler, won't you? I mean, we don't want to impose…"

"No," the old man interrupted, "I insist you sleep in, and if I need anything then, yes, yes I will holler. Fair enough."

The old man did not think it fair enough. His cottage empty for his annual and never failing visit, that would have been fair enough, but a man, even if he was old, did not sleep in the house of a woman who was not kinfolk and did not put a woman and child out in the dark, especially in December.

"You're sure?" the woman asked.

"Yes, sure," the old man answered as he turned to walk back up the hill.

"Well, I hope you'll sleep good tonight, Mr. Caleb. You really are welcome here if you…"

"Thank you, but I must bed down soon now," the old man answered over his shoulder as he strode off into the misty darkness of early evening.

"Did you hear that, Brown Tooth?" the old man asked. "Said I was welcome here, as though she owned the place, as though the cottage was not mine and had not been mine for… how long has it been now? How long, Half Hoof? Fifty years, you say? Yes, fifty years and maybe more. Of all the arrogant things a woman can say! She is a woman isn't she, Pretty Girl? You women are always saying such things, aren't you?"

The old man chose a campsite on the summit of the hill and unhitched Big Head from the goat cart that held most of his earthly possessions. As he was piling kindling for a fire, he heard the child's voice again, this time clearer, louder, and prettier through the night air. He struck his flints and a small flame sprang to life, leaped up, and softened to dim orange, consuming the kindling, crackling for thicker wood. The old man did not go for wood. He listened, not moving a muscle, not breathing too deeply. The child

4

sang songs of ancient days, songs of Christmas, and songs of many other things– songs the old man's mother had sung to him, songs he himself had sung on a ship crossing the sea to do battle when he was a tall, hulking, young man. A solitary tear streaked down his left cheek, left a damp trail in his wrinkles, and dripped into his white beard.

"No fire, tonight, Dog Bit, early sleep tonight. Be still and quiet, and listen now."

The tiny fire withered and died, and the old man rolled out his blanket in the dark, having rolled it out so many times in so many places that no light was really needed. He focused on the twinkling candle in his Christmas cottage and continued to listen as the child sang of fallen heroes and living princes, ancient wars and present peace.

At last, the mother's silhouette appeared in the window. She extinguished the candle.

The child began to sing another song, and the old man knew that it would be the last of the recital, the end of the concert:

> *"Tender Child, Prince of Peace*
> *Born this night to release…"*

"Now, what is the name of that song, Half Hoof?" the old man asked.

Half Hoof did not answer.

"I'll ask about it in the morning," he said.

Sleep never came hard for the Shepherd. Almost as soon as the child was done singing, his eyelids snapped shut, and dreams, old dreams, dreams he had not dreamt in years, paraded themselves across the stage of his imagination. Ever so often he smiled or even chuckled, but mostly he frowned and even cried.

Five hours passed.

The old man sat up quickly, alertly, grabbed his staff, bolted onto his feet.

"No fire! No fire, what was I thinking?" He fumbled through his pouch for his flints, his torch, and his fuel.

5

"Hold on, Lop Ear, I hear you. I hear you too, coward dog. Dogs, is it? I hear you all, yes, every one of you. It is *dogs*, isn't it?"

The old man knew at once that it was not dogs, but he could not fathom it being wolves. There had been no wolves in the region in fifteen years, much less a pack of wolves. He steadied his nerves as best he could and dipped the corner of a wool cloth into a small bottle of oil. He struck the flints, and a small light cut the darkness. He flung the cloth around the tip of his torch and poured on more oil. He held his torch high and nearly fainted at the sight of what its reflected luminescence revealed– eyes, many eyes, sinister, bright, hungry eyes.

"Curse you all, you sons of the devil, and curse me if I don't..."

The old man sprinted toward the closest set of eyes. Down came his staff. Down it came again, and he heard the sound of a skull cracking.

The pain of sharp teeth tearing into the back of his right leg turned him. He screamed, yanked a razor edged knife from its sheath, and cut the throat of the sharp-fanged wolf.

A large, dark shape leaped over the old man's left shoulder, struck the side of his head, and knocked him down.

The old man dropped his gear. He heard low growling, and by the dying light of the torch, he saw immediately before him the eyes– eyes wicked and big and blood-drunk. The old man felt around for his knife or his staff, but he found neither. The wolf did not move. The old man half-stood, dived for his torch, and felt the stalwart jaws of the wolf clamp down on his right arm. He and the wolf rolled twice. Neither made a sound. The old man felt his staff beneath him then. He half rolled, took the staff in hand, and beat at the wolf's snout. The wolf released the old man's arm, turned, ran, and disappeared into the night. The pack had gone. The old man knew it. How far? Not far, never far. How long? He did not know.

The old man felt his arm and leg. Blood and pain, not much of either, but more than enough, he was sure, to require medicine and bandages when he was done medicating and bandaging his flock.

"What's happening? Are you hurt? Where are you?" The woman's voice cried. A bud of candle's light moved up the hill, seemed to float in air.

The old man stood, stumbled, and caught his balance.

"Get back," he yelled, "there may be more. Get back now!"

"More what?" the woman asked.

"More wolves! Get back. Do you hear me? I said get back!"

Presently the old man realized that if the wolves were circling, retreat would be more dangerous for the woman than continuing toward him.

"No, wait. Don't move! No, yes, move. Come here. Come here now!" he shouted.

The woman obeyed. The old man found his dead torch, picked it up, brushed off the dirt, and re-lit it. No more wolf eyes. No more wolf sounds. Only the sounds of scared, injured, or dying sheep and goats.

When the young woman reached him, the old man turned on her and spoke in a tone he seldom used, "What kind of a stupid thing was that to do? You come out here in the dark like a crazy woman? And you've got a child and what would she do when you were eaten alive? What's wrong with you?!"

The woman recoiled, wilted, and said nothing, and her meekness humbled the old man. His steam was now released. As exasperation and anger sank down, diminished, and dissolved in his bosom, remorse and embarrassment rose up, shamed him and darkened his countenance. He felt like a fool.

"I'm sorry, I didn't mean..." the old man began.

"You said you would holler..."

"I said, yes, I said I would holler, and I hollered. I hollered, didn't I? I'm sorry. Sorry I scared you. I'm sorry."

The woman stiffened, inflated, stood erect, and half grinned.

"No, you were scared. I wasn't scared. You were. That's why you hollered. You're still scared."

"I'm not, well, yes, I was scared, but there's no time to talk yet. Come."

With torch and candle, the old man and the young woman searched the hill. They found two dead sheep and one dead goat, three dying sheep and two dying goats, five merely injured sheep but no merely injured goats. The old man ended the misery of the dying animals with his knife, and the young woman sobbed.

"Must be done," the old man said.

"Yes," the young woman forced herself to agree.

Next, they salved with ointment and bandaged the merely injured animals, and as the unlikely pair worked side by side, they heard the first word of a song. As fast as twin hammer strikes, the old man and the young woman turned toward the cottage. No candle.

"Clara?!" the woman shouted.

The singing stopped.

"What, mama?" a small voice asked.

"Where are you, baby?"

"I'm coming, mama."

"No, baby, don't..."

"Stop," the old man whispered.

He stood and held his torch above his head and observed a few sets of eyes on the fringes of the pasture. The woman saw the eyes too.

"My baby, oh my, no, no, my baby..." the woman began to say. She started crying.

With intense sternness Caleb whispered, "Silence!"

The woman's crying trailed off into murmuring and then to a whimper.

The old man cleared his throat and said, "Clara, will you sing for me?"

The little girl stood silent.

"She's shy," the woman said. "She didn't know you were out here, or she wouldn't have been singing in the first place. I've got to get to her!"

The old man caught the woman's shoulder just before she bounded down the hill.

"Don't move," he said.

"My baby... I've got to..."

"Don't move, I said! Clara? There is a Christmas song I love. Maybe you know it. I think it's called *Tender Child*. I don't know.

8

Do you know that song, Clara?"

A long silence and then, "Yes."

"Oh Clara, it's the most beautiful song, but I'm too old to sing, and I was hoping that someone might sing it for me tonight. Would you sing it, Clara?"

A longer silence and then, "Maybe."

"Clara, Clara you make me happy. Oh, how I do love that song! How does it go? Tender Child…"

The little girl laughed at the Shepherd's flat, ugly, and tuneless voice.

"Not like that," she said, "like this." She started singing the song.

"Come," whispered the shepherd to the young woman, "but take this."

The old man handed the young woman his torch.

To the child, and in a loud voice he said, "Come, Clara, sing as you walk."

The little girl's singing moved in the direction of the light. Caleb and the young woman moved in the direction of the singing.

"Quickly now, hurry," he whispered to the woman.

The pair all but raced toward Clara.

"Eyes," the old man said.

The young woman said nothing.

"Two of them," the old man said, racing ahead of his light bearer, "Steady the torch. Hold it. Hold it high!"

Two wolves circled close around the little girl. Without slowing his pace, the old man whipped his staff over his head and twisted his knife to a firm grip. The first wolf lunged and missed the little girl, and for the first time, the old man saw the little girl's face.

Unrelenting and not knowing she had been frightened by anything but a dog's shadow, Clara kept singing. The second wolf lunged and snapped, bit down hard, and caught something in its fangs– the shepherd's staff. The wolf twisted its head, jerked the staff, and shook it and the shepherd, but before it realized that its teeth were not affixed to the little girl's flesh, it felt the shepherd's knife slit its throat.

The first wolf ran away.

The shepherd grabbed the little girl and placed her in her mother's arms, and exchanged her for his torch.

"Come now," he said to them.

At the door of the cottage, the shepherd told the woman he would be accepting her hospitality after all. He closed them in and returned to his sheep and goats.

TWO

Five hours of sleep would have to be enough for the shepherd. There was work, hasty work, and much of it to be done.

The little girl fell deeply asleep soon after her return to the cottage, but for her mother, the night was yet long, and though sleep did come, it brought dreams of terrible things.

Between waking and dreaming, the young woman heard or imagined she heard the sound of someone or something moving about on the roof.

"I must be losing my mind," she thought, and rolled over, tossing the covers of the bed she shared with her daughter.

Clara snored softly, and the young woman touched her face and sighed.

When the faintest glimmer of morning sunlight trickled into the valley, the young woman sat up, wide awake. She left Clara to sleep and donned her work clothes, a brown woolen skirt and a blue cotton blouse. As she buckled her sandals over her woolen stockings, she heard the sound of heavy boots falling hard on the earth before the door of the cottage.

"Just a minute," she said.

Three solid knocks sounded throughout the cottage.

"I said just a minute."

With her sandals buckled, she moved swiftly from the edge of the hearthstone and opened the door.

"Oh, it's you."

"Yes, of course" the shepherd said. "Were you expecting someone else this early?"

Through her mind flashed the face of the sailor, the man she continually hoped but seldom actually expected to see. She answered the shepherd without any reference to her thoughts.

"No, I was just… glad to see you. May I cook you some breakfast?"

"Yes and good and thank you," said the shepherd who delighted greatly in food prepared by hands other than his own when he was lucky enough to get it, "but that's not what I came down here for. Is the little girl all right?"

"She's fine," the woman answered with a smile.

"There was something else I wanted, but I suppose I'll tell you about it over breakfast. You wouldn't be going to town anytime today, would you?" Caleb asked.

"I go to town every day. I work there," the woman answered.

"You walk three miles to work every day? Why on earth?"

"Must be done," said the woman in a tone as solid and final as granite.

The old man dared not ask any further questions about that. He said nothing for a couple of seconds and then, "I was hoping I could give you some money and ask you to buy some things for me, if that wouldn't put you out too much."

"Wouldn't put me out at all," the woman replied. She did not get many opportunities to buy things, and she enjoyed the idea, even if she were buying for someone other than herself.

"Step outside for a minute," the old man said, "and I'll show you why I need your help with buying."

The young woman stepped out into the growing light and saw a pink sliver of the sun's crown working up the edge of the eastern

12

horizon and the shepherd's flock grazing all around the cottage. Nailed to the trunks of the five trees that surrounded the cottage, two oaks and three cedars, hung eleven hides– five sheep's, three goats,' and three wolves.' The furless sides faced out. Dark reddish spots and splotches clung to each hide.

"I'll spend most of the day cleaning them," the shepherd said. "Stay here a minute, and I'll get something for you."

The old man walked around the edge of the cottage and returned holding a large slab of meat in each hand.

"The night was cold, and this will be good for breakfast and lunch and maybe even supper, but you'd better start cooking it now. I wouldn't trust it in another hour."

The young woman's eyes widened. For her, meat was an even rarer treat than were meals cooked by others for the shepherd.

"Yes sir, I'll get right to it."

She took the meat inside, chopped it, divided it, and set herself to the task of preparing it. She built a fire on the hearth, and she hooked some of the meat on an old, rusty rotisserie to roast over the flame. She filled a large black pot with water and a few carrot and potato trimmings and set it beside the hearth to await a long simmering after the breakfast meat finished roasting.

The old man smelled the roasting meat and arrived for breakfast just as the young woman was removing it from the fireplace. He entered the cottage without knocking and felt embarrassed about doing so two seconds after he did it.

The young woman said nothing of it though she did not like it one bit.

As the woman set her table, a rough hewn wooden affair with three good legs and one that wobbled, the shepherd got his first real chance to have a look at her.

Her face looked plain, almost ugly but not quite. If there was anything attractive about her, it was to be seen lower down her frame. Her legs, what he could see of them, appeared shapely and muscular in their beige stockings. Her waist was slender, her bosom full. Her red hair was not well kept. It flamed out, curly and multi-directional, but the shepherd imagined that it might be made to look

13

rather pretty with a little doing in the women's parlors in town. He noticed she wore no ring on the finger where married women wore rings, and he feared it might have meant something contradictory to her talk of a husband and might have been the best explanation for her dwelling three miles outside of town, but the woman was poor and all but a few sailors were poor, and gold was not cheap, and there was a good chance it meant nothing at all.

After he studied her through a number of quick glances, the shepherd sat down at her table.

"Fine improvements you've made in here," he began. "I'm glad to see them– clean all around. Must have taken you half a year."

"Two months," the woman said, not turning from her work and not showing any emotion, good or bad, for the compliment. She was hurrying.

"By the way," the shepherd said, "I don't believe I caught your name."

"Name's Susan," the woman said, briefly curtsying as she placed a hot slab of mutton on the shepherd's plate.

"Pleased to make your acquaintance, Susan," the shepherd said. "Why the hurry?"

"I'll be late for work if I don't get goin' soon. Speaking of which– Clara! Clara get up. Breakfast is ready."

"What kind of work do you do?" the old man asked.

The young woman was spinning about and hastening around the room in early-morning woman-fashion, and she was not yet ready to talk, but she stopped for a second. Her face reddened, but she held her head straight up.

"Mostly washing, sometimes mending, sometimes cooking."

The old man understood her words, understood the expression on her face, and understood the feeling that caused the expression. Susan did housework– worked for women who were too rich or too busy or too lazy or too old to do their work themselves, and maybe she worked for a bachelor or two as well– low paying work, uncertain work, dirty work. He felt guilty, even at that moment, to be a partaker of her morning labor, for the kind of work she did was honorable in one sense and embarrassing in another.

14

Clara came nodding and reeling through the door of the main room– the room that served as foyer, kitchen, and den. She wiped sleep from her eyes as she walked and gave a start when she saw the shepherd sitting in the chair where she was used to sitting.

"Mama, that man is sitting in my…"

"Hush Clara, sit at the end."

The old man winked at Susan, smiled broadly, and said to the little girl, "Is this your chair?"

Clara looked into her mother's eyes for permission to speak.

Susan's eyes smiled, and Clara said, "Yes, it's my chair. It has always been my chair."

The old man moved his plate to the end of the table, stood, and held the chair for the little girl. She climbed into it, and he scooted her close to the table. Clara liked the feeling of her chair moving while she sat in it, and she giggled.

With his eyes, Caleb took in Clara in much the same way he had taken in her mother.

Clara's hair was strawberry blonde, and her face was freckled and sweet– pretty, but not pretty in a way that implied she would break the hearts of men when she was older, just little girl pretty. She was a thin child, and to the shepherd's amazement appeared to be no older than four and maybe as young as three.

"How old are you?" the shepherd asked.

Though other children her age would have held up fingers, pronouncing they were *this many* or *that many* Clara spoke as if she understood the meaning of her age, possibly the meaning of the units by which it was measured.

"I am four years old."

"You're a very smart girl, Clara," said the shepherd, who had a *way* with children not unlike his way with sheep and goats, "and a pretty one too, and you sing as well as a choir."

Clara blushed.

"Where did you learn so many songs?" the shepherd continued.

Clara shrugged.

Susan turned from her labor, the final stages of getting the pot ready for a long simmering.

"Darndest thing," she said, "Clara hears a song once, and she sings it as good or better than whoever she heard it from. And some of the songs I've never even heard before. I think she makes some of them up."

"I wouldn't doubt it," the shepherd said.

Susan joined Caleb and Clara at the table. She had just begun to chew a grizzled piece of goat when the shepherd spoke to her.

"When you're in town," he said, "I need you to buy some salt and some tanner's oil. The salt you can get anywhere of course, and I'll need a great deal of it, but the tanner's oil might be hard to locate. Last time I bought any, I searched half a day, and that's been ten years ago now– found it in a shop that sold fishing poles and bows-and-arrows and all kinds of man trifles. You might ask around."

Susan swallowed her bite of goat.

"If there's tanner's oil in Merrydale, I'll find it," she said.

They continued to eat, and for the shepherd this was a mixed pleasure, as it always was when he was eating of his own flock. Economic necessity demanded that he do so at times, and on such occasions, he had to use all his mental strength and concentration to shut out memories of the beasts as he had known them, to think of the meat merely as meat.

When the trio finished eating, the shepherd volunteered to fetch water from the well and to give the dishes a scrub, and the young woman offered no objections.

As the shepherd was returning with the water pail, he saw a thing that melted him through and through. Caleb almost never "melted," and here he was, having melted twice in less than ten hours. He did not like it.

Susan was setting off toward town with Clara riding piggyback.

"Just a minute," Caleb said, "I haven't given you any money."

He placed the water pail on the ground, reached into his pack, and withdrew a small, cloth purse. From the purse he gathered three silver coins.

"This should cover the salt and oil, and if there's any left over, buy something for yourself and Clara."

16

Susan smiled, but the shepherd had not finished talking. Before breakfast he had been cut short in his questioning of Susan's long daily walk to town, but now curiosity had got the best of him, and he had to have an answer.

"You don't mean to carry her all the way to Merrydale, do you?"

The woman looked offended. "I don't see why not," she said.

"Because three miles is a toilsome walk even if you're not carrying so much as a squirrel's lunch box. You do this very often?"

Susan's face reddened again. "I carry my daughter to town every day, and if you don't mind, I'd like to be goin' now. I'm late as it is."

"Hold on there, Susan," the shepherd said, "I mean no offense. I really do not. Who does Clara stay with in town?"

Susan's face continued to redden to a shade only possible for those with red hair.

"She stays with me, not that it's any of your concern, thank you very much."

"It's certainly none of my concern, but what does she do all day? She must get bored."

"She... she... she listens for songs and plays with other children sometimes, and sometimes she just keeps me company! Now, please, if you don't mind, I must be going!"

A hint of rage had come to the surface, and the shepherd feared continuing the conversation. Susan obviously felt ashamed of her poor woman's life. There was a pride about her, a fiber of being that felt wronged to be poor and probably was not meant to be poor.

The shepherd ventured one more question, "Why don't you leave her here with me?"

Susan shook her head *no* at first, glanced at Caleb, looked him up and down, looked ahead at the winding dirt path, and then looked over her shoulder at Clara. She hesitated and breathed hard as if in indecision or anger– or both. Her back ached as it always did.

"You'd take good care of her? I mean, you think you could handle a four year old? I mean I don't know much of anything about

17

you."

"I've already taken good care of her once if you recall."

"Yeah, you did, didn't you? You'd keep a close eye on her? She wanders off sometimes."

Caleb smiled. "Keeping a close eye on little ones with tendencies to wander off is how I've survived out here for fifty years."

"Well... all right then. I s'pose she can stay with you today."

Clara showed no signs of reluctance to stay with Old Caleb the Shepherd. She might have been a shy child, but the old man seemed to stir in her mind a great curiosity.

Susan started to walk again, but before she had taken five steps, she stopped abruptly, spun around, and said, "By the way, you didn't happen to see... don't think I'm crazy for asking this... you didn't happen to see anything crawling around on the roof of the cottage before day break, did you?"

"As a matter of fact, I did," Caleb answered.

"You *did*? What was it?"

"It was a big, old, hairy thing," Caleb replied.

"A big, hairy thing. Oh my, what was it?"

"It was a big, old, hairy thing, and its hair was all white."

Though he tried to stop them, Caleb's lips started to curl up into a smile.

Susan did not see at first. "I've never heard of... hey, stop playing with me like that. It was you, wasn't it?"

"I'm afraid so," Caleb answered as his smile got full control of his face.

"Why on earth would you go crawling around on top of the cottage in the dark like that?"

"Nails."

"Nails?"

"Yes, nails. I needed them to hang the hides. I climbed up by the chimney and got them out of the shingles of the rooms that are half fallen in. And since you bring it up, I think we'd better look into doing some work on the roof pretty soon. The old beams are holding up pretty well, and I think we could patch it all up right smartly. That would give us three more rooms, and it won't be long

18

before we're getting rained on and snowed on."

"We?" Susan thought, "Did he just say 'we'? Well, that's a man for you, going on yesterday about not having any right to the cottage more than me but now talking as if we lived here together as room mates and will live that way for a long time to come."

"Good idea. We'll have to look into it," she said out loud through a faked smile.

Susan turned back down the path and walked.

"We'll have to look into it," Caleb thought and shook his head, "as if she had any say in the matter. Yes, she's a woman, isn't she?"

Caleb and Clara stood for a moment watching Susan's departure. Clara waved good-bye, but her mother did not see it. Caleb reached down for the pail, but Clara's hands were faster than his.

"I'll carry it," she said.

Caleb did not object so Clara lifted the bucket and waddled toward the cottage, spilling water with every step she took.

They walked into the cottage, and Caleb felt glad for a chance to have a look about and maybe ask the child some questions, but first, there were dishes to wash. He found a dented dishpan in a cabinet and placed it on the table.

Clara climbed onto her chair, stood up, and said she would do the drying. There was more than a hint of timidity in the way she said it. She certainly was shy, but she was active and energetic. Caleb handed her a dishtowel, and she started working.

Caleb had questions, especially about Clara's absent father, and he felt sure he would have opportunity to ask them only after he had established a sort of friendship with the little girl, but Clara introduced the topic herself.

"Do you know my daddy?" she asked.

"What's that?" Caleb asked, taken off guard.

"My daddy, do you know him?"

Caleb understood that the outcome of this conversation would determine much of what he might learn so he thought carefully and proceeded slowly.

"I'm not sure. I know a good many folk. Tell me about your daddy."

"He's got pictures on his arms."

"Pictures on his arms? You don't say. Well, I've known quite a few folk with pictures on their arms. I've got one myself."

Caleb rolled up his sleeve and showed Clara a tattoo so old and blurred that she was not able to make out what it was supposed to be.

"What is it?" she asked.

Caleb looked at the green splotch that had been his tattoo and chuckled.

"It was an eagle and a lion fighting it out. Got it done by a foreign fellow on my way to the war, but doesn't look like much of anything now, does it?"

Clara did not answer. She only smiled.

Caleb continued the conversation. "Now, about your daddy, you say he's got more than one tattoo?"

"Oh yes, lots of them. Mama says he has a new one every time he comes home."

"I see. How interesting. Does he come home much?"

Clara's smile drooped. "Not much."

Caleb went on cautiously, "Well, when was he here last?"

Clara's face darkened. Her nose wrinkled, and an expression of deep thought engulfed her features. The gears of her mind turned hard for an answer.

"Christmas. I think it was Christmas 'cause I got a present."

"A present?" Caleb asked, "Not *several* presents?"

"No, just a present."

"What was it?"

Clara dropped her dishtowel on the table, climbed down from her chair, and ran into her bedroom. Caleb regretted that he had pushed his questioning too far too fast, but before he had time to give himself a thorough rebuke, Clara emerged from her bedroom holding a feathered trinket at arm's length.

Caleb thought, *"Worthless piece of island drivel if I've ever seen it,"* and he had seen it. Merrydale was a seaside town, and "exotic ornaments" were always for sale in the shops.

"It's beautiful," he said. "Bring it here."

Clara walked to the table and held up the trinket. Caleb studied its multi-hued, ink-dyed feathers and blundering wood craftsmanship, and he thought that even a poor sailor should have been able to afford better for his daughter for Christmas.

"*Worthless ship scoundrel*," he thought, but he said, "Thank you, Clara. I had been meaning to have a look at one of those for some time now. It's very pretty. You can put it back now."

Clara did so and returned.

Just then, Caleb heard the approach of a shepherd and his flock. He did not feel overjoyed about this, for he was on the verge of making discovery strides into concerns that were not his own but to which he was drawn like a magnet drawn towards the north for some reason.

Caleb listened. Jerubabel was prone to hum to his sheep, and the humming was unmistakably off key. The shepherd handed the third and final plate to Clara, and he stepped outside the cottage.

THREE

A small mouth and few teeth, a backcountry dialect, and a high-pitched voice made Jerubabel almost impossible to understand at times. Caleb had spent years learning the nuances of Jerubabelese, but even he was prone to say "What's that?" several times during every conversation with the skinny, bald-headed goat herder.

"I shee you know the newsh already."

"What news?" Caleb asked.

"The wolvesh newsh."

"Oh, uh, yes the news about the wolves. Indeed I know. At least I know about the pack that got eight of my stock last night. Miserable thieves! I thought the region was shut of wolves. Where did they come from?"

"Big drought up north. Not rained up there for a year. The Wolvesh an' The bearsh too is comin', followin' the deersh."

"Following the what?" Caleb asked.

Jerubabel, despite having to clarify himself for every human being with whom he spoke, showed irritation, "The deersh, the deersh, with the antlersh and da…"

"Yes, deer. Of course. So the meat eaters are moving south again, eh? In big numbers, I take it?"

"Yesh, big, big numbersh, eatin' up all the world, eatin' chickensh and rabbitsh, eatin' goatsh and sheepsh, and eatin' you too if we doeshn't do shomethin'."

"And I guess you're here to ask me to call a fellowship," Caleb said, not giving Jerubabel a chance to respond. "Sure, I call a fellowship. Send the word. Blow the horns. We'll hold it tonight, right here at my Christmas cottage."

"Ish dish shtill your cottage?" Jerubabel asked.

"What's that?" Caleb asked but not because he had not understood.

"I shaid ish dish shtill your cottage?"

"You'd better believe it's still my cottage! Always has been and always will be, but I know what you're getting at, and I want to ask you some things. What do you know about this woman?"

"I know she sheem mighty shweet to me, and I know she married to a shailor, and I know shomething 'bout that shailor that she don't know."

"And what, pray tell, might that be, and how do you know it?"

"I know 'caushe I hear it 'round town, and I know not a word of it been proved, but I know who shaid what…"

"Out with it, Jerubabel, what do you know?"

"I know that shailor got a looshe tongue and talk about him having another wife shomewhere down the coasht."

"You don't say? A bigamist, eh? But that's just gossip, right?"

"That'sh right, jusht town talk, but where there'sh shmoke there'sh fire, huh?"

"Not always, but I'll look into it. Bigamy's against the law," Caleb said. "What about the woman?"

"She growed up an orphan, and left the home when she wash sheventeen when thish shailor come to town and shay he thought she beautiful and love her and want to marry her. And that'sh not town talk. That'sh the fact. Parshon Riversh told me sho."

"How often does she see the man?" Caleb asked.

"Jusht onshe a year. Hish ship come every year with a big load of trinketsh for Chrishtmash, and then she shee him when he'sh not drinking."

"He's a drunk, huh? Is that everything you know?"

"That'sh all."

"Very well. I've got a thousand things to get done around here today. Send word to the brotherhood, and I will see you all at sunset."

Jerubabel called to his goats, and they ceased their mingling with Caleb's flock, separated themselves in one wave, and followed after him as he walked down the same path Susan had walked.

Caleb thought hard about Jerubabel's gossip and "facts," and he contemplated for more questions, hoping to find the perfect one to start Clara's tongue a'wagging. He opened the cottage's door, glanced around the main room, and said, "Clara?"

Clara did not answer. A stolid silence filled the cottage. Caleb did not like it. He walked slowly to the bedroom that was still covered by roof and peered inside. The room's furnishings were simple and sparse.

"Clara?" he said.

Clara did not answer. Caleb walked fast through the three partially roofless rooms, calling Clara's name twice. There was neither sound nor sign of Clara in the house. A faint shutter of nervousness speeded Caleb's heartbeat and his walking.

He stepped back outside and shouted, "Clara?!"

No answer.

He circled the cottage, glancing high and low. The sun was full and bright, and though the day was cold, the glare was strong. Caleb put his right hand to his forehead to block the sun and scanned the hills. He shouted Clara's name two more times.

Panic almost seized Caleb's thinking, but fifty years of shepherd's experience disallowed panic a place. *If she's walking, she hasn't had time to get beyond the hills,* he thought, *and if she were on the hills, I would see her so I know she's not wandered off.*

Caleb circled the house again. Two windows stood open. He choked down another surge of nervousness and turned his gaze upon the well.

"Oh no," he said under his breath.

He darted to the well. Noon was still a quarter of the day away, and darkness curtained the well's depths. He listened.

Nothing.

He called Clara's name but heard no response.

"If she's down there..." he thought, but he did not finish the thought.

He reached into his bag for his flints and oil. He lit a cloth, let it burn until the flame almost touched his fingers, dropped it, and watched it flutter downward. When the cloth was half way down the well, Caleb could see the water and the clay bottom beneath the water. He did not see Clara at all. His breath returned.

In that moment of relaxation, an idea came. He cleared his throat, closed his eyes, and began to sing, *"Tender child..."*

He walked around the cottage singing, pausing several times to catch his breath and listen for a response. He heard no response outside so he walked through the cottage's front door. As he entered, he heard a repressed snort of little girl giggle. He sang out as loud as he could, sounding every bit like the animals he followed, and for Clara, this was too much. Her giggles increased to out and out gut laughter.

Caleb strode over to the lower kitchen cabinets, opened a door, looked right at Clara, pretended not to see her, and shut the door.

"Where can that girl have got off to?" he asked out loud, "I had intended to introduce her to my flock today. She would have liked meeting Pretty Girl. Guess she'll have to wait until tomorrow, and I'll have to leave without her."

"No, don't leave," Clara said as she burst open the cabinet door and unfolded herself into the kitchen. "Here I am."

"So that's where you've been? I thought you might have gone on a hike in the hills." Caleb did not use a condescending tone with Clara. He spoke to her as though he was speaking to an adult, and she felt very big for it, "And, er, in case you were thinking of wandering off, I must say, I wouldn't advise it. There are wolves about."

"I dreamed about wolves last night," Clara said.

Caleb made no reply. He motioned for her to follow him outside. His sheep and goats were scattered around the cottage, grazing contentedly. Caleb whistled, and the flock grazed toward him, not looking up, not forming too tight a huddle.

"Clara," Caleb said, "this is Pretty Girl. Pretty Girl, I'd like you to meet Clara." Caleb stroked Pretty Girl's wool and invited Clara to do the same. She did so, burying her tiny fingers in Pretty Girl's soft curls. All the world was a great wonder to Clara, and the sheep's coat was as interesting to her as long stories are to grown ups.

"She's so pretty," Clara said.

Clara's lungs were working double time, partly because she was a little afraid of Caleb's animals, especially the goats, and partly because she was overcome with awe. Clara leaned forward and gave Pretty Girl a kiss on the nose. The sheep shook her head and returned to her grazing. Caleb chuckled.

"How would you like to help me with a chore?" Caleb asked.

Clara said she would like to help very much. She had not yet reached the age when chores seemed like chores.

There was very little for her to do. Caleb would use his knife to scrape blood clots and other disgusting sticky stuff from the furless sides of the hides on the trees, and Clara would serve as his "advisor."

"Does this one look clean enough?" Caleb would ask, indicating the answer he expected by the tone he used. Clara would answer accordingly, and Caleb would continue scraping or move on to another hide. When about half the scraping had been done, Caleb told Clara that lunch time had arrived.

They walked into the cottage, and Clara surprised Caleb when she began to set the table.

Caleb found a large wooden ladle in a top row cabinet, dipped into the stew, tasted it, and pronounced, "Oooweee, that's good. Give me your bowl in a hurry!"

Clara surprised Caleb again by walking from the table to the hearth's edge with not one but two bowls. Caleb filled the first for Clara, sent her to the table, and filled another for himself. They ate like a pair of pigs, each having grown very hungry after their morning's entertainment and labor. They said not a word while they ate but managed to glance at one another ever so often.

When Clara was done eating, she sat back in her chair, patted her stomach, which was now protruding, belched prodigiously, and sang:

> *"There once was a sheep named Pretty Girl,*
> *And a pretty, pretty sheep was she.*
> *Her shepherd was a man with white curls,*
> *To match his pretty sheep's fuz-zy."*

Caleb sat back in his chair, scratched his chin, blushed, and smiled. Clara continued:

> *"Pretty Girl liked to go walking,*
> *Eating grass like a pie from a shelf,*
> *And her shepherd liked to go talking*
> *To his sheep and his goats and himself."*

Caleb's faced turned red and went deep crimson. He leaned his chair back on two legs and laughed so hard the chair fell over.

Clara stopped singing and clambered to the shepherd's side.

Caleb reached up, patted her head, and kept on laughing for at least a minute.

Clara thought this a spectacle beyond all spectacles, joined in Caleb's laughter, and hugged him fiercely. Caleb returned the hug, and Clara crawled on to his thick chest. They looked like grandfather and granddaughter. They looked like they had been chums for a long while.

When Caleb had gained a little of his composure, but before all the tears of laughter had stopped flowing, he said, "Clara, please sing that song again."

"What song?" Clara asked.

"That song about Pretty Girl you just sang."

"Oh, I don't think I can." Clara said.

Caleb kept on snickering but managed to say, "You mean it

came and went just like that, huh?"

"I guess so," Clara said.

She had told the truth. The song had blown through her mind like wind blowing through an open window, had been sung, and had gone. She had not forgotten the song, but it was not inside her anymore. She had been a channel for the song, a communicator of things she did not grasp, and she had not fully understood her own words.

"Well that's one fine talent you've got there, Clara. You know what a talent is?" Caleb said, still laughing but regaining more of his composure as he spoke.

"I don't guess so," Clara said, turning up her palms.

When Caleb was in control of himself, he said through a smile, "A talent is a kind of smartness, and you've got one, and I've got a notion that Parson Rivers could use you in his children's choir."

Clara did not know what Caleb was talking about, but she took his words as a compliment and smiled. She crawled off Caleb's chest, and he stood.

"We'd best get busy with these hides. There's half a day's work to do, and we've got a big meeting tonight. Come on," Caleb said.

The two walked outside, and Caleb did not bother to interrogate Clara about her father. He knew that all the answers she could supply would come of their own in their own time now. Caleb returned to scraping the skins, and Clara returned to her advising. Caleb finished his task half way through the afternoon. He watered his flock soon afterward, allowing Clara to hold the bucket as often as she liked, which was quite often until she got tired of sheep and goat sloshings dripping on her hands.

After the watering, Caleb suggested a nap. Clara said she would like to have one so they went inside the cottage. Caleb rolled out his blanket before the hearth, and Clara lay down perpendicular to him, propping her head against his chest. There they slept, snoring like exhausted bulldogs.

An hour or two before sunset, Susan returned. She opened the cottage's door and saw the Shepherd and her daughter resting together. She did not know what to make of the scene, and she did not know if she liked what she saw. She scrutinized the Shepherd's haggard face. His wrinkles ran deep, but a hint of pure youthfulness shined in his complexion. Susan was sure she had not noticed that aspect of his appearance prior to her journey to town, and she wondered if something unusual had happened to him since her departure. She studied him further, observed his rough, calloused hands, his wrinkled brow, and his peaceful sleep. Her feelings ran to extremes. She coughed, and Caleb and Clara sat upright and wiped sleep from their eyes.

"Good afternoon, sleepy heads," she said.

Caleb cleared his throat. "Good afternoon to you, Susan. Did you find my supplies?"

Clara lumbered to her mother's side and gave her a hug, "I got to water the sheep, Mama."

"Good, Clara… Yes sir, I've got the salt and the oil. I hope I bought enough."

"Good," Caleb said, "I'd better get busy now, and if you wouldn't mind helping, I'll sell two of the hides on your behalf."

Susan felt as worn out as a twenty year old wagon wheel, but she said, "Yes sir, I'll do what I can."

Caleb and Susan took down the hides. Caleb showed Susan how to rub salt onto them, and they stacked the hides beside the inside wall of one of the cottage's roofless rooms.

"We'll salt them and leave them for a week or two, and then we'll oil them," he said.

Susan did not like the idea of "a week or two." If she had been asked, she could not have said why, but she wanted the white haired intruder gone as soon as possible. There was something ominous about him, something that suggested the approach of bad happenings, even if he did not seem bad himself.

"Whatever you say," she said, "I'll help anyway I can."

After they salted the hides, they sat down for supper. The stew had simmered all day, and the meat was so tender, a spoon's edge could have cut it. The carrots and potatoes had absorbed salt and pepper flavors, and the meal was delicious.

Three quarters of the way through the meal, Susan heard bells ringing and sheep and goats bleating. The sound started at a distance and moved closer and closer to the cottage. She turned her ear toward a window.

"Susan," Caleb said, "sorry I forgot to tell you; a few friends will be stopping by tonight. We've got to get our heads together about these wolves. Meat eaters are coming in from the north. There's a big drought up that way."

As Caleb finished speaking, someone knocked on the cottage's door. Caleb wiped his mouth, stood, and opened it.

"Well, if it ain't Old Timothy Peg Leg! Man, how are you? Looking better than ever. Flock looks good too. Come on in here, old boy, and have a seat," Caleb said, slapping Old Timothy Peg Leg on the shoulder.

Timothy's hair was gray, but his beard retained rich strands of brown. He looked nearly as old as Caleb, and he limped as he walked.

Susan glanced out the window as Timothy's flock mixed with Caleb's, and she noticed that Timothy's animals wore blue collars with shiny bells.

"Timothy, this is Susan and Clara. Susan and Clara, Timothy," Caleb said.

"Nice to meet you, Mr. Timothy," Susan said.

"Nice to meet you, Susan, and you too Clara," Timothy said, patting Clara on the head as he proceeded to the remaining chair.

"Have a bowl of stew?" Caleb asked.

"Sure, and thank you," Timothy answered.

Susan served Timothy a steaming hot bowl of the stew, and Timothy complimented her cooking.

Before she returned to her seat, she heard another knock on the door. She answered it this time. A short man with big ears stood before her. He was holding a green, wide-brimmed hat in one hand.

"Name's Charley," he said, "looking for Caleb. He here?"

"I'm here," Caleb said, starting toward the door with his right hand extended for a shake. "Charley Bat Ears, get in here, you dwarf. How in the world are you? Still just herding sheep, or have you got big enough to handle goats too?"

Charley laughed, "Still just sheep, you white-haired, old bone. Sheep's for keeps, goats for coats, my pappy always said."

"Your pappy also said the world was flat," Caleb said, elbowing Charley's ribs.

Caleb offered Charley some stew. Charley accepted and sat on the hearth.

Susan shook her head, wondering if any more shepherds were coming. She did not wonder long, for as soon as Charley sat down, four loud knocks shook the door.

"Orfel?" Caleb asked.

"Orfel." Timothy said.

"Orfel!" Charley exclaimed.

Caleb threw the door open. "Orfel Little Mountain, get your big self in here. Been eating well, I can see. You still getting taller? My gosh, what did you have for breakfast this morning, half a bull? No, a whole bull!"

Orfel, who had to turn sideways and duck when he stepped through the door, could do nothing but smile. Though his stature was immense, his mannerism was childish. He shook Caleb's hand.

Susan could not believe her ears when Orfel spoke. His voice was shrill, almost the voice of a small boy.

"Hi Timothy, hi Charley, hi Caleb, hi ma'am, hi little girl," Orfel said.

They all said "hi" in return.

"Say Orfel, you used to sing in the children's choir, didn't you?" Caleb said, "Yes, I remember. A high pitched voice and lungs like coal bellows to power it..."

Before Caleb could finish asking Orfel about the children's choir, another knock came. Caleb opened the door, and Billy and Willy, gray-haired twins of the goat herding persuasion, said "hello."

"Mirror, mirror on the wall, if it ain't the identicalest twins of all!" Caleb said, shaking hands with Billy and Willy. "Come on in and help yourself to some stew."

Susan ran out of bowls when Orfel got his stew so as soon as she and Clara finished eating, she washed their bowls and served helpings for Billy and Willy. They thanked her at the same time. Susan thought about how twins tend to look less and less alike as they age, and she was astonished at how the two gentlemen, at least sixty years old each, appeared indistinguishable.

Caleb never did know which was which, but he did not need to since they were inseparable and weaved their words together as they spoke.

Though she did not show it, Susan started to get irritated. The stew had been depleted, and her Cottage had been overwhelmed. Courtesy has its limits, and if any more shepherds arrived, she told herself she would have a word with Caleb.

More shepherds arrived– Loak the Fat, Nick the Sick, Marsel Long Legs, John the Beer Drinker, Mud Face Richard, and Jerubabel the "what?" (a.k.a Jerubabel the Bald).

Susan had her word with Caleb. The shepherds exited the cottage and built fires, and Susan remained inside. Through the front window, she watched the fellowship grow. Three hours after sunset, when Parson Rivers came, Susan felt sure there would be no more, but she was wrong.

At a great circumference around the cottage, a circle of fires had been built. A thin, brown-haired young man with no beard (and only a small flock of sheep) approached the circle and paused there. Then he approached the main fire near the cottage's front door.

The young man greeted the group with shyness, and Caleb said, "Who might you be?"

"Name's Andrew," the young man said, "I'm new to shepherding. Mind if I join you?"

"Maybe, maybe not," Caleb said, "Where are you from?"

At forty-one, Orfel was the youngest of the shepherds, but Andrew appeared no older than twenty-one. There had been no new shepherds in twenty years or more since most of the young men in those days had forsaken the pastoral life for city jobs, and Caleb and all the other shepherds could not help viewing the young man with suspicion.

"From Merrydale, sir, at least I *was* from Merrydale. Joined His Majesty's Army a few years ago and served in the east until I was discharged with honor, sir. I came back here a month ago and bought this flock. I'm just trying to make a go of it, and I won't stay if I'm not welcome."

"I've run into him a time or two," John the Beer Drinker said. "He seems like a nice kid. I say we let him stay. Won't do any harm, and if he knows how to fight, that's all the more reason to have him around."

Caleb, by default the leader of the Shepherds since he was oldest, consulted Parson Rivers, Jerubabel, and Timothy Peg Leg. They whispered, shook their heads, and agreed.

Caleb spoke, "Andrew, come and join us, but be warned, we expect much of young men like you. Have you seen combat?"

"Just once, sir, a rebel skirmish in the Iragul Province. Got a scar to prove it."

"Well, let us have a look at the scar," Caleb said.

Andrew walked close to the fire and pulled up his shirt. A pink mark ran from his throat to his belly.

"Say you got that in His Majesty's service?" Caleb asked.

"Yes sir," Andrew answered.

"Young man, with a scar like that you are as welcome among us as gold is welcome at a bank. Brethren, I present to you Andrew Scar Chest, youngest of shepherds, His Majesty's Defender, and… I hope… a slayer of wolves." Caleb said.

"Thank you, sir," Andrew said and sat down beside Mud Face Richard.

"We were just discussing how we did it last time," Caleb said, "but since you would have been about six back then, you wouldn't know anything about it, would you Andrew Scar Chest?"

"Actually I would, sir," Andrew said, "We talked about it at school and played like we were shepherds of the wolf war. When I had my choice, I played Old Caleb himself."

The shepherds squirmed and almost laughed, but Caleb raised his hand to silence them. "Old Caleb *himself*, you say? And what stories did you hear of Old Caleb?"

"Many, sir. I heard about how he took on a pack out by Sharpson's Bend all by himself. I heard he was the bravest or maybe craziest of the shepherds. I also heard how he smashed two wolf skulls with one swing of his staff. He was a regular berserker when he was fighting. And not only that, I heard stories of when he was a young man, a soldier in His Maj…"

"Say no more of that, Andrew Scar Chest. You say some folks claimed Old Caleb was crazy?"

"Indeed, sir, crazy as a horse-stomped chicken on a dirt path."

Andrew thought he had made a funny when one of the shepherds guffawed.

"Good description. Best I ever heard. He was a crazy shepherd, wasn't he fellows?" Caleb said to the shepherds.

The shepherds grunted affirmatively, afraid to open their mouths lest laughter escape.

"Did you hear what became of Old Caleb?" Caleb asked Andrew.

The shepherds held their sides now and blew chuckles through their nostrils.

"I don't recall, sir. That was fifteen years ago. He was old then. I guess he died."

"Guess again," Caleb said, "I *am* Old Caleb."

A roar of laughter exploded through the company, but Andrew did not laugh. He hung his head and muttered in regretful tones.

"I didn't mean to… I didn't mean to… I didn't…"

Caleb frowned and felt sorry for baiting the young soldier. He raised his hands again, and the shepherds laughed no more.

"No harm done, Andrew Scar Chest. I am flattered that you wanted to play me when you were a boy. Yes, I might have been a berserker at one time, but not even *these* old men know about that. The stories you heard were playground exaggerations. I never killed two wolves with one staff swing, and I never took on a whole pack by myself, at least I didn't intentionally. All I ever did was what any shepherd would have done, but I'm afraid I'm too old to do much now, and most of the fighting this time will be done by young men like yourself and Orfel Little Mountain."

Caleb broadened his gaze to the entire company.

"Speaking of fighting, gentlemen," he said, "we'd best get our

35

heads together now. One animal from each flock for bait, that's how we did it last time. Hard thing to do, I know, but must be done. Are we all in agreement?"

"Musht be done," Jerubabel said.

"Must be done," Billy and Willy said in unison.

"Must be done," the brotherhood agreed.

"First fight, tomorrow night," Caleb said.

"Aye," said the company, though none of the shepherds liked the idea.

They planned and plotted, broke out wine skins, casks, a keg, courtesy of John the Beer Drinker, and coffee cans. They smoked or chewed tobacco, and one by one, they all fell asleep beneath the stars– except Caleb.

Caleb's pack and blanket were inside. Late in the night, he crept to the door and pushed it open.

The door creaked, and Susan, who was sitting in a chair and dozing, sat upright, and said, "What? Huh? Oh, it's just you again."

Caleb read her annoyed expression, her repressed poutiness.

"Just getting my blanket," he said.

"Caleb?" she said.

"Yes?" Caleb asked.

She shook her head, "Nothing, I'd better get to bed."

Caleb shook his head, walked back into the crisp night air, and slept beneath the moon and stars.

FOUR

Caleb and Parson Rivers, two old shepherds, sat on a log, both half asleep, both sipping coffee and tossing chunks of pine on the morning fire. Caleb cleared his throat several times but decided to put off speaking until he had finished his coffee. Parson Rivers removed a wooden comb from his pack and ran it through his thin gray hair.

The sun's light filtered in through dense fog, but the sun had not yet made itself visible. The other shepherds were rising and stumbling about.

Caleb drained his cup, cleared his throat one more time, and said, "How's a child go about getting a part in your choir for the Christmas Concert?"

"Too late," Parson Rivers said, "the choir's already three weeks into rehearsals."

"Not too late," Caleb said, "this child sings like an angel. She hears a song once, and she never forgets it. She even makes up songs. You need her."

"No, too late, Caleb," Parson Rivers said. "I've assigned the parts already. Maybe next year... but what child are you talking about?"

"I'm talking about the child that lives in my Christmas cottage: Clara. Susan's her mother. Couldn't tell you her father's name," Caleb said.

"I *could* tell you her father's name, and it's a name I don't like," Parson Rivers said.

"What's his name?" Caleb asked.

"His name's Bruker. He's some kind of sailor, I'm told. I never met him, but I know Susan, at least as much as she'll let me know her these days. Can't get her to say more than two words at a time to me anymore," Parson Rivers said.

"Yes, Jerubabel said she was an orphan. You and the sisters raised her, huh?" Caleb said.

"The sisters raised her. Can't say I did much to help. Did what I could. Shepherding every soul in Merrydale that wants shepherding plus shepherding every shepherd in the region, not to mention shepherding sailors down on their luck and shepherding more than just souls, shepherding the church's buildings, the orphanage's buildings, the poorhouse's buildings, the organ, the pulpit, and the pews– takes a lot of time, wouldn't you agree? Susan's the tea leaf that fell through the strainer if you follow what I'm saying," Parson Rivers said.

"I understand," Caleb said, "You didn't have time to be a... well, you know... a father to her. Is that what you're saying?"

"Oh come on now Caleb. I was as much a father to her as I was to any orphan. You better believe it. My office was never closed and is never closed, and not a week goes by that one of my orphans, some half as old as you, doesn't come 'round to see Old Parson Rivers. But Susan. I warned Susan, told her she was throwing herself away, told her not to marry him. Told her she hadn't known him long enough. She wouldn't listen. She was seventeen, too young and too old for listening, and she's a stubborn girl on top of it. How long have you known her?"

"Just met her night before last," Caleb said. "Stubborn is right. Didn't take me long to see that. But about her daughter, you've got

38

to hear her at least. I'm telling you, Parson, I'm telling you. You wouldn't believe…"

"Oh, I would believe. When Susan was Clara's age, she could rip out a tune better than most children twice as old as herself. Next to Orfel Little Mountain, Susan was the best singer I ever trained, but she quit singing when she was just a girl. I think she was nine or ten at the time. Don't know why, but one day she's singing like a lark, and the next we can't get her to open her mouth. Singing runs in Susan's blood, whatever blood that may be."

"You never knew who her mother was?" Caleb asked.

"No," Parson Rivers answered.

"But surely you have your ideas, no?" Caleb asked.

"No. I truly don't have any idea what blood runs in Susan's veins. Her mother never came in. She might have died giving birth for all I know. Susan was left on the front steps, an orphan in every sense of the word. That's as much as I know. I can usually figure these things out, but Susan doesn't look like any family in Merrydale."

"Stands to reason that if you don't let Clara sing now, she might not sing next time around, doesn't it, Parson? Her mother quit. Maybe she'll quit." Caleb said, eyeing Parson Rivers and smirking triumphantly.

"Well, maybe she'll quit but maybe not," Parsons Rivers said.

"Yes, maybe not, but maybe if you get Clara in your choir and get her to do well, Susan will forgive you," Caleb said.

"Forgive me for what? I told you I tried to…"

"Forgive you for being a human being and not God, I could say. At least I think that's what you suspect she's bitter at you about. You think she needs to forgive you for being her father figure but not devoting much time to her, but Susan seems level-headed enough, and she knows something about work and staying busy. No, she needs to forgive you for something much worse than not being God or neglecting her… not that you did neglect her of course. She needs to forgive you for being right and knowing you were right. She needs to forgive you for knowing she knows she was wrong about this Bruker fellow. She's got a pride about her.

That's obvious enough. That's why she lives three miles outside of town. At least that's what I think. She can't stand for people to look down on her so she doesn't give them a chance. But pride or no pride, she loves Clara, and if you want to make amends with Susan, you can do it through Clara. Let her sing in the choir this Christmas. It wouldn't hurt anything. "

Parson Rivers stood and watched the sun climb up through the dissipating fog. He rubbed his round belly and yawned.

"I'll consider it, Caleb," he said, and he walked to the back of the cottage to relieve himself.

Andrew Scar Chest approached the log.

"Mind if I sit down?" he asked.

"Not at all, Andrew Scar Chest, take a load off," Caleb said.

"Listen, I didn't mean to offend you last night..." Andrew began.

"I told you it was all right, didn't I?" Caleb said.

"Yes, but..." Andrew began.

Caleb interrupted, "No 'buts.' If I had a silver coin for every time I ever put my foot in my mouth..."

"You'd be a rich man?" Andrew Scar Chest asked.

"Yes, I would."

"But about the stories of your soldier days... if only half of them are true... I heard them from good..."

Caleb interrupted, "You heard them from friends and family, maybe even your own father, people you trust, sure you did, but who did they hear them from? You believe everything you hear?"

"No, but..." Andrew said.

"No 'buts,'" Caleb said.

Andrew mumbled something and said no more for the time.

The cottage's door opened. Susan walked into the fog, yawned, and stretched her arms, and peered at the sleepy pack of shepherds. She shook her head, motioned for Caleb to come to the cottage, and went back inside.

"Who's that?" Andrew asked.

"Susan," Caleb said.

"Oh, of course." Andrew said.

Caleb joined Susan in the main room.

"Listen," Susan said, "you wouldn't mind looking after Clara again today, would you?"

"No, I wouldn't" Caleb answered, "but I won't be around the cottage after lunch time. We're hunting tonight, and we'll have to set our trap before dark."

Susan squinted and grimaced.

"Oh well, I guess I'll carry her to town. I don't know what you said to my daughter yesterday, but she really liked you. I had my doubts about leaving her, I guess you know, but I've never seen Clara take to anybody like she's taken to you."

"And I like her too, but she's a handful, I guess you know." Caleb said.

"Yes, I know," Susan said.

"But listen," Caleb said, "before you start to town, do you think you could get her to sing for Parson Rivers? I think I've talked him into giving her a part in the Christmas Concert."

"Oh, no. No. No. No! My daughter's not singing for that old buzzard. (Her actual word was not buzzard, but you get the idea.) Over my dead body she'll sing to him."

"Susan, don't talk that way. Clara's got a talent. Parson Rivers can bring it out. It would be good for her. You don't want her to be shy about her singing forever, do you? Besides, what's he done that he deserves being called a 'buzzard?"

"What's he done? What's he done? He's, he's… I don't want to talk about it. She's not singing to Parson Rivers, but I'll think about letting her sing in the concert with the other children… Wait! No, I won't! She'd have to sing for Parson Rivers to sing in the concert. No! She won't be singing. Anyway, she doesn't have anything to wear, and I won't have Merrydale's little rich brats looking down on my daughter."

"Fine, then. Sorry I asked, but I'll tell you what: I'll look after her today if you want. I'll let the boys prepare for the hunt. I'm getting too old for wolf tracking anyway."

Susan studied Caleb for a second. Something was going on beneath those white hairs of his. Something did not smell right, but her back was aching, and Clara liked the old man.

"Thank you," she said. "You can wake her up. I let her sleep late this morning."

"Good, good. She needs her rest. I put her to work yesterday. I let her help water my animals."

"So she said. Well, I suppose I ought to be leaving now."

"Don't work too hard," Caleb said.

Susan grunted sarcastically.

Caleb sat down at the table, and Susan walked out the door. Caleb watched her through the window behind the table. When she disappeared a few yards down the fog-covered path, Caleb moved with haste toward the room where Clara slept. He knocked on the door, announced he was coming in, and did so.

Clara sat up and yawned.

"Want something to drink?" Caleb asked.

Clara smiled, "Yes."

"How about some apple cider?" Caleb asked.

"Apple cider? What's apple cider?" Clara asked.

"You'll see," Caleb said.

Caleb walked outside and said, "Billy, Willy, how's about a cup of that cider you two always have this time of year?"

"Sure. Sure. Don't have much left. Very little left. But help yourself. But have some," Billy and Willy said, intermingling their sentences.

"Be right back," Caleb said.

Caleb went inside, found a cup, and returned to Billy and Willy. He filled the cup with cider, heated the cider on a rock beside the fire for a few minutes, and went back inside.

"Strange," Billy and Willy said to each other.

Caleb thought, *"Nothing like apple cider to warm up the voice box. She's going to sing like a bird for Parson Rivers, and he's going to beg Susan to let Clara join the choir, and, she'll let her."*

Caleb smiled, feeling quite proud, quite clever. What he did not think about was his own motive for sticking his nose in Susan's business– business that had been placed firmly off limits to all interested noses.

42

"Here, sit up," Caleb said.

Clara smelled the cider. She sipped it at first, and then she guzzled it.

"That's the best drink I've ever tasted," she said. "Can I have some more?"

"I'm afraid there is no more," Caleb said, "but I would like you to come outside now. Pretty girl wants to see you."

Caleb exited Clara's room.

Clara donned her little dress, as plain a brown dress as has ever been worn, and joined Caleb just outside the cottage's door. She gave a tiny yelp when she saw the band of shepherds, some of them still half asleep, and she motioned for Caleb to lean down so she could whisper something to him.

"Who are all those men?" she asked.

Caleb whispered, "They're my friends. You'll like them. There's one in particular I would like you to meet."

Caleb took Clara by the hand and led her to the main assemblage of shepherds.

"Where's Parson Rivers?" he asked.

"He left," Mud Face Richard said.

"Left? He was just here! He didn't even tell me goodbye," Caleb said.

"No, he left before the red haired woman left. Said he had things to do. Said he'd join up with us tonight on the hunt," Marsel Long Legs said.

"That old buzzar… er, uh, I've got to see him before then. Marsel, you mind looking after my flock until noon?" Caleb asked.

"Well, I…"

"Good, and much obliged. See you then. Come along, Clara."

Caleb and Clara took the dirt path to Merrydale. Not long after the start of their walk, Caleb realized he would have to carry Clara. He hoisted her onto his shoulders, old shoulders, as indicated by the white hair that rested upon them. He was already stiff from the scuffle on the night he found his cottage occupied, and he knew he would pay for this journey with additional back pain for days, but pain was a toll he was used to paying, for he had been carrying sick lambs and sick kids in similar fashion for fifty years.

"Clara?" Caleb asked.

"What?" Clara asked.

"Can you keep a secret?" Caleb asked.

"What kind of secret?" Clara asked.

Caleb thought hard.

"Well, you see, I was thinking we should get your mother a Christmas present, and presents have to be secret. If you tell her we went to Merrydale today, it won't be a secret. Now you wouldn't want to spoil your mother's surprise, would you?"

"No," Clara said.

"Good," Caleb said, "So you won't tell her anything about us going to town today?"

Clara shook her head *no*.

Caleb could not see her shaking her head *no*, but he could feel her weight shifting from side to side, and he understood.

"Good," he said, "This will be our secret. Do you promise?"

"I promise," Clara said.

Caleb thought a warm up for Clara's voice was in order so he asked her to sing for him. She obliged, and to Caleb, the walk from his Christmas cottage to Merrydale seemed shorter than usual. Caleb knew there was no chance of overtaking Susan in the walk. He was a slow walker at his fastest, and carrying Clara, even if she were small, meant a time consuming journey, even if the minutes seemed to fly by with a song bird on his shoulders.

Merrydale was the place where Caleb traded, where he sold fleeces and skins, and where he bought supplies for his long seasons afield, but he was never at ease there. When he and Clara reached the outskirts of Merrydale, Caleb felt the apprehension he always felt upon entering the town. Caleb was a country man. He felt at home among country people, and town life was a riddle to him. Why people would want to live bunched together "like sheep" he could not understand. He had a few friends in town, some of them quite dear, and "a few" was as many as he wanted since he generally despised the ways of the fast-talking, fast-trading popu-lace of the little town by the sea. He did, however, like Merrydale's

Christmas candles. How many nights he had spent sitting on some deserted hill outside the town staring down at those candles, dreaming, praying, smiling, and transcending his lonely existence he could not begin to count.

Caleb had been visiting Merrydale every year at Christmas time since the beginning of his shepherd days. This year he was arriving early, but he did not intend to stay long. Clara stopped singing as Caleb began to feel apprehension, almost as if the emotion had passed from one to the other like water evaporating into the sky and raining back down upon the earth. Caleb thought her silence an advantage since Susan could have been working anywhere in town.

Susan could be working anywhere in town?! Caleb stopped walking. He had to think about the danger for a minute. He turned off Merrydale's main street, opting for obscure passages between buildings. In case he caught a glimpse of bright red hair and needed to do an about face, he looked in all directions as he resumed his pace.

When Caleb reached the Merrydale Parsonage, he knocked on its door, and Parson Rivers' housekeeper, a stout young widow named Martha, opened the door.

"You're early this year," she said, "What's the matter? Have your sins found you out and you need to confess to the parson?"

"My sin is ever before me," Caleb said, "but I've got no confession to make this morning. I've got urgent business. Where's the Parson?"

"Urgent business, eh? Wouldn't be about his wantin' to loaf off with shepherds on a wolf hunt, would it? At his age, no offense intended, you'd think he'dve outgrown such things. But no, not Parson Rivers, still got too much of a boy's brain in him to've outgrown adventurin'. You should talk to him, Caleb. Y're his senior, and he respects you, but then too, y're as much a single man as he is, and you've got as much of a boy's brain as he does, no offence intended. You, yourself, should've settled down in a room in town years 'fore now, should've married a nice woma…"

Caleb shuttered at the mere mention of settling down in town. He knew that Martha could go on for a long while, and he did not

45

have a long while.

He spoke again, this time in a demanding tone, "Martha, tell me now, where is Parson Rivers?"

Martha acquiesced.

"He's up to the church," she said, and she peered at Caleb as if to say, *"Well, I never!"*

"Thank you," Caleb said.

He felt bad, but he would make it up to her with a bucket of molasses or a jar of jam for Christmas. He had given her enough presents over the years to deserve a direct answer anyway.

Caleb made his plan as he walked. Upon reaching the church, he searched for one of the sisters, and he found Sister Kate.

Sister Kate was as skinny as a hound in August and not much prettier, but she was polite, demure, meek to a fault, and as honest as snow. She stood in the hall of the mid-building, dusting the guestbook table.

"Sister Kate," Caleb whispered.

Sister Kate looked up the hall but did not see anyone.

Caleb and Clara stood with their backs to the wall around the corner from the hall.

"Who's there?" Sister Kate asked.

"Shhhhh, it's me: Caleb."

Sister Kate lowered her voice, "Caleb? Why are you whispering, and why are you hiding?"

"Shhh, come here. I need to ask you a favor."

Sister Kate walked toward the sound of Caleb's voice, and she turned the corner. Caleb looked nervous, and she did not like it.

"Yes?" she asked.

"Is Parson Rivers in his study?" Caleb asked.

"Yes. Why? Is something wrong?" Sister Kate asked.

"I need you to go stand by his door. Don't leave it no matter what. Just stand there until he comes out. He'll be out in a few minutes. Pay close attention to whatever he says when he comes out."

"Mr. Caleb, you've never acted this way. Is everything well with you? Why is Susan's daughter with you? Where is Susan? What is going on?"

46

"Sister Kate, I don't have time to answer just now, and I'm sorry. This is very important. Will you please, please help me?"

Refusing to help an old man with a tone of pitiful desperation in his voice was something Sister Kate was not capable of doing, and Caleb knew it. She agreed to help and asked no more questions.

Caleb walked Clara into the sanctuary of Merrydale Church, the single largest room in town, a room with stone walls and high ceilings, a room designed for the magnification of the human voice. Caleb sang the first note of *Tender Child*, which with his voice was not the first note of *Tender Child* at all, and Clara giggled.

"Well, you sing it then," Caleb said.

Clara obliged. She had heard her own voice in the wind over the fields. She had heard her voice in dumpy, wooden washrooms. She had heard her voice in the confines of the cottage, but she had never heard her voice echoing from the surfaces of a thousand carved stones, doing so almost imperceptibly, echoing tightly so as to increase the fullness of each note but not to confuse the subtlety of the inflections. Caleb saw Clara the moment she caught herself up in her own singing. She stood rigid, and the church exploded, flamed, blazed with the sound of her song. She played with each note. She struck out with ear-shattering volume at times and whispered as if calling to a frightened kitten at others.

Caleb joined silently in her rapture, and the same kind of tears that had dripped down his cheeks on the night of her "recital" gushed with severity now.

Parson Rivers pushed open the door of his study.

"Who is that?" he asked to no one in particular, "I've never heard singing like that in all my life! Amazing!"

He saw Sister Kate and continued, "Did an opera singer come in on one of the boats? You know anything about this? We're doing that song in the concert, you know. Is she one of ours? And why are you just standing here in the hall like that, anyway?"

Sister Kate did not answer. She had a faint idea why Caleb had asked her to stand near the Parson's study and hear what she had just heard. She pointed to the church sanctuary and followed the parson.

47

Parson Rivers rushed to the ethereal, heavenly, divine, celestial sound. He stepped inside the church sanctuary and nearly fainted when he saw its tiny instrument.

Clara stopped singing.

"Well, what did he say?" Caleb asked Sister Kate as he wiped his eyes. The tone of his voice implied that he had just gotten the best of the parson in some way and that her repeating what the parson had said would seal his victory.

Sister Kate hated conflict. She sighed and threw her hands up in the air, "I don't know what this is about, and I don't want to be in the middle of it, whatever it is, and if..."

Parson Rivers interrupted Sister Kate. He said, "Yes. Yes. And again I say, yes! And no, not too late. And yes, you were right, Caleb. She may have a part in the Christmas concert, and not just any part. She'll have the part she was singing just now, the principal part. We're performing *Tender Child* I guess you know. I suspect she learned it by overhearing our choir rehearsals since *Tender Child* is a new song, and nobody in Merrydale has the music to it but me. Bring her in this afternoon. I'll just have to tell the mayor's daughter that someone will be taking her part. And as for Clar..."

As Parson Rivers spoke, he, Caleb, Clara, and Sister Kate heard a violently loud, thunderous, booming bang. BANG!

FIVE

BANG! The main door, an ancient oak slab adorned with ornate carvings of the twelve apostles, crashed open and slammed into the stone wall to which it was hinged.

Susan entered. A vein near the center of her forehead pulsed, and her lips curled into a snarl. Her face showed hurt, anguish, and rage, but she said nothing.

Behind her walked a tall, big boned, broad shouldered man. Beneath his large black top hat, he sported long, blonde hair that had been pulled back to make a ponytail, and he wore a thick moustache that covered his top lip. He wore no shirt under his green silk vest (the better to show the many tattoos that covered his arms, Caleb thought). He wore white pants that were at least two sizes too tight and black, high-heeled boots with silver chains dangling around the ankles. Shiny rings and polished studs of various shapes and sizes hung from various parts of his body. Thick, chunky bracelets encircled both his wrists, and matching necklaces enveloped his neck.

Caleb disliked the man immediately, partly because of his

bizarre appearance but mostly because he knew the man was Clara's father, a giver of worthless island drivel for Christmas presents and perhaps a polygamist. The man spoke, and the eloquence of his voice surprised Caleb. His words flowed with something like eloquence.

The man extended his hand, saying, "I say there, Parson, you are the parson, yes? Yes, of course, and I do believe your name is Caleb, yes? Yes, good. And, could you be anyone other than Sister, ahhh, Kate? Of course you are Kate. I've heard about you. I am Bruker, Susan's husband and Clara's father, and I am certainly pleased and honored to make the acquaintance of such a fine, upstanding trio of citizens of this fine town of, er, Merryvil..."

"Dale," Susan finished the town's name correctly, for she felt sure that Bruker could not, and she did not want him to sound foolish.

"Yes, Merrydale," Bruker continued, "jewel of the coast, handsomest town by the sea, and home to (he grinned, proud he was about to sound charming) the prettiest two girls in the world if I must say so myself."

Clara clung to the right leg of Caleb's pants, scrutinized Bruker for a few seconds to make sure he really was Bruker, went to him, and called him "Daddy."

Susan smiled as though she had won a hand of a low stakes card game, but she continued to say nothing.

Bruker resumed his speech, "I hear kidnapping is a serious charge in this region, but we discern that you three were not kidnapping. At least we hope we discern it. It wouldn't do to..."

Sister Kate shook her head and stomped her left foot.

Parson Rivers, who on ordinary occasions was quite the talker, moved his lips like a fish out of water, but he could not form words.

Caleb stepped forward, looked Bruker dead in the eye, clinched his fists, drew a deep breath, released it, and stepped back, whispering, "For your daughter's sake, young man, for your daughter's sake..."

"You transport our daughter without our consent. You convey her to this place in direct violation of my wife's revealed wish. She did tell you she did not want Clara singing for the parson, sorry Parson, no offense intended, did she not? You step forward but step back to control your anger over my words, and you do it for my daughter's sake? How kind of you, old man, how very kind of you. I don't suppose you really wanted to hit me, now did you? Assault on top of kidnapping? Besides, you're an old man. What could you have done to me?" Bruker said with a chuckle.

Bruker glanced at Susan, and she tried to join him in his chuckle but was not quite capable of doing so.

Caleb observed her effort to raise the corners of her mouth. The return of her man gratified her, Caleb saw, strengthened her pride, made her feel she was as good as any other woman and maybe better than some, but he also saw that Bruker's unnecessary remarks embarrassed Susan.

Parson Rivers placed his right hand on Caleb's left shoulder as if to calm him and spoke, "No offense taken, Mr. Bruker. It's just that your daughter has a gift."

"I am fully aware of what my daughter has, preacher man, and if you are aware of the laws of this region, you will do well to keep your distance from her. Oh yes, I know things about the activities of this place, things my wife has told me, things that you and the good sister would not want anyone else to know. Now if you will excuse me."

Bruker bowed slightly as though he had just finished a rousing speech and was receiving a round of applause. Susan took Clara by the hand and with Bruker marched up the center aisle of the church and through the main door. As they stepped over the doorsill, Caleb thought he caught a glimpse of Clara's tiny hand waving goodbye, but then he thought he might have seen nothing more than the child lifting her arms in gladness for her father's return from the sea.

"What did he mean by 'the activities of this place?'" Caleb asked.

"I don't know," Parson Rivers answered.

"And what do you know?" Caleb asked, turning to Sister Kate.

"I don't know anything," Sister Kate answered.

"You're sure?" Caleb asked.

"Yes," they both answered and gave each other a furtive glance.

"Hmm," Caleb said, "Cat's got both your tongues, I see. You two, you aren't, you know, you aren't...?"

"What? Oh no, definitely not, no, no, not at all." The answer came from Sister Kate's and Parson Rivers's lips simultaneously, and they each took a step in the direction opposite the other.

"Then, what?" Caleb asked.

"For the common good, some things are best kept secret, Caleb," Parson Rivers said, "and if memory serves, you told me that yourself once. You said something about burying the past and keeping it buried..."

"That is enough," Caleb said, "your point is well taken. Sister Kate, what do you know about this Bruker fellow?"

Sister Kate cleared her throat. She had not regained enough of her composure to be able to speak clearly so what she said came out in a combination of breathy, forced, mumbling groans.

"I know only what I'm told. By the time Susan met him, she was no longer our child, no longer a child at all for that matter. She slept here still, ate here, studied here, and did her chores here, but her life, her true life, the life of her choosing, she carried on in the streets and public houses of Merrydale."

"No!" Parson Rivers said.

"Yes!" Sister Kate said, raising her voice so much she surprised herself.

"Why didn't you tell me?" Parson Rivers asked.

"Because you know nothing about a woman's heart," Sister Kate answered. "You would have come down on her even sooner than you did, and you would have pushed her away–out of Merrydale altogether. She would have taken to the sea. She would have run from us. You certainly came down on her hard enough once you found out about her wedding plans."

"I would not have needed to come down on her if I had known in time," Parson Rivers said, "I would have talked her out of marrying him."

"Sorry, parson," Caleb said, "but I've got to agree with the sister on this one. You shepherd your flock with a heavy staff any time you think there's need. You would have come down on Susan, and it would have driven her even further away. Now, go on, Sister."

Parson Rivers mouthed silent opposition to Caleb's opinion, and Sister Kate continued, "She was seventeen when his ship, The Dogfish, entered our port. The ship hauled livestock from down the coast. In their spare time, the crew sold trinkets and whatnots for Christmas presents: ornaments, bizarre paintings, bone handle knives, and such. I saw Bruker once with a gang of his friends at the market. He was barking to passers-by about 'rare, exotic gifts for your loved ones, and his voice rang out with so much charm that many a gullible soul stopped to listen to him or buy his rubbish. I thought to myself then that he looked like a fool, a clown of sorts, but a dangerous sort of clown, a man with a happy face painted over a mad and evil face.

"I never saw him again after that, but I'm a grape on the local vine if anybody is, I guess, so I heard things. I heard about the trinket seller who sang in the pubs. I heard how his singing was so pleasant and strong that people said he cast spells with his voice. Of course that was just town talk, you understand. I thought little of it until word got back to me that one of our own had fallen under the spell. I felt bad, felt like it was my fault she had fallen for the man, but I reminded myself that if it had not been him, it would have been another. Sooner or later, she was going to break from us. I knew that. Anybody who paid even the slightest amount of attention to Susan knew that. As I do more often than I should, because I don't like disagreement I guess, I purposed in my heart to say nothing to Susan or to the parson or to anyone else. I held it in as long as I could, too, but a day or two before their wedding, I broke down and told the parson."

"And it was too late by then," the parson said, "you should have told me sooner."

Sister Kate lowered her eyes but offered words of defense: "I could not have told you much sooner, Parson, even if I should have. They courted for less than two weeks, and for her it was too late long before she met him.

"There's more that I know, Caleb," she said, "things I wish I didn't know, or at least things I wish I'd never heard. Who's to say what's true and what's not…"

Sister Kate began to ramble, but Caleb guided her back to the subject of Bruker by mentioning Jerubabel's gossip.

"Oh, yes," Sister Kate said, "I've heard all about the wives. I've heard Bruker brags to the boys in town about having wives all around the world though that can't be possible since ships like his run the same route each year. Still, I doubt that Susan is his only wife and that Clara is his only child. I've heard other things too. He's no young man, but he's fond of women that are practically girls, and if all of what I've heard is true, some that actually *are* girls. 'The younger the better,' he says, or at least that's as much of what he says as I'll repeat in this church.

"I've heard he likes to fight, especially when he's drinking. He can't hold his liquor. The happy paint melts off the mad man's face when the alcohol runs down the clown's throat. Two mugs of ale and Bruker turns into a rabid dog biting everything he sees. Folks steer clear of him."

"Did you say 'steer clear?'" Caleb asked.

"Yes, why?" Sister Kate asked.

"That's a sailor's saying. Sailors talk about steering their ships clear of rocks and reefs and sandbars. When I met Susan, evening before last, she offered to 'steer clear' of me. I don't think it's a coincidence she would say that, but I don't know what it could mean. Maybe nothing at all. Go on," Caleb said.

"Clara was born during the September after Bruker's first visit to Merrydale. Susan had moved out of the orphanage to stay at the Mayor's house and clean for his wife, but she put her pride away long enough to come back here to give birth. At first we thought she was going to ask us to keep the child, but she told us that she had come here only because there was no other place she could afford. Her husband, she said, would be back to Merrydale with a chest full of money, and we would see, yes, we would all see then, and then she would be able to afford to stay anywhere she liked. That's been four years ago, and we still haven't seen that chest of money.

"Every December, it's the same thing. His ship sails into port.

His big talk excites Susan. He stays here until just after Christmas, and his ship sails. Susan thought that this town's good people felt sorry for her and that this town's scorners laughed at her so she moved out to your Christmas cottage this past October, Caleb. I've never known anyone with as much pride as Susan. Must be something that runs in her blood, whatever blood that may be."

"That's all you know, huh?" Caleb asked.

"That is all," Sister Kate answered.

"And neither of you are going to tell me anything more about whatever it was that Bruker meant by 'the activities of this place?'"

Parson Rivers and Sister Kate glanced at each other and shook their heads *no*.

"At least tell me this. Is it something that would be scandalous to most people, but you feel like you understand it in a way they never would?"

They glanced at each other again and shook their heads *yes*.

"I can understand that," Caleb said, "I can truly understand that. I'll be going now. May I expect to see you at the wolf hunt tonight, Parson?"

"I wouldn't miss it for a bag of gold, Caleb," Parson Rivers said.

Sister Kate rolled her eyes.

Instead of exiting the church through the rear, as he had entered it, Caleb stepped outside the front this time. He knew he needed to hurry back to the brotherhood of shepherds, but more than anything else, he felt he needed to speak with his sheep and goats. Caleb thought he could straighten out even the most confusing of circumstances by speaking it aloud to his animals. He walked up Merrydale's main street.

Through the corner of his eye he caught a glimpse of commotion in a dirty side alley. His first thought was that he should ignore it and continue walking. After all, he had big, important business to carry out with the brotherhood, but he could not resist having a second look. Without much concentration, he paused and turned his head sideways to get a better view, and he did a double take because of what he saw. A large crowd had gathered and many more were cramming into the tight space between the buildings.

Bruker's loud voice filled the alley:

"Step right up, and you shall witness,
a match of sailors' strength and fitness.
A silver coin is all it costs
To see who'll win and who'll be tossed
On his head to bleed and cry
To scream for mercy or to die."

"In this corner, Mean Dog Moe.
In that corner, Killer Joe.
They're great big men, for what it's worth,
And from the meanest spots on earth.
Moe's from the desert, dry and hot.
Joe's from the swamp, full of rot."

"They'll kick and claw, and bite and tear,
They'll stomp and bruise, and pull out hair.
They'll break and bust, and jab and poke,
They'll punch and wound, and hold and choke.
They'll knock and sock, it will be rough,
Til one or both has had enough."

At the end of each verse, Bruker emphasized the rhyme, and the crowd laughed as he did. Caleb realized that at least part of Clara's ability with words and rhythm came from Bruker's blood, for Bruker seemed to be quite the colorful talker. However, the greater part of her giftedness, Caleb judged, came from Susan's blood, whatever blood that may have been, because Clara's singing communicated something more than a mere ability to rhyme words. Even when she sang a happy song, there was something in Clara's voice that told of things profound and deep and weighty, things inscrutable, sad, and beautiful. In Bruker's chatter, Caleb heard the rhythm of the world, but in Clara's singing, Caleb heard rhythms older than the world.

The man has not yet lived who could resist watching a good

fight so Caleb, though he knew he needed to get back to his flock and to the fellowship, dropped a silver coin in the hat of the sailor who stood at the front of the alley to collect the entrance fee and joined the crowd.

Bruker howled on and on until so many bodies had pressed into the alley that Caleb feared he would be unable to breath.

"*Like sheep*," he reminded himself, "and *here I am, just like the rest of them.*"

Bruker rang a cowbell. His rambling ceased, and the rumbling began. Mean Dog Moe, a tall red haired man with a fat belly, charged out of his corner and into the center of the alley. Killer Joe, a brown bearded man of average height and far above average weight, met him there, and together they danced. Killer Joe tossed Mean Dog Moe against the alley's back brick wall. Mean Dog Moe fell down on his head but got up looking meaner than ever. He tackled Killer Joe, pulled his left arm behind his back and bit his hand. This seemed to infuriate Killer Joe so he rolled over, ignoring the pain in his arm, kicked off Mean Dog Moe, flipped onto Mean Dog Moe's stomach, and pinned him to the ground.

Mean Dog Moe stretched his neck so hard that Caleb thought it would break, but just when his head would reach no further, his object came into view, and he bit down again, this time on the inside of Killer Joe's arm. Killer Joe yelled and released his grip, and Mean Dog Moe tossed him aside. Mean Dog Moe stood and kicked Killer Joe. Killer Joe rolled onto his side and struggled to stand, but Mean Dog Moe kicked him again. The third time he attempted a kick, Killer Joe grabbed his foot, tripped him, and threw him to the ground. Killer Joe stood and leaped into the air like a bird. The weight of his body went hurling toward Mean Dog Moe's body, but just before Killer Joe crashed into him, Mean Dog Moe rolled, and Killer Joe landed flat on his face.

Caleb did not think they could continue to fight like that very long, but they did. They did everything Bruker said they would do and more.

Unlike most of those in the crowd Caleb did not stay caught up in the excitement. He studied the fighters. As he did, he saw what was truly happening. The shadows of the alley provided just enough cover to obscure the particulars of the combatants' motions. They were not really hurting each other. They were just entertaining the crowd. Caleb laughed, and as he did, he noticed Bruker staring at him. He stared back, and Bruker turned his head.

Killer Joe *won* the fight, and many of those watching handed money over to others in the crowd: money that had been placed as bets on Mean Dog Moe.

"*A scam*," Caleb thought, "*nothing but a scam.*"

He lingered in the alley as the crowd dispersed. He looked around for Susan, hoping to say something to her to justify his defiance of her wish that Clara should not sing for Parson Rivers, but he did not see Susan in the alley. Surely Bruker had not sent her back to work, had he?

"Greetings, old man," Bruker said.

"Old man," one of Bruker's mates said, "what are you looking for? It is not safe to look too closely at things in this alley."

Caleb turned his head to see who had spoken, and in an instant, Bruker's mates surrounded him. Killer Joe stood to his left. Mean Dog Moe stood to his right. The hat holder stood behind him, and two others stood in front of him.

Laughing, Killer Joe said, "Maybe not everything I did to Moe was real, old man, but everything I'm going to do to you will be."

Joe did not know the danger to which he exposed himself, for as he spoke, Caleb slowly moved his hand to the hilt of the knife he always carried concealed in his garments, and if Caleb had drawn the knife, Joe would have said no more words, no more words at all, to anyone, ever.

"Wait!" Bruker said. "I don't think this one is here to complain about losing a bet. I think he wishes to see me. Don't rough him up, boys. Allow him to address me if he wishes."

Joe and Moe stepped away from Caleb, and Caleb breathed a sigh of relief. They thought the old man must have been glad to have avoided a beating, but in truth, Caleb was glad he would not have to explain to the sheriff of Merrydale that he had cut their heads off in self-defense.

"Where's Susan?" Caleb asked.

"Susan is no concern of yours," Bruker said in a tone more serious than he had been using. "Leave things alone, and you'll be better off."

"What did you mean by 'the activities of this place' back there in the church?" Caleb asked.

"Oh, it was really just nothing. I've told Susan to get over it, but you know how women are. They never get over anything. You know how church people are too, don't you, old man? They'll carry unspeakable guilt for half their lives over the smallest things. You bring those things up, and they shut their mouths and surrender to you. My little strategy in the church worked, didn't it? Our visit was short and sweet, and for that, you should be thankful. Listen, I have no dispute with you, old man, so why don't we be friends, or better yet, why don't we be strangers?"

Caleb shook his head, sighed, turned, and walked from the alley.

"You will be all right, old man," Bruker yelled, "Just remember, when you see me or mine, steer clear."

"Steer clear," Caleb thought, *"Yes, steer clear. Better yet, why don't we be strangers? Perhaps Bruker gives the best advice. I should steer clear."*

Caleb walked out of the town of Merrydale and back into the country. As he ambled along he thought about Clara, but as soon as he did, he buried the thought. Noon was drawing on, and the brotherhood would be waiting for him to begin what had to be the ugliest chore of all.

SIX

"I hope my sheep and goats didn't say anything cruel about me while I was gone," Caleb said.

"They talked to my animals a plenty," Marsel Long Legs said, "but they didn't talk to me."

"Have all the shepherds made their decisions?" Caleb asked.

"I think so," Marsel said, looking down and contorting his face as if he had been forced to say something obscene.

"One animal from each flock," Caleb mumbled.

He then made *his* decision. Because he had three young ones, three unnamed ones, three to which he had not yet grown fully attached, the choice was not as difficult for him as it had been for some of the shepherds.

Caleb called for the brotherhood to gather. The shepherds formed a circle around him, and he went over the battle plan one last time:

"We will leave our flocks about a mile from here, inside Farmer Quigley's fences. Jerubabel spoke with him this morning, and Farmer Quigley agreed to allow us to use his pens, or at least he agreed to allow *something*. The way Jerubabel talks, there's no telling what he thought he was agreeing to."

Jerubabel said, "Hey, shtop that," and all the shepherds laughed.

Caleb continued in a softer voice, "After leaving our flocks at Farmer Quigley's, we will travel as fast as we can to Holder's Creek Valley where we will each depart in a different direction. We will lead away the animals we've chosen. We will walk for three hours, warning every person we meet along the way that a wolf hunt will be held tonight. At the end of our walk, we will cut our animals, and we will lead them bleeding back to Holder's Creek Valley.

"When night falls, the blood trails will lure the big meat eaters into the valley. The bleeding animals will be herded together and tied to stakes in the valley's center. The meat eaters will crouch toward the flock, but we will be waiting with bows and spears. Any questions?"

Andrew Scar Chest spoke up: "What about guns? When I left the army they let me keep my gun. Can I use it?"

"Absolutely not," Caleb said. "The noise would ruin the hunt. Our two best weapons will be blood and silence. Anymore questions?"

No one spoke.

For December, the air was warm. The midday sun competed with no clouds, and every stone, tree, cottage, and field exulted in its light. The Shepherds marched to Farmer Quigley's in near silence. They abandoned their animals to the protection of Farmer Quigley's fences and collected silvers to pay Farmer Quigley for the use of his pens. They marched toward Holder's Creek Valley, groaning most of the way.

The shepherds chose paths and directions.

Choked with sadness, Caleb whispered, "Blood trails. Back here at dark. Go."

The shepherds departed, and Caleb lowered his head and set out to do his duty.

To a sheep that would be dead by morning, Caleb could tell many secrets: secrets so old, so painful, and from so deep inside himself that he seldom allowed them to pass from his heart to his mind, much less through his lips. Would a sacrificial lamb not bear the secrets away?

Caleb spoke of the most agonizing thing of all. He spoke of love. Caleb had loved once, but as he spoke to the little lamb, he would not allow himself to repeat the name of the woman he had loved. Even then, fifty-one years after he had loved her, the memory of love stung his soul more than all other memories, more than morbid memories of war, or mournful memories of his mother's departure, or mixed up memories of what he had buried beneath the cottage's chimney.

Caleb could not speak of love for long. He registered a few grievances and complaints, and the lamb listened but did not reply.

The time for sacrifice came. Caleb cut the nameless sheep's right hind leg and led it back to the valley. By the time he reached the appointed place of wolf slaying, most of the fellowship had gathered on the sand beside Holder's Creek. Only two shepherds had not returned: Andew Scar Chest and John the Beer Drinker.

"I bet I know what'sh takin' John sho long," Jerubabel said.

"Beer, of course. Makes him move slower than a dead cow in a creek," Charley Bat Ears said.

"What do you think is taking Scar Chest so long?" Timothy Peg Leg said, "At his age, he should have been the first one back."

"I'm pretty sure I can answer that," Caleb said. "Having never bled a sheep before, he probably cut too deep, and now he is dragging the corpse behind him."

"That's got to be it," Marsel Long Legs agreed.

Parson Rivers met the soon-to-be wolf hunters when only the faintest hint of the sun's light remained to caress the hilltops. As he greeted the men and prayed for their safety and success, Andrew Scar Chest and John the Beer Drinker returned.

"Been drinking, John?" Caleb asked.

"Uh, eh, yeah," John stammered.

"Parson, take John with you," Caleb said with a wink, "we need a man like him on the high side of the valley."

"Very well," said the parson. "You'll be coming with me a little later on, John."

"Yeah, uh, yeah, goo, goo, good," John said.

"Scar Chest, looks like your sheep bled to death before you got here. Did you cut it too deep?" Caleb asked.

"Yes," Andrew answered, "but that's not the only reason I'm late. Farmer Hunley insisted that I take supper with him."

"And with his fat and toothless daughter too, huh?" Mud Face Richard teased.

Andrew snickered and said, "Well, yes, but there was something else. After supper he claimed he had to show me something, and he said he wished Old Caleb could see it too. He poured some load and powder down the barrel of his gun and led me to the back of his pasture. In the soft dirt near the fence row, I saw it. Farmer Hunley didn't even have to point it out. It looked as big around as a barrel head."

"What barrel? Did he mention a barrel?" John the Beer Drinker asked.

"Hush, John," Parson Rivers said as he tugged on John's shirt-sleeve, "let him finish."

"What I saw," Andrew continued, "was a bear track. When I was in the army, I went on bear trapping expeditions in the north region of the Iragul. I've seen some big bears before but never one that left tracks the size of what I saw in Farmer Hunley's pasture. If the track size is any indication, this bear stands eleven feet tall."

The members of the brotherhood did not dare show any signs of concern over the story of a novice shepherd.

"We're sure there are some big bears in the region," Timothy Peg Leg said as he patted Andrew Scar Chest on the shoulder, "but you will be fine. We won't let them eat you."

The members of the fellowship laughed and elbowed one another. Only Caleb did not join in their joking. He observed the sincerity of Scar Chest's face. Though Caleb did not defend Andrew's estimation of the giant bear to the rest of the brotherhood, he took Andrew's words seriously.

"Time to divide up," Caleb said. "I'm the oldest so I'll pair off with Scar Chest, the youngest. Peg Leg, you're the second oldest so you'll pair off with Little Mountian, the second youngest. Billy and

Willy, you two make one team no matter what. Everybody else, keep matching oldest to youngest until the ages meet in the middle and nobody's left. Come on Scar Chest, we'll take the boulder on the edge of the valley's stone face. The rest of you find rocks and position yourselves on them. Remember, three claps and the torches blaze."

Caleb and Andrew hiked around the rim of the valley and lowered themselves onto the smooth surface of the largest rock protrusion, a boulder the size of a small house. They rolled out their blankets and lay prone on their stomachs with their feet to the valley wall and their faces toward the sacrificial flock.

Andrew whispered: "How long before they come?"

"I'm not sure," Caleb said, "but probably when the moon is high. Do you have your gun in your pack?"

"Yes," Andrew said, "Why?"

"Can you put its pieces together in the dark?" Caleb asked.

"Of course I can. I had to learn to do that in my early training," Andrew said, "Didn't you?"

"Not every soldier used guns when I was in the army," Caleb said, "Guns were heavy and awkward back then, and they missed more often than they hit. I used a spear and a sword, but never mind that. I think you spoke sincerely about the bear track at Farmer Hunley's. Put your gun together and load it, but don't use it unless I tell you to."

Caleb heard Andrew rummage through the contents of his pack. He heard iron parts clanking one against the other and the muted clunk of wood parts being shoved into place. He heard clicks, thumps, and thuds. For a few seconds, he smelled oil and gunpowder, but the cool north wind wafted the odors away almost as soon as Caleb recognized them.

After less than a minute's work, Andrew said: "Finished, sir."

Caleb chuckled.

"Good work, Scar Chest, but don't call me *sir*. We're members of a brotherhood. There are no *sirs*. If any meat eaters come, sling the gun over your shoulder, but don't take it off unless I tell you to, and I seriously mean it."

"Yes, sir, I mean, just yes. Yes," Andrew whispered.

Caleb chuckled again. Andrew Scar Chest reminded Caleb of himself when he had been a young man, and Old Abel Nearly Blind had been the oldest of the shepherds. Caleb could not believe it had been fifty years since Old Abel had questioned him in much the same way that he had questioned Scar Chest on the previous evening.

For a few moments, Caleb lost himself in reminiscing and pondering. He wondered what Old Abel must have thought about him on his first wolf hunt as they had sat on this same boulder. The world had changed since then, but the boulder had not. For Caleb, this was a comforting thought somehow. Would the world go on changing as fast as it had in his lifetime? And what about himself? Would he ever change? Would he ever make up for so many lost years? He fended off the question. The years had passed, sure, but not all the time had been lost. He might not have had *her*, but he had had a few friends, and…

Caleb stopped his mind from thinking. Now he doubted his decision to tell the love secrets to the nameless sheep. It had been a bad idea, yes. Better to forget some things entirely. He tried to forget. He could not so he settled for merely burying his thoughts as he had done countless times before.

Overhead, a golden quarter moon floated upon an ocean of silver starlight, but the valley, for the most part, remained dark.

The Shepherds had finished positioning themselves, and except for the cheerless moan of the wind upon the rocks and the occasional weak whimper of a frightened sheep, silence had prevailed.

Caleb sat still and listened. Though his ears had grown old, his hearing had remained sharp. He could hear Andrew breathing. Time passed.

Caleb reminded himself not to think too much about days long gone. He rolled onto his side, then back onto his stomach, then back onto his side. He feared the blood trails might have been in vain. He heard no wolf sounds: no growling, no grunting, no panting. Then something changed. Caleb felt it. Something or some things had entered the valley. The sheep stirred. A lamb cried out. Then nothing. Silence. Time. Nothing.

Then... the flock screamed. Caleb rolled onto his stomach and clapped his hands three times.

In an instant, Andrew Scar Chest sprang to his feet, and Caleb said, "Here, give me your hand. Help me up."

Like red and orange flowers blossoming on a black wall, the shepherds' torches flared upon the valley rim. As Andrew helped Caleb find his balance, a sharp pain ran down Caleb's back and into his right leg, but for the moment, Caleb could not bother about that. He lit his torch, and Andrew drew his sword. They climbed off the boulder and hurried down to the center of the valley.

"Thish way, the wolvesh comin' thish way," Jerubabel yelled.

The shepherds near Jerubabel tightened the circled on the side of Holder's Creek opposite Caleb.

The wolves turned and splashed through the shallow water, and the shadows of wolves filled the valley.

Marsel Long Legs released an arrow, and being careful not to raise his voice too much, he said, "got him," as the arrow lodged in the wolf's hip.

The wolf yelped and snapped at the arrow's shaft but to no avail, and Andrew Scar Chest stabbed the suffering brute through the rib cage.

The pack scattered, and the brotherhood fell upon each wolf with the necessary violence. The shepherds killed five wolves and left the bodies to lie where they fell.

They returned to their places and extinguished their torches.

The night wore on. Two or three times, Caleb heard Andrew begin to snore, and when he did, he prodded him with the torch handle, and Andrew's entire body would jerk and quiver.

Twice Caleb clapped three times, and twice the Brotherhood killed wolves: twenty-three in all.

The third time Caleb clapped, the brotherhood killed two medium sized black bears.

The fourth time Caleb clapped, the shepherds' torches blazed, the circle tightened, and they saw: nothing.

At a steady pace, the hunters moved close to the center of the valley and to the flock of sacrificial lambs, most of which had died by that time.

Nothing.

They examined both the dead and living animals, and among them, they found something unaccounted for, a thing quite unprecedented and unexplainable.

A sheep's leg remained tied to its stake, but the rest of the body had disappeared. It was gone, taken, but by what? When? How? They examined the soft dirt beside Holder's Creek, and after a short search, they saw what Andrew Scar chest had seen at Farmer Hunley's: a giant bear track. They scratched their heads in disbelief, partly because they could not believe that a bear so large had entered the region but mostly because they could not believe that such a creature had slipped past them and had taken one of their sheep without being seen or heard.

All at once, the gravity of the situation struck the fellowship. It was out there. A monstrosity of a bear was out there, somewhere just beyond the reach of their torchlight. Without saying one word, the shepherd brothers moved close to one another. Facing outward, they formed a ring.

"Well, which way did it go?" Caleb asked.

No one wanted to move from the comfort of the ring, but someone had to. Andrew Scar Chest followed the bear's tracks for a few seconds and pointed toward the south ridge: the high side of the valley, the place where John the Beer Drinker and Parson Rivers were likely to be asleep.

"Let's go," Caleb said, "Must be done."

"Must be done," Billy and Willy agreed at the same time.

The fellowship scampered up the steep wall of the valley's high side. They saw the bear lean over John the Beer Drinker's body and nibble his shoulder. They howled and screamed, and the noise surprised the bear, and John, quite sober after having slept most of the night and having been roused from sleep by a bear bite, got up and ran toward them.

The bear turned to Parson Rivers, but the parson never so much as stirred in his sleep.

68

"Quick, shoot it, Andrew," Caleb said.

"I can't. I might hit the parson."

"Then shoot straight up," Caleb said. "You might scare it away."

Andrew shot his gun into the air.

The parson awoke and looked into the huge bear's mouth. He smelled and felt the bear's foul breath. He tried to shout, but he could not. He could make no noise at all. He could not move.

When the bear heard the shot, it turned from Parson Rivers. It stood on its hind paws, and Timothy Peg Leg released an arrow that hit it in the center of its body. The bear roared in pain and swatted at the arrow, and the arrow dislodged and fell to the ground.

"Move, parson," Caleb said. "Get away from it."

The parson did not move.

"Andrew, fire again," Caleb said.

"I can't. My powder's in my sack." Andrew said.

"Then go get your sack."

"I'll need the torch."

"Here," Caleb said. "Take it, but give me your spear."

Andrew took the torch and sprinted toward the far side of the valley.

The shepherds with bows and arrows joined Timothy in shooting at the bear. The arrows bothered the bear, but they did not seem to hurt it much. The shepherds continued releasing arrows until they had only a few left, and then they looked to Caleb for direction.

Caleb did not wish to say it, but he had no choice: "Spears and swords. Let's go. Now!"

The shepherds circled the bear. Those holding torches lifted them high. The spear and sword wielders moved toward the bear and the parson. The bear growled, roared, and turned around twice.

Suddenly the parson grabbed one of the broken arrow shafts and stabbed the bear on the leg.

"Stop that," Caleb yelled. "Get away from it!"

The parson crawled out of the circle. Caleb could see the bear clearly now, a mass of brown fur, twice as tall as Marsel Long Legs, three times as broad as Orfel Little Mountain. The bear's head looked as big around as a washtub. The white of the bear's teeth contrasted with the dark red blood that dripped from its mouth. The bear's eyes and ears were small, almost hidden.

"Tighten the circle," Caleb shouted, and the brotherhood, each member trembling and groaning, moved toward the bear.

Mud Face Richard pricked the bear's neck with the point of his spear, and the bear slapped the spear away with cat-like speed. Mud Face circled behind the ring of shepherds and picked up his spear fifteen feet beyond them.

The bear charged at Loak the Fat, but as it did, the shepherds moved close to Loak, poked the bear with their spears and forced it back into the center of the ring.

"We won't hold him much longer," Caleb said. "This one's seen battle. We're not wearing it out. It's wearing us out and looking for our weak spots. Andrew! Where are you? Get back here."

Andrew did not answer, and as Caleb spoke, the bear lowered itself to all fours and charged. Caleb had not intended to do any of the fighting. At his age, he felt he should be doing the torch holding and the instructing, but now he had to fight.

Old reflexes took control of Caleb's hands and arms. He gripped the sword, stood motionless, and sliced at the bear's broad side. The bear stopped, stepped back, and got onto its hind paws, covering Caleb with its shadows

"Andrew! Get back here with that gun!" Caleb shouted.

He knew he could not fight this bear, not in his old age anyway. If he were twenty years younger, perhaps, but not now.

Arrows had done little harm. What, then? No time to think.

"Run, all of you," Caleb shouted. "I'll hold him off, and you run. He's too big to…"

The bear opened wide its mouth and with great speed and force, lowered its weight onto Caleb, knocking the old man on his back.

Caleb heard Andrew's gun then. The bear backed away from Caleb and got back onto its hind paws. Caleb breathed out a quick prayer and crawled toward Andrew Scar Chest, who stood reloading his gun. The fellowship had not run away as Caleb had instructed, but they had clustered in one place, assuming a more defensive posture.

"I had to fire in the air again. Couldn't risk hitting you," Andrew said.

"Just reload," Caleb said, "and the rest of you, spread out."

Caleb took the torch from Nick the Sick's hand, and he and Andrew drew near to the giant bear.

"It's us or him, Andrew," Caleb said, and Andrew fired.

Blam! The sound echoed around the valley. The Bear's body turned and fell to the ground. The bear roared and growled and even whimpered, but it did not lie still. Instead, it got up and ran away, and the shepherds could do nothing to stop it from going.

With much emotion and volume, Parson Rivers voiced a prayer of thanksgiving.

John the Beer Drinker's body lay curled and trembling on the ground, and Mud Face Richard stooped to examine him.

"He's bleeding real bad," Richard said. "I think we're going to have to burn him."

John did not respond. Though he had not lost consciousness, he had lost awareness of what was happening. Mud Face thought this a good thing.

"Come here with the torches," he said, "and somebody burn him. He'll die if somebody doesn't burn him."

"Well, I for one, can't do it," Nick the Sick said, "why don't you do it, Mud Face?"

"I can't do it either," Mud Face said, "but somebody's got to do it."

Most of the shepherds shook their heads *no*, and Caleb said, "Give me your torch, Mud Face. Must I do everything?"

Caleb stabbed John's shoulder with the tip of the torch, and a quiet but horrible sound came from John's throat.

The shepherds turned their heads.

Caleb stabbed deeper, driving the fire into John's flesh, scorching, charring, and searing. He yanked the torch away.

"That should do it," he said, "but we'll have to watch him close."

The night passed. The Sun rose, and the shepherds did the nor-

71

mal thing that people do after times of great distress and danger. They made jokes, and since they had slept little since the previous morning, most of their witticisms seemed very funny.

"Good thing the bear bit you, John. Made the poor thing so drunk it couldn't fight back," Billy said.

"If it had bit the parson instead of you, John, we'd all be dead now," Willy added.

John could not take such insult without answering back: "Yes, and if the bear had eaten one of you but not the other, what would it have mattered? Nobody needs two of the same thing unless it's gloves or shoes."

Billy and Willy laughed.

"Say, parson, no praying this week. You skinned your knees too bad crawling away from your hairy girlfriend," Nick the Sick said.

"Oh, leave him alone," Marsel Long Legs said, "the parson BEARly survived."

"Yes, but the parson is always preaching on BEARing one another's burdens," Nick argued.

So forth and so on the shepherds joked until at last Caleb said: "Enough of this! It's become unBEARable."

Except for the bear's escape, the shepherds counted their hunt a success, and even the action against the giant bear had not been a complete failure. They studied its tracks and saw that Andrew had managed to blow off part of its right front paw. They worked until noon, skinning wolves, bear, and sheep. They agreed that Caleb should receive the largest bear hide, and he thanked the brethren for their consideration of his age.

After lunch, the brethren rolled out their blankets for a nap.

Caleb fell asleep fast. He then fell into a deep sleep. Then he fell into the deepest sleep he had known in years, but even that sleep got deeper. In that final, very deep sleep, he dreamed a clear dream, a deeper dream than any of the dreams that made him cry on the night he listened to Clara's singing.

He dreamed of things he had mentioned to but had not discussed at length with the sacrificial lamb. He dreamed of that which he feared, of things far more terrible than any bear, of things capable not only of ripping and devouring the flesh, but of ripping and devouring the soul as well. He dreamed of love, of course.

The dream began, as it always did, with *her* eyes.

SEVEN

Brown eyes, dark but shining, liquid but fiery, friendly but questioning, sweet but forbidding, sad but smiling. Sometimes her soul seemed to reside thousands of miles behind her eyes in a place where no one but she had ever gone or ever would go. At other times her soul seemed to reside immediately behind her eyes, or rather, seemed to *be* her eyes. The dream always began with her eyes, just her eyes.

Then the eyes vanished from the dream, and a flurry of visions of Caleb's early life followed: his father's death, his mother's being forced to move out of the country cottage and into the village, his going to work at age ten to help his mother put food on the table, and his beloved activities in the church.

The visions subsided, and a dream as vivid as real life (or perhaps more vivid if such a thing is possible) followed:

He saw himself as he had appeared more than fifty years ago during his late teen years, a tall young man with black hair, a square jaw, broad shoulders, muscles like living rocks, and a long crooked nose.

Young Caleb sat on a bench in the little chapel behind Merrydale Church waiting for Old Parson Glick to come lead the weekly young people's early morning prayer service, except there were no young *people* there. Early mornings and young people did not mix, and as was the case every Wednesday, only Young Caleb bothered to attend. He rubbed his hands together several times and shifted in his seat. It was past time to begin. Where could the old man be?

The door opened, but to Caleb's astonishment, another young person entered. She must have been new to Merrydale, he thought, because he had never seen her. Caleb noticed her pleasant brown eyes first of all. Then he noticed her well-sculpted face, her long brown hair, her thin body, her delicate pink lips, and her innocent smile. She wore modest clothes: a yellow dress and brown shoes. She looked sweet, not overwhelmingly glamorous but definitely attractive. For this girl he did not feel "love at first sight" or anything like it, but he did feel a sort of "softness at first sight," an immediate desire to protect her, though he could not imagine why he should feel such a thing.

He smiled and said, "Hello."

"Am I late? Have I missed the prayer? I'm always late for everything, and I apologize. My name's Angelica by the way. What's yours?" she said as she sat down beside Caleb.

"Caleb's my name," he answered, "and I don't guess you're late since the parson hasn't come yet, and no, you haven't missed the prayer since the parson hasn't been here to say it."

"Good. Nice to meet you, Caleb." she said.

Silence followed. Caleb looked around the room several times. He wanted to talk with her, but he could not think of anything to say.

Fortunately she started the conversation: "So what is there to do in this town?"

"Well, there's...uh... well, there's church." Caleb said and abruptly changed the subject. "Where are you from?"

She looked uncomfortable, as if Caleb's simple question had been too private in nature, too penetrating.

"I'm from up the coast, and you?" she asked.

"I'm from here, born and raised just outside of town," he said. "What brings you to Merrydale?"

Angelica squirmed in her seat. She shook her head and sighed.

"Mother said people would ask, and you're the first person I've met. Guess she was right, huh?"

"What? I'm sorry, I... have I asked something wrong? I apologize, seriously I..." Caleb started.

"No," she said, "you haven't asked anything wrong. I wasn't ready for it yet, that's all, but here goes anyway: my father left us, plain and simple. Mother grew up in Merrydale, and she moved back last week so we could live with my grandparents, and that suits me fine because I love my grandparents very much. That's the story. That's what brings me here."

"I'm sorry to hear it," Caleb said.

"Well, don't be," Angelica said, "he was a liar, and he was lazy. Mother says we're better off without him."

The possibility of anyone being better off without his father was a concept that had never entered Caleb's thoughts. The idea seemed strange.

"Oh," he said and changed the topic again. "Look! The sun is coming up. You won't see the east window any prettier than you will see it in a couple of minutes."

They watched the growing glow in the window to their right. The numerous colors of the stained glass brightened, opened, and intensified. Illuminated by the early morning sun, the resurrection scene depicted in the glass, though not remotely realistic in style, seemed to present the truth of life conquering death in a way that no other medium could.

"Wow!" Angelica said. "Gives me chill bumps."

"Makes me feel warm all over," Caleb agreed.

As do most church buildings, the little chapel amplified noises, and their almost whispered words came out of their mouths as swelling sounds. Therefore they spoke in tones that gave their conversation a feeling of intimacy though they kept the topics light and upbeat. Caleb liked Angelica from the start. He felt as if he had known her for a long time. He felt, even then, that he had met a true friend or at least someone who could become a true friend.

Caleb's dream skipped ahead three months. He saw Angelica and himself sitting beside Holder's Creek, buttering bread and eating it with honey. So vivid was the memory of the flavors that if any of the shepherds had been awake, they would have seen Old Caleb licking his lips and drooling between snores.

"Angelica," he said in the dream, "you're one of the best friends I've ever had. In fact, I think you *are* my best friend. I feel like I can tell you anything."

"I feel the same way," Angelica said. "I've never had a friend like you before. You're a good person, Caleb, and everybody knows it. You're Parson Glick's right arm, I guess you know. If he didn't have you to do the handiwork on the buildings, the church would fall to pieces. Great things are in store for you, Caleb, many great things."

By the time Angelica finished speaking, Caleb felt a new sensation. After his father's death, he had closed his heart to everyone except his mother and Parson Glick, but during their picnic beside Holder's Creek, he opened it just enough to allow Angelica inside. He embraced her in his soul, and the embrace was more than a friendly embrace. Caleb began to love her as a man loves a woman, but he did not tell her that. He thought he should wait until he could look into her eyes and see the love of a woman for a man.

Caleb smiled in his sleep, and the dream became a stream of thematically connected but chronologically disjointed visions of Young Caleb and Angelica. He saw himself with her, walking upon lush, green hills in summer, through rich golden hayfields in autumn, over glistening, white snow in winter, and among pink, blossoming flowers in spring.

He dreamed of the way they laughed at their many little inside jokes. He dreamed of their talks about their fathers. Those had been the most personal talks of all. Angelica admitted that even if her father were a lazy liar, she missed him and wanted nothing more than to see him again.

Caleb, who usually buried his feelings, said that sometimes he wanted to die so he could go to Heaven to see his father. He cried on Angelica's shoulder, and she cried on his shoulder. They shed many tears together. They embraced from time to time. They got to see each other as often as they wished, but they wrote each other letters anyway, and they both signed them with love.

"But what kind of love?" Caleb wondered after almost a year had passed.

Every day Caleb looked into her eyes, hoping to see the love of a woman for a man, but he did not think he saw it. But how could it not be there? If love existed at all, how could it not be there?

"Surely she loves me," he thought, *"but..."*

Over the course of months, he saw many lights in her eyes, sweet and beautiful radiances, but he also saw deep and mysterious shadows, dark places he could not reach, inscrutabilities that captured and enslaved him.

Caleb felt that if he did not speak his true love to Angelica, the fire at the core of his being would burn him to death. He had to tell her. He built up his courage. He told himself that she must love him as he loved her. Yes, he convinced himself of it.

The dream slowed down. The proceedings of mere seconds seemed to transpire over the course of years, ages even: a late summer day drew to a close. Caleb and Angelica stood beneath the enormous limbs of an old oak tree in a field on the outskirts of town. The sun was setting.

Old Caleb could see it all too clearly. He knew what was coming but he could not stop it. He could not wake up.

"Angelica, you know I care about you very much, maybe more than I've ever cared about anyone or anything," Young Caleb said, "and I would like for us to be more than friends. I would like to be your boyfriend, and I would like you to be my girlfriend."

Her lips, so delicate and so precious to Caleb, twisted themselves into a mixed expression of distaste, sadness, and sorrow. Her eyes frowned. The dream halted. That look on her face froze in his memory and lasted forever.

Caleb mumbled and cried in his sleep.

Parson Rivers, who was sleeping not far from him, woke up,

looked at him, and thought Caleb must have been dreaming about the giant bear. The parson shook his head, rolled over, and went back to sleep.

Angelica spoke: "I don't know, Caleb. That would be awkward."

The dream halted again, and though she said it once, he heard it a million times: "I don't know, Caleb. That would be awkward." Again, again, and again, like a rusty old knife plunging into his heart, stabbing, ripping, and devouring every happy thing, the words persisted: "I don't know, Caleb. That would be awkward."

Caleb groaned out loud, and the Parson and Billy and Willy woke up.

"He's having a bad dream," Billy said.

"He's having a nightmare," Willy said.

"He's probably dreaming about the bear," Parson Rivers said.

"I agree," Billy said.

"I think so too," Willy said. "Should we wake him?"

"No," Parson Rivers said. "Let him get it out of his system. Dreams are good for us that way."

The dream returned to a somewhat normal speed. Caleb's and Angelica's relationship hobbled along on broken legs for a few months after he revealed his true feelings to her, but instead of loving her less, he loved her more, and if Caleb had felt that he was losing his mind before he asked Angelica to be his girl, he felt that he was sinking into the depths of hell itself afterward, not merely losing his mind, but having his mind burned by a merciless fire. Torment, agony, sadness, and darkness devoured his internal life. He often prayed to die. To love her dearly and to be close to her without being able to express the depths of all the love he felt for her crushed him. He began to run, to sprint, scuttle, scamper, scurry, dart, dash, hasten, and hurry everywhere he went. He ran through open prairie. He ran by the sea. He ran up and down the streets of Merrydale. He even ran through forests where tree limbs slapped and smacked his face until he bled. When he ran, he came close to forgetting, but he could not run all the time, and he could not banish her from his mind.

When he could stand the pain no more, he sat down at his mother's table and wrote Angelica a letter.

"Dear Angelica, I loved you once, but I wasn't good enough for you, was I? All you wanted was some kind of friend and a shoulder to cry on. You did not want me as the man that I am. Well, I am a man, and you will love me as a man, or you will not love me at all. I cannot stand being around you anymore. You are no longer welcome at our house. Do not come here again. Do not speak to me again. In fact, I never want to see you again. Love, Caleb"

His conscience told him not to give her the letter, to burn it and to forget it. Giving her such a mean spirited letter would constitute wickedness and immorality. It would stand contrary to every good thing he had been taught. His heart pounded so hard he could hear its beat and feel its throb in his head. He tried to silence the voice of his conscience, but he could not. He would give her the letter, yes, he would give the ungrateful little strumpet the letter she deserved.

He delivered it to her in person. He knocked on her door, and when she answered, he placed the letter in her hand, and he stomped away without seeing her reaction.

If he had not left, he would have seen that his words hurt her more than he would have imagined, that his words cut her heart in much the same way that her words had cut his heart, maybe even deeper. He would have seen tears running down her cheeks. He would have seen that she loved him more than he could have believed, maybe more than he loved her, even if she did not love him as a woman loves a man.

No, she did not love him the way he wished. If she could have forced herself to love him that way, she would have done so without hesitation or second thought, but she simply did not love him as woman loves a man. This was unchangeable and it was not her fault.

"This is the way of love" said a disembodied voice in Caleb's dream, "If love for a man burns in the heart of a woman, many waters cannot quench it, but if a woman does not love a man, he may give all the substance of his house for her heart, and his offering will be rejected and scorned."

Caleb recognized the saying and rolled about on his blanket, screaming like an insane man.

All the shepherds rose and stood around him.

"This is no good," Timothy Peg Leg said. "We've got to wake him up. He'll hurt himself if we don't."

"No," Parson Rivers said, "the bear must have scared him awfully bad. He's got to dream the fear out of his mind. He won't hurt himself, I promise. Don't touch him."

The dream broke up into flashes of memory.

Young Caleb vowed a terrible vow: He swore he would make something great of himself. He would earn immense fame. He would perform deeds so illustrious and grand that many would celebrate his name. Exalted, splendid, and lofty he would grow.

Angelica would know of his greatness, and she would be sorry, and she would love him.

Caleb saw himself enlisting in the King's Army. He saw himself crossing the sea to do battle. He saw himself stabbing, slashing, spearing, stomping, slitting, and slaughtering. He saw the Caleb that, in accordance with his vow, became the topic of legend, the brave, bloody, berserk soldier of the big war.

The dream skipped ahead a year, and he heard his commander's voice: "You have fought with valiance. You have fought as bold men. You are not like these wretched dogs who cower behind the walls of their castle. You are men who labor with the sword, and today your labor shall be finished and rewarded. Today we take the castle!

"As I have told you before, slay all the enemy, but spare the enemy king. He must remain alive, for he knows much that our king wishes to know. Take not his life or his royal treasures, for they shall become the property of our king, but of whatever else you find, you may take as much as you desire."

Caleb saw himself amid a company of his fellow soldiers heaving a battering ram against the castle's gate until it burst open. In they poured, and Caleb led the battle. He stormed about the court-yard, slaying all he met. He broke through doors and entered cham-bers. He chased down and killed as many of the enemy as would not surrender. At last he entered the royal chamber, the throne room of the king. No other soldier walked with him as he entered.

The old king, arrayed in his finest attire, sat upon his throne.

"Though I do not welcome you, I yield to you. Your king's armies have defeated my armies. You may send word to your com-mander that our war is over and that I wait in my chamber to for-mally surrender." the king said.

Young Caleb stood still a moment and considered his circum-stances. He remembered Angelica's eyes, and he remembered what he had never seen in her eyes. He remembered that he did not fight for king or country, but for honor and glory. He devised a plan.

He closed the chamber door behind him and approached the throne.

"Young man, I know the long standing orders of your king. My life must be spared. Now go and speak to your commander." the king said through a nervous smile.

Caleb laughed. Instantly he hated the arrogance in the man's voice. He hated the man too, even more in person than he had hated him in story, and that would justify what he planned to do.

"Never mind my commander," he said. "Surrender to me, Caleb of Merrydale."

The king laughed at him, and when he did, Caleb chopped off his head and finished the first part of his plan.

The dream skipped ahead. A military transport vessel docked at the Port of Merrydale, and Young Caleb disembarked. He threw his pack over his shoulders and walked, head high and chest out, down Merrydale's main street.

Today would be the happiest and brightest day of his life. He would make a donation to the church. He would see his mother, and Angelica, he felt sure, would become his girl. Surely she had missed him. Surely she had seen the error of her ways by now, but even if she had not, he had a way to win her heart. Surely no woman could resist, he thought. Many eyes turned to watch him as he strode along. The people whispered to each other stories of his greatness, stories that had sailed back across the sea before he had, stories that had grown more glorious with each retelling. He heard their whispers. He saw their expressions of wonder and awe, and he could not stop himself from smiling.

He then heard something different in their whispers and saw something different in their expressions. Some people shook their heads. What was this? He stopped. His heart sank. He knew.

He ran to the church.

"Parson Glick, Parson Glick!" he shouted, and the echoes of his shouts filled the church building.

Parson Glick did not appear, but a young man wearing parson's garb walked into the church from a side door.

"May I help you?" the young man asked.

"Who are you?" Caleb asked.

"My name is Rivers. I'm the new parson here. Now, how can I help you?" the young man asked.

"Where is Parson Glick?" Caleb asked.

"Were you a friend of his?" the young man asked. "Oh, I understand. You want to see the grave marker, don't you?

"What do you mean? What are you talking about? Has Parson Glick died?"

"Oh, you didn't know? I'm terribly sorry. I didn't mean to..." The young man started speaking but stopped suddenly.

Caleb dropped his pack, sat on a pew, and buried his face in his hands, and young Parson Rivers sat beside him. This was bad, but could this have been the very bad thing he had seen in the faces of the townspeople? He hoped so, but he did not think so.

"He was like a father to me," Caleb said.

A look of understanding and dread came upon the young parson's face, and he said, "You wouldn't happen to be named *Caleb*, would you?"

"Yes, why?" Caleb said, but he did not have to ask. He knew. He knew the death of the old parson was the beginning of the day, not the end of it, and certainly not the worst of it.

"I will be right back," the young parson said.

He returned with the young Sister Kate who held a glass of water, a warm washcloth, and a towel.

The moment the two of them stood before him, Caleb said, "My mother is dead, isn't she?"

Sister Kate and Parson Rivers glanced at each other and shook their heads *yes*.

Caleb wept, and Sister Kate offered him the washcloth and the towel. He refused them both, lifted his pack, rose, and trudged out of the church, his head hanging, his legs shaking. He walked alone for half the day. He screamed at the sky and shook his fists and fell down more than once.

When he had all but lost his voice, he said: "I will find consolation in the arms of my true love."

He walked to Angelica's grandparent's house and knocked on their door. Nothing in the world moves faster than big news in a small town so all of Merrydale, including Angelica's grandparents, knew of Caleb's wild conduct. Angelica's grandmother barely opened the door.

"Where is Angelica?" Caleb asked.

"She no longer lives here," the old woman said.

"Where does she live?" Caleb asked.

"She lives with her husband," the old woman said, and she slammed and locked the door.

Caleb's body convulsed, and he cried out in his sleep. Jerubabel extended his hand to wake him, but Parson Rivers grabbed Jerubabel's hand.

"I said don't wake him. I know about dreams, and I know Caleb. If we're standing here when he wakes up, he's not going to be happy. Come on everybody, back to your blankets. If he wakes up, pretend you're asleep," Parson Rivers said.

The shepherds obeyed, and the dream continued.

Caleb saw himself in a small field on the edge of the forest north of Merrydale. The day had not ended, but the yellow sun would soon drop behind the tree line. He thought of killing himself, but he did not believe he could do it.

"Oh God," he prayed, "Since I was a boy, I have served You. I have not served You very well, I know, and I have done many wong things. I am ashamed of what I am about to ask You. Lord, I believe in You, but please help my unbelief. Please do something, anything, to show me you're there and that you love me. Send me a sign. Anything. I just want to know that You love me. Oh God, please help me."

Young Caleb thought of a number of ways God could answer the prayer. Perhaps a kind hearted forester would emerge from the trees and say that things would get better. Perhaps an angel would descend and embrace young Caleb in its wings. Perhaps God Himself would speak out loud.

Nothing happened.

He cried so hard that crying hurt. His eyes and face muscles ached. In his heart, he gave up on living, but he could not bring himself to turn his sword upon his own flesh. He would have to go on, but he would not believe in God or love anymore, and he absolutely would not believe in hope. But then...

He stood to walk back to Merrydale to rent a room for the night, and just after he got on his feet, just after hope evaporated, and just after he felt emptied of all goodness and happiness, he looked up.

High above him in an overcast evening sky shone a rainbow.

The rainbow communicated the presence and love of God to him. In his heart, he called it a miracle. Had the laws of nature been suspended to produce the rainbow? Probably not. Was the rainbow anything but a natural occurrence, the interaction of water and light? Probably not. But the timing of it, the perfect timing of it: *Sometimes a miracle is in the timing of things*, Caleb thought.

Mysterious are the ways of Providence, far beyond the searching of human understanding, Caleb thought as he dreamed. Who has known the ways of God? Who has understood? All things are from His hand. There is timing in it all in the joy and in the pain. The Almighty is working out the plot of a great story, and we sense it. We know it. Sometimes he leads us through a dark valley to show us the strange and beautiful flowers He has planted there. Sometimes He leads us upon a sunny hilltop only to show us the mangled carcass of a fallen eagle. Strange are the ways of God. Strange they are indeed: Just enough miracles to disallow unbelief. Just enough hurt to disallow an absolute and perfect faith.

Old Caleb saw young Caleb digging a hole beside the chimney of a country cottage. He flung dirt high in the air and tossed clods of earth as fast he could. Dirt stuck in his hair and on his face. He sweated and breathed hard, but otherwise he worked silently beneath a full moon.

Jerubabel said: "He shtill looksh nervoush, but I believe he'sh calmin' down shome."

"Yes," Parson Rivers said, "the bear is going away now."

Old Caleb saw young Caleb drop something into the hole, and Old Caleb knew what it was. Young Caleb looked in every direction as he filled the hole. No one had seen, and he felt better.

The dream continued, Old Caleb rested easier, and even the nervousness seemed to depart.

Jerubabel said, "I guessh you're right, parson. He looksh like he'sh gonna be all right."

The shepherds returned to their blankets.

Caleb dreamed one last scene, a scene that was not a memory of things that had happened. No, the last scene, the one with which the dream always ended, was pure fantasy, and it was Caleb's least favorite and most favorite part of the dream.

EIGHT

Caleb's dream ended with this scene: Angelica, the only girl he ever loved, his greatest loss, his greatest hope, his greatest agony, and the most painful secret of his soul, stands in a golden field. Warm sunlight creates a halo about her face and hair. She smiles at him.

Caleb cried out loud in his sleep, and all the shepherds heard. He shouted Angelica's name. He whispered it too, and he said this out loud, "Angelica! Oh Angelica, Angelica. My sweet Angelica. Why did you go, Angelica?"

"Who is Angelica?" Marsel Long Legs whispered to Parson Rivers.

"I don't know," Parson Rivers said, "and don't ask him. Caleb's a private person, and he wouldn't appreciate any questions about his dream. Don't even let him know we knew he dreamed. Let's try to get some sleep."

The brotherhood slept. They awoke late in the afternoon and walked to Farmer Quigley's to retrieve their sheep and goats. They took their flocks and parted, each agreeing to blow his horn to alert the entire brotherhood should he discover any evidence of the great bear.

Caleb had been aching to speak with his animals since before the wolf hunt so as soon as he was out of hearing of the rest of the shepherds, he began: "When you get old, you're supposed to lose your memory, aren't you Brown Tooth? Yes, of course you are, and I'm losing my memory, or at least parts of it, but not the parts I'd like to lose. I can't recall half of what I do these days, but things I did fifty years ago are as fresh on my mind as morning air on a mountain.

"Go on, Pretty Girl; ask me something about what I did three days ago. What's that? Want to know what I ate for breakfast? I can't recall. Which hill did I sleep on? Oh, I'm sure you remember, but I don't.

"What's that you say, Dog Bit? Why am I acting upset and worried?

"Why should I tell you? Telling secrets is what opened up my mind for a troublesome dream, and I shouldn't tell anymore of them.

"What's that, Swallowed Medicine? You say if I would tell the secrets I wouldn't have the bad dreams about them? Say I need to confess all, huh? Should go have a talk with Parson Rivers, eh? Yes, and maybe he should confess to me…"

Caleb heard a rustling noise in the brush beside the trail. At once he stopped walking and talking, and his hand shot into the folds of his clothes. He pulled out his knife. He backed away from the place from which the sound came. He removed a roll of twine from his pack, unwound some, and cut a length of it. He wrapped the twine around the handle end of the staff and the knife's grip and secured the two together, making a spear of them. He reached back into the pack for his torch and oil.

The light of the setting sun flowed over the tops of the bushes and trees beside the trail, but shadows and half-darkness clotted in the brush beneath their twigs and branches. Caleb lit his torch with two purposes in mind: to see what he might see and to defend himself if necessary. In his mind, he pictured the monstrous bear rising from the brush to seek revenge for its hurt paw, roaring, growling, charging, and devouring his flock and himself.

"No, no," Caleb whispered to his flock. "It's probably just a thrush."

He heard the noise again, and this time it was louder.

"Who's there?" Caleb asked.

No one answered, and Caleb said, "Whatever it is, Dead Eye, it's not a person. Probably just a thrush, don't you think?"

Dead Eye did not answer.

"Well, let's find out."

Caleb stooped and thrust both his spear and torch toward the edge of the trail. He struck the underbrush with the spear, and a raven cried out, beat its wings, rose into the air, became a silhouette in the sunset for an instant, and flew away.

"Like I said," Caleb continued, "only a bird, not a thrush but a raven, and that's close enough, don't you think?"

He extinguished his torch.

"Now, where were we? Oh, you wanted to know about the dream, eh, Big Head? It's not important, or probably it is important, that is to say I don't think the dream came for no reason, but I don't think it came for its own sake. Something's happening inside me, and I don't fully know what it is, but I fully don't think I like it."

"What do I mean, Pretty Girl? What do I mean? Hmmm. What I mean is: I'm torn asunder and divided up like a side of beef in a pen full of badgers. First, there's my cottage, and it is *my* cottage even if I don't hold the title to the land it sits on. If I went to the title holder and told him about the situation, he would bounce this Susan annoyance right out of there. And why shouldn't I? She has no business out here. This is shepherd territory, the outer reaches, and it's not always a safe place. I need the cottage for you sheep and goats, it being a fine place to shut you in at night. I need it for myself too. After all, I'm an old man with a tired back. I shouldn't have to sleep outside like an animal during this dark time of year. Furthermore, you all know that something is buried beneath the chimney of my Christmas cottage. You don't know what it is...

"Eh? What's that Brown Tooth? No, I will not tell you what it is, and you know better than to ask. As I was trying to say, you don't know what it is, but you know it must not be found. The idea of Susan staying in the cottage scares me, scares me for my sake, sure, but scares me for her sake too. No one saw what I did to the king and no one saw what I buried beneath the chimney, or at least I've always told myself that no one saw. Who knows for sure? Buried things have a way of unburying themselves, and words whispered in closets are eventually shouted from rooftops. That my secret has remained such for this long time borders on being miraculous, don't you think, Big Head?

"Get rid of the Susan problem, and be done with it, Lop Ear, that would be easy enough, just send her packing, but I can't do that. There's the little girl to consider. Susan's pride is no good for Clara, and I should do something about it. Clara needs to sing in the Christmas concert, deserves to sing in the Christmas concert, and will sing in the Christmas concert if I can help it. But that's just it! I can't help it. That's the problem. I tried to help, and look where that got us. Now I'm banished from seeing the little girl, and that's a sad fact in and of itself. I'd intended to be good to her, maybe get her a nicer Christmas present than the island trinket her father gave her, something nicer than anything her mother can afford. The hides, er, sorry to, uh, talk about them like this, but the hides could go far toward buying a Christmas present. I could get two silvers for each of the wolf hides and four for each of the... well, you'd prob- ably rather not hear about your relatives like that.

"Of course there's Bruker to think about, Dog Bit. I'm not sure who he is or what he's about. I know I don't like him, and I know I've heard bad things about him, but what does that mean? Half of Merrydale doesn't like me, and all of Merrydale's heard bad things about me. Maybe he's not so bad. No! What am I thinking? Of course he's bad. The rigged alley fight proves he's bad, but how bad is he?

"It's none of my business, is it, Big Head? I should just forget about all of it. Who cares what Parson Rivers and Sister Kate are keeping quiet about Susan's upbringing? Who cares that I don't have a cottage this year? Maybe the problem will be gone by next year, or at my age, maybe I'll be gone by next year. Who cares if the little girl sings or doesn't sing in the children's choir? It's not like she will know what she's missing.

"Most of all, Lop Ear, who cares about this Susan character? Sure, she's had a hard life, but haven't we all? She's made her bed. Let her lie in it, right, Pretty Girl? That's what people say, isn't it?"

Caleb stopped walking. He heard another commotion in the brush beside the trail. This time it was much louder. He relit his torch with haste, and he swung his spear and slapped the underbrush.

"Probably not the bear," he mumbled.

The noise grew louder. Caleb backed to the other side of the trail. Opposite the spot where he stood, a thick clump of bushes concealed the source of the sound.

"A bear *could* hide in there," he said.

He saw something move at ground level, something large and noisy.

"Is that a bear's foot, Big Head?"

Caleb gripped his spear and held his torch sideways at arms length.

"Come out of there, whatever you are," he said, and a tremor of nervousness and fear rolled through his body. He swallowed several times.

He shouted: "Come out of there!" And something did come out. A fat, brown jack rabbit hopped onto the trail for a moment and darted off again as soon as its big feet touched the bare, foot-worn path.

"Turns out to be nothing after all, Swallowed Medicine, and isn't that always the case? These people and situations that are eating at me, well, they're all nothing to me. 'Do unto others as you would have them do unto you,' the Bible says, and so I will. I would have people leave me alone, and I'll leave them alone. I'll forget these problems, but I'll keep an eye out for my Christmas cottage. You can believe that."

He extinguished his torch and continued to walk toward the decrepit little stone building under which his big secret lay buried.

As he walked he felt his heart harden, and it felt normal. That he had allowed softness to creep in was abnormal, even if it was softness for an impoverished little girl.

"I've got plenty of friends," he said to his flock, "and I don't need anymore of them."

"What's that you ask, Brown Tooth? How do I define 'friend?' Why do you ask? Because you wish to dispute my claim to having plenty of them? And you wish to join him, Pretty Girl? And so do the rest of you? Very well, a friend is someone you like.

"What? That's not a good enough definition? Why not, Big Head? Because it's easy to like people we barely know, huh? You say I count Parson Rivers' housekeeper a friend but barely know her, and you want to know why I'm so sure she's a true friend. Hmm, you make your point. I will try again. A friend is someone you know fairly well but like anyway. How's that? Still not enough, huh? Why not? Because I know John the Beer Drinker very well, like him very much, but would not trust him with two measly copper coins, you say?

"Again, you make your point. Trust must be a part of it. Very well, a friend is someone you know fairly well, like anyway, and trust fully. How about that for a definition? Say you won't accept it because I've still not said anything about the importance of sacrifice to a friendship?

"Ahh, I'm getting tired of all this. What are you trying to tell me? What's that? No! I have not closed the door to my heart. Yes, I let people in. I'm just careful, that's all. Take Parson Rivers: He's a friend in every sense of whatever definition you are trying to get out of me.

"What's that? You say it's sad when a man's only true friend is his parson and that I'm a weak soul, and you want to know how I've been hurt so badly..."

Caleb heard another rustling in the brush, and it snapped him out of his conversation.

"It's even louder this time," he said.

Only a little light remained in the sky so his torch became a dual necessity, a light and a weapon, and not one more than the other.

"I hope it is the bear, Dog Bit," Caleb said, "I'm tired of this ridiculous talk. A bear, that's a problem for a man to solve, not this silly friendship riddle. Step aside animals, and I'll flush out whatever it is."

Caleb felt confident that another small animal had taken cover in the brush so his eyes grew large and his mouth fell open when he heard a growling sound emanate from the exact place where he heard the rustling.

"Oh my," he mouthed but did not say out loud as he retreated to the far side of the trail. "That's no bird or rabbit."

He stood perfectly still and listened. The thing in the brush stirred, and Caleb recognized the sound of something heavy shifting about on the ground. He continued to listen. He heard slow, even breathing punctuated by an occasional growling sound.

He smiled a little and said, "Whatever it is, Pretty Girl, it's asleep, and I hope it stays that way."

He built up his courage and inched toward the sound being careful to maintain a firm grip on his spear and to keep his torch high. Through a gap in the brush he saw a patch of thick, brown fur.

The thing lying in the brush released a grumbling growl, and Caleb said, "It's a bear alright, and I'm going in on it."

Holding his torch in his left hand and his spear in his right hand, Caleb sprang off the trail, and onto the brush. As he did so, he aimed his spear at the brown patch and drove it down with tremendous force and speed. And then...

Caleb yelled, "Oh, no!" just before the spear struck its target.

At the last fraction of a second, he moved the spear tip aside and landed flat on the chest of Killer Joe!

Thinking he had been attacked, Killer Joe woke up screaming. The torch had fallen to the ground and gone out so all Killer Joe knew was that a large, heavy, furry, creature was upon him.

"A bear!" he screamed. "Aarrgghh!"

Killer Joe beat and clawed at the "bear," and Caleb had no choice but to beat and claw back.

"It's not a bear," Caleb shouted. "It's Old Caleb, the shepherd you met in town."

Killer Joe recognized the voice, but having set himself in motion, he could not discontinue his feeble efforts at fighting off the attack.

"I'm sorry for threatening you, old man. Please don't hurt me anymore," he said.

"And they call you 'Killer,' eh Joe? You're as weak as a day old sheep. What do you kill? House flies?"

They continued to roll about and grapple.

"I'm not weak," Killer Joe protested. "I'm just drunk."

"I suppose that explains why you were sleeping beside the trail, does it?"

"You bet it does."

The fighting slowed, and the conversation picked up speed.

"What are you doing out here?" Caleb asked.

"What's it to you?" Killer Joe smarted off.

For good measure, Caleb punched him in the stomach one last time but not hard enough to knock the wind out of him.

"That's for ripping off the townspeople in Merrydale with a fake fight," Caleb said, "and I will tell you *what it is* to me. In case you haven't noticed, you're not in town anymore. This is shepherd territory, and that means it's *my* territory, and everything that happens out here is something to me, and you will answer me. Now, again, what are you doing out here?"

"Going to see a friend," Killer Joe said.

"Bruker?" Caleb asked.

"Yes."

"In a cabin?"

"Yes."

"With his wife?"

"Yes."

"Hmm, since you're here like this, you may as well tell me all about Bruker," Caleb said.

"Don't make me, old man," Killer Joe pleaded, "He wouldn't like it. Hey, how about I pay you? I've still got some money from the fight."

"I wouldn't want your dirty money, you scoundrel. Now tell me about Bruker."

"I can't do it, old man."

Caleb rolled him onto his stomach, twisted his arm behind his back, and yanked Killer Joe's little finger so far backward that it almost broke.

"Let go," Killer Joe howled.

"I can't do it, young man," Caleb said and pulled Killer Joe's little finger harder.

"Ohh," Killer Joe yelled, "Please don't break my pinky. Ohh, please don't. I'll tell you whatever you want to know."

"Good," Caleb said, releasing some of the pressure on Killer Joe's little finger. "How many wives does he have?"

"Not many," Killer Joe answered.

Caleb reasserted the pressure on Killer Joe's pinky.

"Wow! Stop! Three, I think. Just three. That's not many. Please don't tell the red haired one. She's his Christmas wife."

Caleb slapped him across the back of the head.

"Hey, what was that for?" Killer Joe asked.

"A man ought to be ashamed to talk that way about a woman," Caleb said. "How many children does he have?"

"Who knows? A lot of'em, I guess, ten or more." Killer Joe answered.

Caleb slapped him again.

"What was that for?" Joe asked.

"That was because you called him your friend earlier, and anybody that calls a man like that his friend deserves more than a slap across the back of the head," Caleb answered. "Don't you know what a friend is? A man like Bruker couldn't be a friend to anybody. Where's he from?"

"A town called Pranville. It's down the coast. We both grew up there."

"Who is his father?" Caleb asked.

"He ain't got no father. His mother was a sailor's woman, any sailor's woman, any old time, not that I understand how. She's a fat, ugly cow of a woman, not that I would tell Bruker that." Killer Joe answered.

"You mean she didn't teach him to treat women better than how she had been treated?" Caleb asked.

"Good heavens, no," Joe answered. "She petted him, always let him have his way. Spoiled him."

"And you persist in calling such a man your friend?" Caleb asked.

"Hey, I've got to call somebody my friend, don't I?" Killer Joe said.

"I don't know, and that's a different conversation altogether." Caleb said.

Brown Tooth bleated.

"Anyway," Caleb continued, "What I really want to know is: Would Bruker break more than Susan's heart? Would he hit her? Would he hurt the little girl?"

Killer Joe, who was lying on his stomach with his face shoved toward the ground, turned his head to the side, looked away, and refused to answer.

"Answer!" Caleb said as he pulled back on Killer Joe's little finger. "Answer, or you'll eat dirt. Will he hurt them?"

"I don't know," Killer Joe said. "It depends."

"On what?" Caleb asked.

"How much he's had to drink for one thing," Joe answered.

"And?"

"And what?"

"What's another thing?"

"I can't explain it," Killer Joe said.

Caleb pulled back on his finger and said, "Try!"

"All right, all right, Bruker gets in a mood sometimes. Like him or not, at least he's usually fun, but when he gets in this mood, you'd better steer clear."

"When he's in the mood, does he tell people to steer clear?" Caleb asked.

"Yeah, come to think of it, he does. He always says that when he's nervous, or trying to hide something, or just plain mad. When his other friends and I know he's getting in the mood, we tell one another to steer clear of him."

"Anything else you've got to tell me about him?"

"Nothing you couldn't figure out for yourself. Bruker's no saint, but he *is* my friend, and I would like to go see him now."

"Sorry," Caleb said, "change in plans."

"What do you mean?"

"You won't be going to see him tonight. You'll be heading back to your ship to sleep. You're not welcome at the cottage. In fact, you're not welcome outside of Merrydale."

"Says who?" Killer Joe demanded.

Caleb wrenched his knee into the small of Killer Joe's back.

"Says me."

"You're lucky this time, Old Man, but give me time to sober up, and you won't be so lucky. I'll have the advantage, and you won't be telling me where I can and cannot go."

"Oh, maybe not by myself, I won't," Caleb agreed, "but listen to this…"

Caleb released his hold on Killer Joe's little finger but kept his knee in the small of his back. He reached into his pack and removed a short, polished bullhorn. He blew one short, sharp note on it. Within three seconds, Killer Joe heard horns answering from many directions.

"That," Caleb said, "was a note telling each shepherd within hearing to reveal his location. If I blew three sharp blasts followed by two long ones, you would be dead within the hour. Like I told you, this is shepherd territory. We're the next best things to deputies out here, and we watch out for one another. You'll do what you're told, or you'll endure our punishment. Now, if I let you up, are you going to behave yourself?"

Killer Joe shook his head *yes*.

Caleb picked up his spear and stepped back.

"Get going," he said.

"All right, just give me a second to catch my breath," Killer Joe said.

"No, get going," Caleb said as he popped the backside of Killer Joe's left leg with the blunt side of his spear's knife blade.

Caleb removed a small, blue handkerchief from his pack and

wiped his brow.

"They've been calling me old since I was a young man on account of my hair starting to go gray after the war, but now I really am starting to feel old," he said to no particular sheep or goat.

He continued up the trail until he drew near to his Christmas cottage. He stopped walking at a distance from the cottage that would allow him to remain unobtrusive and inconspicuous yet would provide a good view. There he built a fire, and there he slept until early the next morning when he heard Susan screaming like a crazy woman.

NINE

Susan's voice rang out clear in the December morning air. Caleb got on his feet, picked up his spear, started walking toward his Christmas cottage, but suddenly stopped moving.

"What am I doing, Half Hoof? Her screaming is no concern of mine. Steering clear, that's what I'm supposed to be doing. Susan wanted it that way, didn't she? Besides, I don't even really know Susan.

"No, Pretty Girl, there's no way she's screaming because of the bear. The windows aren't broken. No more of the roof has crumbled, the door opens outward, and it's still in place. The bear's not in the cottage. It's probably just a mouse.

"What, Big Head? You say Susan's a strong woman and would not scream that way about a mouse? You're right. It's probably not a mouse.

"Yes, I know, Brown Tooth. She could be in trouble with Bruker, and she might need help, but what's that to me? She *chose* him. The thing about people who need help is: They DON'T WANT to be helped, Brown Tooth. Don't you know that?

"But you say Clara could be in trouble, Half Hoof? Yes, she could be."

At a faster pace, Caleb resumed his walk toward the cottage.

"Well, if it's Clara in trouble, I'll help out, but if it's just Susan, I don't care if he's knocking her teeth out, it's none of my concern, and I won't do anything about it."

At first, Caleb passed near the cottage but did not stop walking.

He heard Susan say: "How could you bring that thing in here?"

Bruker answered, "Why don't you just shut up, relax, and come back to bed? I'm still sleepy. At least you could have enough courtesy to let me sleep."

"Courtesy? You wannna talk about courtesy? You bring a thing like that into my house…"

"*Our* house," Bruker *corrected* her.

"Uh, yeah, our house. You bring a thing like that into our house without tellin' me, and you have the nerve to speak to *me* about courtesy?" Susan said.

"Aw, come on honey-sweetie-sweetie, relax and come back to bed. It didn't hurt you, did it? It's not even the dangerous kind." Bruker said.

"Well, that's good to know now. Wish I'd known before I woke up with it on my arm." Susan said.

"The warmth probably woke the poor little thing up." Bruker said.

"Get rid of it." Susan said.

"Aww, I don't want to do that. I brought it all the way back from the Islands. I was thinking about giving it to Clara for a Christmas present."

"You'll NOT give my daughter that thing!"

"*Our* daughter," Bruker reminded her.

"Yes, our daughter," Susan continued. You will not give her that thing. Throw it out."

Bruker giggled. "If these things weren't lying around everywhere in the islands, free for the taking, I wouldn't do this, woman."

Caleb saw the bedroom window's shutter open. Something

green dropped out the window and fell to the ground.

He started to tell his sheep it was no concern of his, but curiosity got the best of him, and he did not bother. He approached the thin, green object, which was lying still, lifted it with the tip of his spear and said: "How about that, Dog Bit? A snake. Never saw one like this before."

In the coolness of the morning air, the snake lay torpid, and he tossed it aside without much thought.

"See. It's better not to get involved. Turns out to be hardly anything, not that I would call waking up with a snake on *my* arm 'hardly anything.' Makes me wonder… what sort of grown man carries a snake around in his pocket? I mean I know Bruker's no angel, but a snake in his pocket? To my way of thinking, that's just strange. I wouldn't blame Susan if she threw him out the window with his pet."

Just then, the door opened, and Susan exited the cottage. She looked at Caleb. He looked at her. They rolled their eyes, turned their heads, looked away, and grunted. Neither said a word or acknowledged the other. Susan walked toward Merrydale to work, and Caleb walked in the opposite direction.

"The gray haired old fool," Susan thought.

"The red haired young fool," Caleb thought.

When Susan was out of sight, Caleb circled back around the cottage being careful to keep his distance but remaining close enough to hear any loud noises coming from it. He told his sheep that his only reason for staying near was that the cottage belonged to him, and he had to keep an eye on it, but he thought his sheep and goats suspected otherwise.

At lunchtime, Caleb walked close to the cottage to draw water from the well, but he quickly retreated to a rock on the hillside. He sat down, removed a wooden box from a pack in Big Head's goat cart and lifted its lid, unfolded a towel, unwrapped some bread, cut a slice of cheese, and scooped out some apple jelly.

When Caleb was almost finished with his lunch, Bruker opened the cottage's door, stepped outside, yawned, stretched, and walked to the well to fetch some water for coffee.

The noon sun glowed brilliantly on Bruker's blonde hair. Just before he reached the well, he saw Caleb.

He coughed and in a morning voice said, "Didn't I tell you to leave us alone, old man? What is your problem?"

"You're not in town anymore, Bruker," Caleb said.

"Yeah, so?"

"So out here you don't have your friends to help you."

"I don't need help, old man."

Caleb laughed, "I know what you are. You're a big mama's boy."

"Old man, I will break your neck," Bruker said, throwing out his hand and pointing his finger.

Caleb secretly wished that Bruker would start a fight, but then he remembered how he had sworn off fighting after leaving the army and had not fought anything but wild animals since then. He pretended to yawn and pat his mouth.

"Oh, I'm sure you will," he said.

Bruker looked puzzled. His bold warnings had sent many men cowering, but this Caleb did not seem concerned, much less afraid. He approached Caleb's rock and sat down.

"So, who are you, old man?"

"You know my name. It's Caleb."

"I'm not talking about your name, although it seems I remember it or a name similar to it being important to some of my friends. What I'm talking about is your intentions. What are you about?"

"The way my back is hurting, I feel like I'm about a hundred," Caleb said and tried to chuckle.

"Well then what do you want with Susan? Why did you try to impress her by getting the little girl into the choir? You got a *thing* for Susan?"

"Absolutely not," Caleb answered.

"So it's just this old shack then? Hey, I can understand that, and I'll move Susan and Clara out of it at the end of month if you'll promise to steer clear and not talk to either of them."

"Really? And where would you take them?" Caleb asked.

"I wouldn't take them anywhere. I'd just make Susan move

back into the servant's quarters of whoever it is she cleans for. Her living out here is as much a shock to me as it must have been for you when you found her here."

"And you think you could *make* her move back to town?"

"I could *make* her do just about anything, old man. I can always get people to do what I want, except for you it seems, which is all right with me so long as you…"

"I know, so long as I *steer clear*. I'm getting sick of the expression. Now let me ask you something: What have you got to hide from me? Even though nobody has the heart to tell her the truth, everybody but Susan seems to know about your claming to have other wives, and you know everybody knows it so that can't be it. You barely know me so what is it about *me* that troubles you?"

Bruker tried to act like the question did not bother him, but Caleb saw intense worry pass across his features for half a second.

"You don't trouble me. All you do is inconvenience me. What is mine is mine," Bruker said, trying to smile but not quite doing it.

"Oh, bother!" Caleb said, "I do want my cottage back."

"If you'll steer clear, you'll get it back," Bruker said.

They sat in silence for a few seconds. The conversation had reached an end.

Then Bruker started another conversation: "Hey, that name *Caleb*, I believe my pirate friends used to tell a story about a soldier named Caleb.

"I wouldn't know anything about that." Caleb said a little too swiftly and abruptly.

"I see," Bruker said as if he made a mental note of Caleb's reaction.

They sat in silence awhile longer, and Caleb said: "Promise me something."

"What's that?" Bruker asked.

"Promise me that you won't hurt Clara, and that you'll keep your friends away from her."

"Old man, I am insulted. Do you think I would hurt my own flesh and blood?"

"I have no idea. Just promise."

"Sure, all right. I promise."

"What?"

"I said I promise."

"Huh?"

"I said I... you understood me... I promise. Why this promise? You heard something about me that you haven't said, old man?"

It was plain to Caleb now why Bruker did not like him. Caleb looked straight into people's faces, and Bruker felt that Caleb looked inside him.

"No, and I don't need to. I *see* what you are. Now, you will keep your promise or the hurt you render will be returned on your own head a hundred fold, and this too is a promise."

They sat in silence until sitting felt awkward.

Bruker took his water jug and went back inside the cottage.

Caleb stood and continued walking.

As Caleb walked, he wondered where he would spend Christmas. Having Bruker thrown out would have been easy enough to arrange with the owner of the land surrounding the cottage. Though sailors were a big part of what kept the money flowing through Merrydale, they were somewhat of a scourge, and the owner would surely have preferred to provide lodging to a shepherd rather than a sailor. However, if Caleb got Bruker thrown out, Susan would follow him, but not on board the ship, for Bruker would certainly not allow that. She and Clara would be forced to live in someone's "servant's quarters," which might be a most oppressive arrangement, and maybe even a place of misery for Clara. Most likely Clara would not be allowed to sing at night.

Caleb pondered the impossibility of the situation, and a thought came to him: Though he was an old man, and though he hated leaving the Merrydale countryside, there was something he might be able to do. He could make a journey down the coast. He could locate Bruker's other wives, obtain the appropriate court documents, and put an end, legally and maybe even practically, to Susan's illegitimate marriage. If he could do it, if he could drive a wedge between Bruker and Susan, perhaps he could save Clara a lifetime of agony, and maybe with Bruker gone, he would be able to talk Susan into allowing Clara to sing in the Christmas Concert, which for some reason seemed to Caleb an immensely important thing.

The sheep could not read Caleb's mind, but that did not keep him from saying: "Yes, yes, yes Brown Tooth, I should do this thing."

Having no idea what Caleb was talking about, Brown Tooth looked at Caleb with puzzlement.

Caleb continued, "But every girl needs her daddy, even if he's a polygamist. Isn't that right, Pretty Girl?"

Pretty girl agreed.

"What do you say, Dog Bit?"

Dog Bit said nothing, but just then Caleb witnessed a series of small events that completely made up his mind. He saw Bruker exit the cottage with Clara running clumsily behind him to keep up. Bruker walked to the well, and as he walked he mumbled something about his head hurting. He used words that no child should have heard, and that was bad enough, but what settled the matter in Caleb's mind was this: Every time Clara would reach up with her tiny hands to gesture for her daddy to pick her up and hold her, in a disinterested tone of voice Bruker would say things to the effect of: "Cut it out, you. You're big enough to stand on your own two feet. No, I won't pick you up."

That did it. That was the last straw. Caleb made up his mind. He walked from the general vicinity of his Christmas cottage toward Farmer Quigley's house. Though he never made much money as a shepherd, he was old and frugal, and he had more than enough to provide "room and board" for his sheep for more than enough time to take care of his planned business.

About a third of the way to Farmer Quigley's he passed by a rocky hill that bore a few tall sprigs of rich green grass.

Andrew Scar Chest lay on the hill's summit with his head propped against a log. Caleb reached down and picked up a gray, slightly blue tinted pebble that looked just the right size for throwing. He threw it side-armed, and it spun in the air and landed near Andrew's feet.

Caleb intended only to wake Andrew so he was quite surprised by Andrew's response. At the sound of the pebble popping against the hillside, Andrew sprang up like a deer. As he rose, he grabbed his gun, and in less time than it takes an owl to twist its head around from one side to the other, he stood at full attention.

"Who's tha… Oh, it's you," Andrew said.

"Yes, it's me," Caleb said, "but if I had been a wolf, I wouldn't have thrown a stone to wake you before I ate at least one of your sheep. You sleep hard for a shepherd, but you'll learn."

Caleb was only teasing of course, but what he did not know was just how much Andrew looked up to him as a kind of legend. Andrew frowned and turned his head to the side.

The young man had been a soldier so Caleb felt surprised that he did not take the joke better than that. He did not know what to say so he changed the subject.

"Say listen, you're from Merrydale, aren't you?" Caleb asked.

"Yes sir," Andrew said.

"You don't have to call me *sir*," Caleb said. "I want to ask you about something. There can't be too many years between your age and Susan's age. Had you never seen her before the other morning?"

"Well, yes, I had seen her but never up close. She's a year or two older than I, but once you said her name I remembered who she was, or at least I remembered her reputation." Andrew said.

"Let me guess," Caleb said, "Redhead Susan, the wild little orphan girl, name your pleasure, and she'll give it to you. Is that about right?"

"That's about right," Andrew said, "or at least it used to be right. That was her reputation before I finished school. It's been six or seven years since I heard a word about her, but I will tell you something else: She had another reputation too. She couldn't stand being in tight places. When you told me her name it made sense to me that she lived in a field so far out of town. One of my older cousins was teasing her on the school yard one day. He liked her, and she liked him too, or so he said. Well, you know how awkward boys are in the bud of manhood. He pretended that he was only having fun when he put his arm around her from behind, and she went crazy, screamed like a panther, and bit a hunk of flesh right off my cousin's arm. She said she was sorry afterward, but my cousin never touched her again. According to what I've heard, that wasn't the only time something like that happened. When Susan got cornered, Susan went crazier than an ape."

"Glad you warned me," Caleb said, "and by the way, I was just thinking. I'm getting too old to go traveling alone, and I'm about to make a trip down the coast. How'd you like to come along?"

"I don't know. I've got my sheep." Andrew said.

"No worries," Caleb said. "I'll pay Farmer Quigley to put them up with my flock while we're gone."

"All right, I guess I'll go," Andrew said, "but I'll have to tell my grandmother we're going. She'd worry herself sick if I stayed away from her cooking for more than a day."

"What about your parents?" Caleb asked.

"My mom's dead, and my dad's a traveling merchant. There's no telling where in the world he is," Andrew answered.

They led their animals to Farmer Quigley's, and Caleb paid for two weeks' keeping for both flocks. Only Big Head did not remain at Farmer Quigley's. Caleb wanted to have his supply cart along on the journey, and he thought a strong goat would do a better job at pulling it than he or Andrew Scar Chest.

Andrew said his grandmother lived in a brown stone house beside a grove of pecan trees a quarter mile south of town. Caleb said he had passed by that house a few times but that he had never met Andrew's grandmother.

They walked along the outskirts of Merrydale. As they topped a slight rise in the path, they saw the house in the distance. Smoke puffed out its chimney, and Caleb remembered that little old ladies felt cold most of the time. He remembered the way his grandmother used to wear her shawl even on the warmest, sunniest days. Caleb had always enjoyed and preferred the company of the aged, and he looked forward to meeting Andrew's grandmother who was sure to be a sweet lady, the kind of lady whose grandson meant all the world to her. He looked forward to assuring her that he would keep an eye on young Andrew as they traveled.

As they ambled up the path to the house's front door, Caleb asked, "What is your grandmother's name?"

"Beatrice," Andrew said, "and she gets mad when anybody calls her 'beat-rice.' You would be surprised how often that happens. She'll sign a receipt, and some shop keeper will pronounce her name the way it's spelled."

Caleb had never heard of a woman named *Beatrice* being called "beat-rice," but he made a mental note to himself to be extra careful not to do it all the same.

When they arrived, Andrew knocked on the door, his grandmother opened it, and Caleb said: "Pleased to meet you beat-rice." Then he smiled, feeling every bit like a drooling fool, and he thought: *"Mental notes are too often misread. Why did I just say that?"*

The woman looked almost exactly like Caleb thought she would look: thin, white haired, a little decrepit, and slightly stooped, but there were a few things about her that he had not anticipated. He had not anticipated her response to his mispronouncing her name, for he had not anticipated mispronouncing her name. He had not anticipated the way she was dressed. She wore the clothes of a young woman. Her arms, which were not without some muscle, she crossed in front of herself, and Caleb felt shocked that a woman her age had the nerve to go sleeveless, exposing her limbs for anyone to see. Besides, she was supposed to have been shivering cold.

"So," Beatrice said, "You think my mother was a fool?"

"No," Caleb said, "I don't think that at all. I never met your mother."

Andrew looked at his grandmother with an expression that pleaded for mercy upon the ignorant, and he looked at Caleb and shook his head, not able to understand how anyone, especially the most respected of the shepherds, could have made the mistake that Caleb had made.

"Well, you must think my mother was a fool," Beatrice continued, ignoring her grandson's pleading gaze, "because only a fool of

110

a woman would have named her daughter 'beat-rice.' 'Beat-rice' isn't even a name, and whoever heard of anyone beating rice? It's just not done."

"I'm terribly sorry," Caleb began to say, but Beatrice interrupted him.

"Beat-rice! I ought to beat your rice for saying such a thing."

Caleb could not help but smile, "No ma'am, please don't. I am sorry, and besides, I'm old. The mind plays tricks. Andrew just warned me not to call you that name, and I got confused.

Beatrice pinched Andrew's left ear between her fingers and twisted.

"Oww," he shouted.

"That's for putting thoughts into an old man's head," she said, "and it probably doesn't take much to confuse an old man that looks as ragged as this one."

Caleb wanted to protest the old woman's instantaneous judgment against the orderliness of his appearance, but he had to admit to himself that he had never felt as ragged and confused as he had felt in the past few days. It was as if ten horseflies were whirring and buzzing about his head at once. His simple and unsurprising life had been disturbed, and he knew the old woman saw it on his face.

After Beatrice finished her speech, Caleb took a quick glance at her from head to toe. For a woman who looked nearly as old as himself she cut a striking figure. Even in the defeat and decay of old age, something about her appearance remained pretty. This made Caleb want to leave her house and never come back. There were three things that he considered dangerous: wolves, bears, and women who struck him as pretty. And not necessarily in that order.

"I stopped by to tell you that I'm going down the coast for a few days, Grandmum," Andrew said.

"Why?" Beatrice asked.

"As a favor to Caleb here," Andrew said, and Caleb nodded at Beatrice as if to tell her it was nice to make her acquaintance. "He's the oldest of the shepherds, and he's asked me to go along."

She turned her eyes to Caleb, "What business do you have down

111

the coast?"

He thought he might begin by telling her that his Christmas cottage had been occupied and eventually work his way up to the part about exposing a seafaring polygamist, but he did not wish to waste time.

"I need to check some old court records," he said. "Family matters, you know."

Beatrice raised one eyebrow as if to say that something did not ring true about his answer. She glanced at Andrew.

"You must have dinner with me before you leave," she said. "I was expecting you tonight, and I've spent half the day cooking it."

Now Caleb understood why a fire burned in her fireplace and why she wore no sleeves.

"And you can eat too," she said to Caleb, "but I'm afraid I'm fresh out of beaten rice."

She tried to keep a straight face, but her eyes smiled, and her mouth followed suit. Caleb shook his head and smiled too. Now they were being friendly, and Caleb did not like it, but he smelled what she had cooked for dinner, fried pork chops with pepper sauce, fresh garlic bread, and stewed mushrooms, and he said: "Thank you, Beatrice. It will be my honor to have dinner at your house."

Lonely goats in unfamiliar territory are prone to wander so Caleb removed a rope from Big Head's cart and walked him over to a pecan tree to tie him there.

When he was far enough away from Beatrice's house that he would not be heard, he whispered, "I'll be right back, old fellow." He added, "Stop looking at me that way. I will most certainly be right back. Don't say that, Big Head, I'm telling you I will be right back."

Big Head did not seem convinced.

TEN

Beatrice's food gratified Caleb's senses of smell, touch, and taste. The aroma watered his mouth. The feel of the food in his mouth warmed his body, and the taste tickled his appetite. The eating of the food almost completely satisfied his appetite, but before he had filled his stomach, Beatrice said, "Save some room. I've got pie in the oven."

Caleb drew a breath through his nose and smelled custard, and he smiled because he liked no other desert more than custard pie. Beatrice removed the pie from the oven, and the smell nearly intoxicated Caleb. One's mouth seldom waters after one has eaten, but Caleb salivated like an old horse, and the custard turned out to be every bit as delicious as he hoped.

"Ummmm, ummm, umm" he said. "Ohhh, this is so good."

Almost embarrassed by Caleb's enthusiasm, Beatrice smiled and said, "Thank you," and she almost laughed, for Caleb seemed to enjoy the pie more than any man had a right to enjoy pie. He ate like a man who had been starving, offering compliments that sounded more like animal noises than words.

When Caleb finished eating he leaned back in his chair and said, "Beatrice, I thank you for your generosity, and I'm very sorry we have to be leaving."

"You can't be leaving now," Beatrice said, "Dark is falling, and you'll be caught by it."

Caleb looked out a window on the far end of the table. The sun had fallen, and the day had begun to whisper goodbye.

"It's true," Caleb said. "We'll have to make camp outside."

"Nonsense," Beatrice said, "I've got two spare rooms, one for each of you."

"Ma'am, a man does not spend the night in the house of a woman who is not kin," Caleb said.

"But Andrew is my kin," Beatrice said, "and you're his guest, not mine."

Caleb opened his mouth to say something to contradict her, but he could think of nothing so he accepted the invitation.

"Let me get my things," he mumbled.

He walked outside and saw Big Head chomping some grass. Before the old goat had a chance to spit out the grass and say anything, Caleb said, "Shut up, shut up, and, no, you were not right. It was getting dark anyway."

Big Head did not say anything in reply. He did not need to, but Caleb said, "Shut up," one more time just for good measure.

Caleb gathered some personal items from Big Head's cart: a change of clothes, his washing cloths and soap, and his beard clipper. It had been far too long since his beard had been trimmed, Caleb reminded Big Head, but Big Head looked at him sideways, it seemed to Caleb, as if to question the timing of the trimming. Surely the old man wasn't trying to make a good impression on the old woman, now was he?

"Shut up!" Caleb said again, "I'm too old for that kind of nonsense, and you know it, but it doesn't hurt to make friends, does it?"

The goat did not answer.

Caleb began to walk back to the house, but then he remembered that, unless it had died of the gunshot wound, a giant bear now roamed the Merrydale countryside, not to mention stray wolves and

114

lesser bears. He pondered the situation.

"I will come for you later, after we turn out the lights, and that should not be very long from now," he said. "You know how old ladies like to go to bed early. I'll be listening for you until then. One frightened bleat, and I will be right out."

Beatrice, contrary to what Caleb thought, did not like to go to bed early. When she had company, she liked to stay up late telling stories of days long passed, talking about life, or talking about nothing at all, just talking. When Caleb re-entered the house, Beatrice led him to his bedroom for the evening, and she asked him if he would need anything more than what he saw, maybe an extra pillow or perhaps an additional blanket. Caleb assured her that the accommodations were sufficient. He thought she would say *good night* and leave him in the room then, but she did not.

"Put your stuff on the bed and come into the sitting room," she said.

Caleb did as he was told, and if she had promised to bake him another custard pie, he would have jumped through hoops for her.

Caleb, Beatrice, and Andrew sat in the sitting room, and Andrew dozed off almost immediately. This made the atmosphere uncomfortable for the old people. They chatted, but the talk remained small, and it led nowhere until by chance Beatrice hit upon a way to break the ice. At just the right point in the struggling but otherwise polite attempt at conversation, with an impish grin she asked a question that required more than a simple answer.

"If you had a chance to go back and start over, what about your life would you change?"

Caleb sat up straight in his chair.

"I've thought about that many times," he said, "I take it you've thought about the same thing?"

"I have" she said, "Has the old person lived who has not? But I asked first."

"Yes, you did," he said.

A long silence followed, and Beatrice did not dare interrupt it for she saw the wheels turning in the old man's head.

"Well," he said, "I would have given it back."

115

"You would have given what back?" Beatrice asked.

"Oh, I'm sorry, I can't tell you that," he answered.

"But you brought it up," she said.

"Even so, I cannot tell you what *it* is," he said.

"I take it you still have *it*?" she asked.

"Yes, I'm afraid I still do," he answered.

"Then why don't you give it back now?" she asked.

"I am afraid that giving it back is simply impossible," he answered.

"Who gave it to you?" Beatrice asked.

"You mean: From whom did I take it?" Caleb said.

"Yes, from whom did you take it?" Beatrice asked.

"I'm afraid I can't tell you that," Caleb said.

Beatrice saw that pushing her questions further would lead to no answers so she said, "Very well, you've answered my question, not in detail, but you have answered. You stole something, and you never returned it."

"I said I took something," Caleb said, "I didn't say I stole it, not exactly, not unless it's possible to steal from the dead."

Caleb covered his mouth with one hand. He knew he had said more than he had meant to say. Beatrice recognized the gesture and respectfully stopped pushing Caleb's side of the conversation further. She switched over to her answer to the question.

"You have answered," Beatrice said, "and I will answer in kind. If I could change one thing about my life, I would change the way I treated members of my own sex. I always made friends with men easier than I made friends with women, and now I have few friends because most of the men I knew are either married or dead. If I could go back, I would make myself less of a tomboy, and I would make a greater effort to win some female friends because I could sure use some. It gets lonely out here sometimes."

"But living this close to town, you must have many friends?" Caleb asked.

"No, only a few," Beatrice said, and that was when the conversation began in earnest, for they each started going through their mental lists of friends, relatives, and acquaintances, mentioning

116

them out loud, and sometimes hitting upon the same person. When they discovered a mutual acquaintance they talked about that person, praising the humble, laughing at the scoundrels, and shaking their heads and smiling about those who were simply good to know. Dead mutual friends came up from time to time, and they said things like, "Pity he's gone." As they talked, the conversation grew warmer and almost took on an air of intimacy.

"I'm surprised we never knew each other before now," Caleb said. "We know more than a few people in common."

"I'm *not* surprised," Beatrice said. "I am from Merrydale, but I haven't lived here my entire life. I married a ship's captain when I was still in my teens, and he moved our family rather often. My daughter settled down here to raise Andrew and have some more children, but no more children came. She died when Andy was just a boy."

Tears came to Beatrice's eyes, spilled over, and moistened her cheek. Caleb felt embarrassed when people cried so he looked away.

"You don't have to look away," Beatrice said. "I'm not ashamed, and I never really get finished crying about it. I cry for the loss of my daughter, yes, but more than that, I cry for the loss of Andrew's mother. Oh Caleb, if you had seen the way the poor little boy behaved after my daughter passed. He's still a lonely young man, and I believe it goes back to the death of his mother."

She paused and sobbed sincerely. Caleb felt an instinctive desire to hold her, but he repressed the feeling. After a short while, she regained her composure.

"I fear for him," she said, "No disrespect to your profession, but the world has changed since you took up shepherding. Few young men choose to herd sheep and goats now days. There's no money in it, and I believe he did it only because he's got a gentle and sensitive soul, and he wishes to place it out of harm's way. I look out for him all I can, and I know you'll look out for him on this trip the two of you are about to make. I only wish someone could look out for his heart."

Caleb did not know what to say so after an appropriate amount

117

of silence had passed, he gently changed the subject. He told Beatrice about the mission he was intending to fulfill, and since she had lived upon and traveled the coast, she told him a few things he needed to know about the towns he intended to visit.

"Beware of Loaden," she concluded, "Of all the places you'll visit, Loaden is by far the worst. It's as if a wicked spirit inhabits that place. Everyone knows that it has been a nasty and wicked place since long ago, even since before Elias the Traveler passed through it on his journey to the Castle of Wisdom. Now it's worse. It's a sprawling web of rot and gloom. I don't like the thought of Andrew visiting Loaden, but your mission sounds noble enough, and I would not keep him from assisting you in it. Just promise me you'll watch him better than you would your favorite sheep."

"I will," Caleb said. "I promise I will."

Beatrice continued to instruct Caleb about the particulars of his mission, describing in detail the places he needed to visit to find the information he sought: churches, courts, and city offices. She also mentioned a few·scenic stops not to be missed along the way like the high cliffs south of Loaden and the hot springs of Pranville.

"Beatrice," Caleb said after a time, "how long has it been since you traveled down the coast?"

"Five years," Beatrice said, "Why?"

"Because I want you to come along with us. Your knowledge would help me get through this journey faster."

"Oh, I couldn't do that," Beatrice said, "I'm too old."

"I'm too old too," Caleb said, "but I'm going anyway. Seriously, you should come along."

Beatrice thought about it for a short time and answered, "Well, at my age, what have I got to lose? Yes, I will go along, but you must allow me some extra time in the morning to pack up some essentials."

"Of course," Caleb said.

Beatrice rose and touched Andrew on the shoulder. She woke him but not completely. In a trance-like state, he stood, and she led him by the hand to his room, turned down the covers on the bed, and helped him get into it.

"Goodnight," she said to Caleb as she passed back through the sitting room.

"Goodnight," Caleb said.

He went to his room and lay down on the bed, but he did not go to sleep. He waited until silence reigned in the house, and then he went and stood beside the door to Beatrice's room. He listened, and he heard the slow, even breathing of sleep as well as faint snoring. He went for his goat.

Finding one of his animals in the night was no challenge for Caleb. Fifty years of shepherding had developed the ability to a level that bordered on genius, plus he remembered the spot where he had tied the old goat. He retrieved the animal in complete silence and in near complete darkness since the moon had not yet come out. He led Big Head back to his room intending to return him to the tree before earliest light.

Big Head lay down beside the bed, and Caleb stroked his fur with hopes of calming his old friend and putting him into a sound sleep. When Caleb was sure that Big Head was asleep, he stopped petting him.

When Big Head was sure that Caleb was asleep, he stood up and began to munch on the bed's covers. He then munched the curtains hanging over the window. Not feeling satisfied, he put his big head to use and pushed open the door. He entered the house's sitting room and munched the pillows on the couch, the curtains on the wall, and the throw rug on the floor. He entered the dining room and munched the tablecloth, the dishtowels, and the room's curtains. All night long the goat munched, and munched, and munched.

As he had planned, Caleb woke before dawn. He yawned and reached out his hands to raise himself, and he felt stickiness and roughness on the edge of the covers at the same time.

"*Uh oh*," he thought.

"Big Head?" he whispered.

He heard no sound. He bounded out of bed.

"Big Head?" he whispered again.

By the small amount of light that the now risen half moon shined through the nearly curtainless window, Caleb saw that the door had been opened. Many thoughts flooded his tired mind. Had Beatrice heard the goat chomping on her furnishings, and had she released him, or had the goat released himself? The latter seemed more likely since even the slightest sounds other than those made by his animals tended to wake him. Caleb chanced lighting a candle, and with it he ventured into the sitting room, astonished and horrified by what he saw. He entered the dining room, and there sat Big Head looking quite content and happy.

"I'm sorry I didn't leave you out for the bear to eat you," Caleb whispered. "Now what do I do?"

Caleb ran his fingers through his hair and stroked his beard. He felt knots twisting in his stomach. He felt pain in his lower back. He felt most of the bad feelings that a person can feel. He felt gripped by his old secret thought that things just didn't work out for him like they did for other people. He felt cursed. He felt ashamed and out of place.

"I can't confront this," Caleb said to his goat. "I know it's not the manly thing to do, but I'm going to leave a note and get going."

He tore a piece of paper from a half-chewed pad in Beatrice's sitting room. He found a pencil in a cabinet and wrote:

Dear Beatrice and Andrew,

    I am sorry for this, and I accept full responsibility. I promise I will pay for all the damage as soon as I can, and I will not trouble you further. Andrew, you may leave your animals at Farmer Quigley's and take some time off to relax if you wish. I am leaving without either of you, and I will be back as soon as I have completed my task. I will then try to set things aright in regards to the damage that has been done. Please forgive me.

Sincerely,
Caleb

He left the note on the dining room table. He gripped Big Head by one horn, led him outside, and hitched him to the goat cart. He returned to his room and gathered his belongings, keeping as quiet as possible. When all was in order, he departed without looking back. After he had put at least a mile between himself and Beatrice's house, the first silver light of morning peeped over the edge of the sky, and only then did he pause to wipe his brow and rest. He breathed, shook his head, cut a glance at the sky above as if to ask why his life had to be the way it was, and then he continued walking south, grumbling to the goat.

He reached the ocean at about the same time he felt he could walk no more without eating some breakfast. The sun had risen to the east over the water, and the sparkling, shining, glittering reflection of the fresh daylight cast a spell over Caleb, as did the rhythmic roar of white-topped waves crashing upon sand and rock. He found a smooth-topped boulder just off the seashore path, took some food from Big Head's cart, and sat down to eat. As he chewed his food, he looked out across the water and saw three ships sailing together toward Merrydale. He thought little of it until he saw that none of the ships flew a flag, and then he swallowed a mouthful of bread in one unchewed lump because he knew that meant the ships carried pirates.

"Well, there's nothing I can do about pirates, Big Head, so I won't bother turning back. Maybe in shepherd's territory I could hold them at bay, but not in town. I would be useless in town so I think I'd better stay with my plan. I'm too old to fight pirates anyway. They're not my responsibility. I've got a journey to make."

Caleb finished his breakfast and continued down the path.

ELEVEN

The cool December air was perfect for a long walk, and even though Caleb ran out of breath more than once and felt more than a little bit tired most of the way, he completed the first part of his journey in three days on foot, no small accomplishment for a man his age. He drew near to the outskirts of Pranville in the middle of the day, and he began his search for information about Bruker and Bruker's other wives half an hour later when he arrived at the center of the town.

The first place he inquired was the local church, and he could not have picked a better place to start because Parson Wilson of Pranville knew Parson Rivers of Merrydale. The two of them corresponded from time to time so he had a vague idea of who Caleb was. Parson Wilson had little information to offer Caleb about Bruker, however, but he volunteered to go with him to the Pranville Courthouse to search for the correct documents. Since the court registrar knew and respected Parson Wilson, he offered to help search for the documents too, and in an hour's time, Caleb had learned as much about Bruker as the legal documents of Pranville had to tell.

Bruker turned out to be a polygamist indeed. No more doubt about that. He had a wife in Pranville named Rosalyn.

Because the law forbade polygamy, the Pranville Registrar was most interested in learning about Bruker's other wife, Susan. After hearing Caleb's story, he sent official correspondence to the registrar of the Merrydale Courthouse to be signed and returned to the High Judge of Pranville, and he signed a stamped a copy of Bruker's marriage certificate and gave it to Caleb. Caleb smiled about the registrar's legal actions because deep inside, Caleb liked the idea of ruining Bruker's life almost as much as he liked the idea of improving Clara's life.

Caleb's next move was to locate Rosalyn. The Registrar provided her address, and Caleb went out to search for her. On a dirty off street, Caleb found the tiny shack that served as Rosalyn's house. He knocked on the door though doing so was not necessary since the holes in the wall provided a clear view of him the moment he approached.

Five filthy children ran about in the street, screaming, cursing, and crying.

"Hey, old man!" one of them yelped at Caleb.

"Hey, you stupid old man!" another said, and the gang of children snickered.

Not to be outdone, a third child screamed: "Hey, you stinking, stupid, old, ugly man!"

Caleb shook his head.

Rosalyn opened the door. Though her hair was blonde, she bore a striking resemblance to Susan.

"What do you want?" she said. "If you're here to collect, I'm telling you, I ain't got no money right now so you may as well get lost."

"I'm not here to collect anything," Caleb said. "I'm here to give you some news about your husband."

"He's drowned at sea? Please tell me he's drowned at sea," Rosalyn said. "Please tell me that worthless bum is dead!"

Caleb relaxed because he knew that what he was about to tell her would not be taken as bad news but would actually make the woman feel happy. She would be glad for her freedom.

"Bruker is a polygamist," Caleb said. "He's married to you, and he's married to a woman in Merrydale named Susan. I believe he's also married to a woman further down the coast, but I do not yet have proof of that. You're free of him if you like. The Pranville High Judge will annul your marriage as soon as he receives the appropriate documents from Merrydale. Shouldn't take more than a week."

Rosalyn smiled but not completely because she did not know for sure that the old man was telling her the truth.

"Can you prove this?" she asked.

"Not at this time," Caleb said, "because I have only your wedding certificate and not the other lady's, but go and have a word with the Registrar if you like. What I am telling you is true beyond question."

Rosalyn recognized that Caleb was speaking completely sincerely, and her smile broadened. "Sir, I don't know who you are or why you've done it, but you've brought me the best news I've heard in years. Thank you. Thank you. Thank you."

"You're welcome," Caleb said, and not knowing what else to say, he turned and walked away, pleased that his efforts to ruin Bruker were going smoothly so far.

Caleb was ahead of schedule on his journey. The sun had not yet set, and he decided to spend the night in Pranville. He worked his way through the streets of the city until he located an inn that overlooked the sea. He paid for one night's lodging and walked back outside to lead Big Head to the stable behind the inn.

The stable was large, sturdy, and secure, and many animals stood in its stalls: horses of high breeding, mules of even higher breeding, and several donkeys.

Caleb felt no apprehension about leaving one of his most valued creatures in the stable. If anyone decided to steal one of its animals, Caleb reasoned, Big Head would be their last choice. He removed most of his supplies from Big Head's cart, propped the cart against the far wall of the stable, and went to his room on the

125

inn's second floor.

In the room, he took off his shoes and stretched himself on the bed. He rested, but he did not feel sleepy. As he let his mind wander, he remembered Beatrice's advice that he should not miss seeing Pranville's hot springs.

Since he did not feel like sleeping he put his shoes back on and went back downstairs. He asked the clerk where the hot springs were located, and the clerk told him that he would find them in the hills behind the town.

Toward the hills he walked, and he had no trouble finding the hot springs since many people were on their way to them. Caleb made pleasant conversation with his fellow pedestrians as they moved along the green crests and spring-watered valleys of the hilly area. Some of the people walking to the springs were locals who often went for baths, but most of the walkers were travelers, visiting the hot springs of Pranville for health benefits.

The more Caleb walked, the greater his curiosity grew. The hot springs seemed more and more fantastic with each step he took. The sun floated low in the sky now, but that did not matter. There would be no need to hurry back before dark. Lamps shielded by glass globes cast slightly green hues, and red and orange torches burned on the tops of poles along the main trails that led to the springs. The springs were surrounded by torches and fires, and the atmosphere glowed with festivity. The crowd of bathers seemed full of careless fun.

When Caleb reached the first spring, those walking with him invited him to go for a splash. Feeling quite uncomfortable with the idea of taking off everything but his underclothes in public, he declined the offer and walked on to another spring.

The second spring's pool was much larger than the first's, and bathers of many shapes and sizes rolled and paddled about in its steamy waters. Caleb saw everything from white haired men and women who looked older than himself, their faces crimson with the heat, to youngsters so small their parents had to hold them to keep their heads above water. Again the bathers invited Caleb to join them, but Caleb refused and walked to a third pool.

The third spring differed from the other two in that it was smaller and its surface was much steamier. A sign stood beside the pool warning would-be bathers to consider the heat of the water before plunging into it. Caleb felt the heat of its waters even before he drew close enough to kick off his shoes and stick his toes in to sample the pool's temperature. A slightly sulfuric odor rose from the spring, but Caleb's nose adjusted to it, and after a few seconds he did not smell it anymore. Through the steam, Caleb saw the faces of the few bathers who braved the third spring. The bathers looked almost as red as cooked lobsters.

Night fell, and Caleb contemplated walking away from the pools, but then he reminded himself that a man has but one life and that it passes too fast and that he might never have another opportunity to experience anything like the hot springs.

He disrobed down to his underclothes and eased the weight of his body into the third spring.

"Ow, ow, ow," he panted as his body sank into the heat.

The steam soaked into the hair on his head and face, causing it to droop limply down on his shoulders and chest.

"Wow, this is hot!" Caleb said to his fellow bathers, but they paid him no attention. They each held their eyes shut, concentrating on not feeling the heat. Caleb ducked his head underwater and came up breathing hard.

"Sorry fellows, but I believe I'm a little too sensitive for this pool. See you later," he said.

He climbed up the steps that lay along the edge of pool and picked up his clothes and shoes, and he walked as fast as he could back to the second spring. Despite the warmth of the fires that burned along the edge of the path, when the cold air of evening caressed his skin, goose bumps pimpled his body.

When he arrived at the second spring, he did not hesitate before sliding off the walkway and into the water. The water was hot but not nearly as hot as the water in the third spring's pool.

Caleb sighed and breathed in the steam. He closed his eyes for a few seconds, and the heat relaxed him so much that he could have fallen asleep, but after a few more seconds, the heat stopped relaxing him and started invigorating him. His heart beat faster. His pores opened, and he began to sweat. His mind began to race, and he found himself thinking about many odd subjects. He felt sure that the vapors rising up from the water were responsible for the things going through his head, but he did not feel bothered about that fact. He enjoyed the new sensations, and he drew a deep breath and sank himself all the way down into the pool, baptizing himself in the moment.

When he emerged, he used his feet to push himself to the far side of the pool. A group of six people who looked as old as himself were leaning against the wall there in pairs, and he hoped they would accept him into their company for some pleasant conversation.

They did not disappoint Caleb. They seemed as eager to speak to him as he was to speak to them. Their conversation rambled quickly from one subject to another, and they laughed more than they spoke.

"I'm Captain Henry Jake," one of the men said, "formerly of his Majesty's army."

"I'm his wife," the woman beside him said.

"I'm his girlfriend," another woman said and burst out laughing. "No, seriously," she continued, patting the bald head of the man beside her, "I'm this man's wife, but maybe the captain's wife will be so kind as to accept a trade."

The third old man and woman leaned with their arms wrapped around each other, and their cheeks rubbed.

"We're newlyweds," they said, holding up their dripping hands to show their matching wedding bands.

"'Til death do us part," the old man said.

"And that might not be a long time from now," the old woman added with some humor and a little seriousness.

"My wife died last year," the old man said.

"My husband died the year before that," the old woman added.

"We felt like it was time to move on with our lives," the old man said. "They say you're never too old to start over."

The old man continued to ramble, but Caleb did not hear him.

The one phrase, *"you're never too old to start over,"* stuck in Caleb's mind and repeated itself several times. *You're never too old to start over. You're never too old to start over.*

Caleb felt strange stirrings in his soul. He reminded himself that it was probably just the vapors and the steam playing tricks with his mind, but he did not resist because if the stirrings were tricks, at least they were good tricks. He let his thoughts go, go, go, but then he began to guide them back into line. He tried to dismiss the idea of beginning new things, shaking his head and reminding himself not to get carried away. He leaned back against the edge of the pool and passed the rest of the evening chatting with his fellow aged bathers. He let his new companions do most of the talking as he kept telling himself to forget about the possibility of changing some of his comfortable and long established habits and practices.

When he climbed out of the pool, he felt certain that his unusual new thoughts would soon go away, but they did not. He stood beside a fire to dry his underclothes, and the new thoughts persisted. He put his clothes back on, and the thoughts continued. The thoughts followed him along the path and all the way back to his room. When he reached his room he felt certain he would want to go to sleep, but he did not. He felt refreshed and wide awake. After the hot bath, the cool air had energized him. He opened the room's single window to hear the roar of the ocean and feel the cool breeze, and he built a coal fire in the stove at the foot of the bed to provide warmth.

He lit every candle in the room, and he removed his knife from his pack. He sharpened its blade until it would have sliced falling tissue paper. He wet his face, lathered it with soap, and began to do something he had not done in more than fifty years.

He began to shave, not merely clip, his beard. Close against his skin he dragged the knife until his face nearly shined with smoothness, and he used his beard clipper to trim his eyebrows.

He held a small mirror over his head and angled it downward as he sat in a chair facing the room's full length mirror, and after some consideration he gave his hair a good trimming. When he was satisfied that he had removed enough of his curls, he parted his hair on one side, and he opened one of the boxes from the goat cart and removed his white church clothes. He put them on and stood before the mirror. In the reflection of the flickering light of the candles, he saw himself as if he stood in a more beautiful world than his own.

"To be my age," he thought, *"I don't look half bad."*

Caleb was not speaking immodest words or thinking immodest thoughts. His words and thoughts were far *too* modest. The figure that stood before him in the mirror was a handsome old man, not a frail old man or a shriveled, weak old man. Beneath and behind his white hair, Caleb had aged well, and though he was in his early seventies, he thought that if he had passed himself on the street he might have mistaken himself for a healthy man in his middle fifties.

He moved the chair to a position in the room where he might feel both the cool wind blowing from the ocean through the window and the heat radiating from the coal fire in the stove at the same time. He listened to the sound of the waves rolling onto the shore, and the sound of the coal burning, and he thought about the future instead of the past. When his eyelids finally began to feel heavy, he removed his church clothes, hung them at the foot of the bed, turned down the covers, climbed between the sheets, went to sleep, and dreamed good dreams all night long.

When Caleb awoke, he knelt beside his bed and prayed as he used to do in the days of his boyhood when he slept, not on tops of rocks or in caves or in tents, but in a bed every night. After giving thanks for the good feelings of the previous night, he went downstairs for breakfast. With an appetite made large by the walking and the bathing, he ate three eggs, four pieces of toast, two pieces of bacon, two pieces of sausage, and half an orange. He washed his breakfast down with black coffee, and he left a big tip for the young woman who served his table.

"If you don't mind," Caleb told the inn-keeper "I'd like to wait a couple of hours before I clean out my stuff. I need to take care of some business in town."

"Take your time," the inn-keeper said. "This is not the busy time of year for Pranville, and I have many vacancies."

Caleb walked back to the Pranville Courthouse. There he located the Registrar who had been friendly enough to help him locate Bruker's wedding certificate the previous afternoon.

"Hello Caleb," the registrar said. "Are you looking for another document today?"

"No," Caleb said. "I would like to ask you a question about the law."

"If it is about Bruker, I assure you his multiple marriages are entirely illegal."

"It's not about him. It's about a friend. My question is: What happens to a soldier who disobeys a direct command?"

"Military law is not my specialty," the registrar said, "but I can tell you that cases are tried individually, and punishments may range from slight to severe depending on the seriousness of the crime. Can you be more specific about the crime?"

"I can't repeat much of what my friend has entrusted to me, but I can tell you that he killed more of the enemy than he was supposed to have. He buried the evidence, and to this day he's scared someone will find what he buried."

"The way you say *to this day* raises a question: During which war did your friend commit his crime?"

"The Big War," Caleb said.

"The Big War?" the registrar laughed. "Then your friend has nothing to worry about. That was fifty years ago. The statute of limitations has run out."

"Statute of limitations?" Caleb asked. "What's that?"

"It's a law that says you can't be tried for crimes committed in the distant past. The limitation for some misdemeanors is as few as five years, and the limitation for all but the worst felonies, murder and kidnapping, is thirty years so your friend has been in the clear for at least twenty years. Tell him he has nothing to fear," the registrar answered.

"Are you sure that disobeying a direct order and killing an enemy isn't one of the worst felonies?"

"Yes, I'm certain of it. Crimes committed during the course of war are not ranked among the worst felonies. Even a case of a killing in violation of a superior's command may not be brought to

131

trial at this late date."

Caleb smiled much more than he should have. His grin stretched from ear to ear.

"Thank you for telling me that," he said to the registrar as he reached out his hand for a shake. "My friend will be more relieved than you would believe."

"Oh, I think I would believe," the registrar said with a wink and a nod, and Caleb knew that the registrar had seen through him.

"By the way," the registrar added, "I like the haircut. It becomes you."

Caleb walked back to the inn feeling so light of heart that he could have danced the entire way, but he did not. He contented himself with smiling at passers-by on the cobble-stone streets. He retrieved his stuff from his room and walked to the stable behind the inn. He hitched Big Head to his goat cart and led him to the center of Pranville. He tied Big Head to a post, strolled among the shops, and bought provisions to refurbish his supply: bread, cheese, jam, honey, dried beef, and other food items that were not likely to spoil during the long foot journey to Loaden.

All of his life, Caleb had heard stories about Loaden, and none of them had been good stories. For centuries, Loaden had been labelled "the wildest city in the world."

Caleb did not know what to expect when he reached Loaden so as he walked he tried to prepare himself for anything.

TWELVE

Caleb entered the city of Loaden just before dark on a cold, wet day. The on and off drizzling reminded him of his Christmas cottage's roofless rooms, and that reminded him of the hides he stored in one of them. He hoped that rain was not falling on the hides. For Clara's sake, he hoped that rain was not falling on the cottage at all because the cottage tended to get damp, even in the rooms over which the roof remained intact.

Since night was falling, Caleb made finding a room his first goal, and since Loaden was a port city, there were many rooms to be found. Still, Caleb had heard stories of bizarre things happening to travelers in Loaden so he made an extra effort to get a room in a respectable inn, and that was not easy so his search lasted for almost two hours.

As he walked the streets of Loaden, women wearing scarlet dresses and holding silk fans in front of their faces to cover all their features except their eyes presented themselves to his attention. Caleb knew what the women were about so he avoided eye-contact with them as he walked from the front of one inn to another.

Most of the inns catered to sailors. They bore names like *The Silver Sail*, *The Trade Winds*, or *The Albatross Nest*. None of these appealed to Caleb so he searched until at last he found one named *The Oaks*. *The Oaks* offered expensive lodging, but since Caleb intended to stay for no more than a night, he gladly paid the higher price. Apart from wanting to distance himself from the partying and occasional violence that was said to crop up in Loaden's sailors' inns, his reason for chosing *The Oaks* was that it offered good shelter for animals. Caleb shut Big Head into one of the stable's many stalls and paid one of the keepers to feed the goat some corn. He paid another keeper to take his stuff to the room.

He walked around the inn to its front entrance, went inside, and sat at a table in its dining room.

The table was set with elegant silverware and china, and Caleb felt reluctant to lean back in his chair and relax. He sat up straight and looked around the room.

Blue velvet curtains hung from brass rods over the windows, and matching carpets covered the entire floor except for a wooden walkway in the center of the room.

Caleb ordered a steak and potato supper. When the supper arrived, he stuffed butter into the potato and smothered the steak in a spicy, tangy sauce. Several times during the meal he had to remind himself that he was not in an open field or among shepherds and that he had to mind his manners: no smacking, no taking large mouthfuls, and no gnawing on the steak bone after he chewed off the meat. He washed his supper down with a glass of sweet iced-tea with extra lemon and stood to leave, but his table maid laughed and told him to wait for dessert.

"But I don't have any room for dessert," Caleb said.

He patted his stomach.

"You will find room," the maid said with complete confidence and a pat on Caleb's shoulder.

"Oh yeah? What's for dessert?" Caleb asked.

The table maid sat down beside him and put one hand on his arm.

"Well," she said, "We've got the thickest cheesecake you've

ever seen or tasted, and you get your choice of toppings: strawberries, cherries, or blueberries. What'll it be?"

"I'll have the strawberries, please," Caleb said. Caleb looked up when the woman stood. In an earthy sort of way, the woman looked pretty. She had curly brown hair, large brown eyes, and a full figure.

He watched her as she bounced from table to table with more energy and exuberance than a rabbit in spring. She flirted with all the men in the room, Caleb noticed, and he thought there should be a word for the likes of her. She was not quite what the women in the street were, but the way she offered false affection in hopes of getting more money was not very different from the way they sold themselves, and maybe it was more dishonest. To have called her what people called the women of the street would have been unfair, but to have called her innocent would have been even more unfair. Caleb shook his head. *"Tableharlot"* came to his mind, but it was not a real word.

The table maid returned with a slice of cheesecake on a white saucer and placed it before Caleb. Sliced strawberries covered the top of the cheesecake, and strawberry juice dripped down its sides onto the saucer.

"You'd better put this on," the table maid said.

She rubbed Caleb's shoulders and smiled at him as if she would like to be his girlfriend. She flung open a folded bib and tied it around Caleb's neck.

He did not protest, but he continued to think there should be a word for the likes of his table maid, a woman who offered false affection in hopes of receiving large tips. Caleb guessed that her falseness proved effective on most of her customers, especially lonely men who secretly hoped the table maid felt genuine affection for them, but Caleb would not allow her flirting to work on him. He left her no tip at all.

He walked upstairs to his room and washed his hands. Upon the room's stove rested two steaming kettles. Mixing the hot water from the kettles with the room-temperature water from a tall blue urn, he gave his face a good clean shave and took a warm bath in a porcelain tub that stood on four stubby legs.

He opened the room's window. The rain had stopped falling, and the city smelled cleaner than it did when he arrived. The temperature outside had dropped considerably so Caleb closed and latched the window.

"I'm going for a stroll," he told himself, "and I don't care if I do get robbed or killed. I won't take much money with me, and at my age, I don't have much *life* left."

He sorted through one of his boxes and found a heavy overcoat. He put it on over his regular clothes, laced up his boots, and left his room. When he entered the street, the first thing he noticed was the sound of exciting music coming from a few blocks behind the inn. He wanted to see the source of the music so he walked toward it. When the music was so loud that he knew it was being played just around the corner, he glanced up and saw a sign that read *Sailor Street*.

Most of the bad stories he had heard about Loaden were set somewhere along Sailor Street, but the place did not seem so dangerous now that he was there. A few drunks staggered down the sidewalks, and a few half-dressed women danced on the balconies, but policemen stood guard on most of the corners, and the lights of many candles and lamps behind gold, green, and purple shades scattered away most of the darkness. Caleb felt sure he had little to fear.

Careful to stay near its center, he walked down the street. The buildings looked pretty in the reflections of the candles and lamps, and the colors of the shades created a pleasant atmosphere, a feeling in the air that said: "Take your time and enjoy."

Caleb did take his time, and he enjoyed more than a Christian man should have. Several times his eyes lingered on the dancing women on the balconies, and impure thoughts entered his mind. He had learned as a young man that while these thoughts brought a brief happiness to the body, they left a lonely pain in the soul, but he did not bother to think about what he knew to be true. The moment seized him.

As he walked he patted the side of his leg to the beat of the music. Before he realized what he was doing he turned into an ale-house and took a seat. A table maid who did not bother to act as charming as the one from the inn stopped at his table and said: "What'll ya have, sailor?"

"I'm not a sailor," Caleb politely corrected her.

"Well, I couldn't care less what you are," the table maid said, "but the question is: What'll you have?"

"I'll have a glass of ale," Caleb said.

"I'll be right back then," the table maid said.

Caleb liked this table maid better than the one from the inn. Though she worked in a less respectable place, and though she acted with more than a hint of rudeness, she seemed honest at least.

The table maid returned, and Caleb sipped the dark beverage she placed before him. He relaxed his mind, but he did not allow himself to get too relaxed. Sailor Street did not seem as dangerous as he had been told, but the presence of the policemen on most of the corners reminded him that danger could come at any moment.

Hanging on the wall behind the ale-house's bar was an ancient painting of a perfectly vicious looking old pirate. Tattoos covered the pirate's body, rings hung from every imaginable place on his skin (and a few not so imaginable places), and his long white hair flapped in the wind. The pirate held a sword over his head and grinned with rage.

"I would hate to meet up with a character like that," Caleb thought, but then he remembered that he had met Bruker, and that Bruker looked something like the pirate. At that thought, he nearly choked on a gulp of ale. Bruker was living in his Christmas cottage, the only place in the world that almost felt like a home to Caleb.

"Can't do a thing about Bruker tonight," Caleb reminded himself, "but tomorrow I'll take him down another notch." The thought helped Caleb smile, and he continued to relax.

As he sat sipping his ale, he overheard the conversation at the table next to his.

Two young men were discussing going to a hog-catch. One of the young men had never been to a hog-catch, and the other was explaining what happened at a hog-catch.

137

"They let the hog out of a cage on one end of the pen," the young man said, "and they let the bulldog out of a cage on the other. The bulldog runs and catches the hog by the throat and throws it on its back. The hog squeals for its life, and then a team of men jump in and pull the dog off the hog before the dog can do any serious damage. Most of the time they have to use a stick to pry the dog's jaws open. The dogs that take the least amount of time to catch their hogs move up at the end of each round, and at the end of the night, the fastest dog is declared the winner."

Caleb had heard about the *fun* to be had at a hog-catch, but he had never been to one. Against his better judgment, he turned to the young man who was describing the hog-catch.

"When is the hog-catch?" he asked.

"Tonight," the young man answered. "Starts in about half an hour."

"Where are they holding it?" Caleb asked.

"Two blocks over," the young man said, "on a lot behind *The Albatross Nest*."

"Thanks," Caleb said.

He wanted to see the hog-catch. Since neither the hogs nor the dogs actually got hurt very badly, he did not see anything wrong with taking part in the excitement. He reminded himself that he was in Loaden, but he further reminded himself that Loaden had turned out to be less dangerous than he had been led to believe. He decided to go watch the hog-catch. Watching it would give him some good stories to tell the brotherhood when he returned to Merrydale.

Locating the hog-catch required almost no effort. Scores of people were walking in the direction the young man had indicated. Caleb tried to comfort himself with the idea of there being safety in numbers, but when he took time to observe the appearance of most of those going to the hog-catch he could not feel at ease. Though a few well dressed men and women walked toward the lot behind *The Albatross Nest*, the great majority of the walkers looked like they had crawled out of Hades.

In the throng, Caleb saw a man with gold teeth that looked life knife blades, and he wondered how it felt when the man bit his tongue.

He saw a man who had two silver hooks instead of two hands, and he wondered how the man wiped after... well, he wondered how the man did many things.

He saw a woman wearing a dress cut low in the back to show off her tattoo. The tattoo was a portrait of her that showed her face from the side but showed a full view of her back. The tattoo of herself had a tattoo on her back, which in turn showed another portrait of herself. Caleb wondered just how many tattoos of herself were inside the tattoo of herself, but he did not get close enough to count.

The odor of strong drink and strong tobacco blew in the wind. The more Caleb walked, the louder the crowd sounded, and the more apprehensive he felt. Maybe going to the hog-catch was not such a good idea, but he did not feel that he could turn back now. The crowd almost seemed to carry him along. He could not get a seat close to the pen so he sat high on a makeshift wooden bleacher that swayed with the motion of the restless drunks who occupied most of its planks. After he had caught his breath, he tried to adjust to this new environment.

The men and women in the crowd howled and screamed, and the noise sounded as much like pain as it did pleasure.

On an elevated stage on the opposite side of the pen, a tall, skinny man with a funnel-shaped tube to amplify his voice strutted about barking to the crowd. He wore red pants, white shoes, a black tuxedo jacket, and a straw hat. As he walked back and forth, he shouted something that Caleb could not comprehend. From time to time, the man lowered his amplifier and grinned and moved his head up and down in a large, sweeping *yes* motion, and the crowd howled with excitement every time he made the motion.

Behind the man the fattest woman that Caleb had ever seen sat on what appeared to be a throne. She wore a tarnished, costume gold crown, and in her right hand, she held a matching scepter topped by a huge, cracked, fake jewel. She sipped beer from the largest stein Caleb had ever seen and chomped on a fat fried chicken. Grease dripped down the sides of her face, and she wiped her hands on her bare legs.

139

Caleb winced at the site and continued to doubt that it had been a good idea to come to the hog-catch.

When the hog-catch did not begin at the appointed time, the crowd grew angry. Empty bottles flew through the air, and shouts erupted.

The crowd was on the verge of starting a riot when the skinny barker turned to the fat lady and bowed to her. She used the throne's side arms to balance, and she stood.

She snatched the amplifier from the barker and yelled, "SHUT UP!"

Her voice rang out so deafeningly loud that the entire crowd hushed all at once.

She smiled, wiped grease from her face, and said: "Listen up, morons, the tall drink of water's got something to tell ya!"

She handed the amplifier back to the barker, and he said, "Ten dogs and thirty hogs. That's how it starts tonight. At the end of the first round, four dogs will be eliminated. Two dogs will be elimi-nated at the end of the second round, and then one dog at a time will be eliminated until we have a winner. The easiest-caught hogs will be eliminated too. The Queen will keep time. You may place your bets anytime you like. Also, you won't want to miss the open dog-challenge at the end of the hog catching competition. Two hundred silver pieces will be awarded for a successful challenge."

Caleb could not imagine what the "dog-challenge" was all about, but he did not have time to think about it. When the barker stopped talking, the crowd cheered, and a team of handlers led a bulldog toward the cage on one end of the pen.

The crowd hushed as the dog trotted from one end of the pen to the other, and those wishing to place bets studied the dog carefully. When the dog was secure in its cage, the handlers placed a fat boar in the cage on the other end of the pen without parading it through the pen.

Caleb noticed that the boar's tusks had been trimmed.

Spectators placed bets at a booth where four club-wielding policemen stood guard, and some placed bets among themselves. When the flurry of bet making settled down, the Queen grabbed the barker's amplifier, not that she really needed it, and yelled: "Attention!"

She stretched the word out for what seemed like a minute.

"In the cage to my right, there is a hog," the queen said.

"Sitting on the throne, there is a hog!" an anonymous spectator shouted back.

The crowd laughed and whistled at first. Then it booed the remark.

The queen pretended she did not hear. She continued: "And in the cage to my right there is a dog named Iron Jaw. Ready, Iron Jaw, get set and GO!"

Iron Jaw, a black bulldog with white specks and spots on it back, bolted out of his cage and darted toward the opposite end of the pen.

Because the dog moved with confidence, Caleb sensed that Iron Jaw had seen combat many times.

The hog stood bewildered for a moment after its cage opened. Then it saw the dog coming, ran out of its cage, and tried to reach the stage side of the pen, but before it could get so far as halfway to the fence, Iron Jaw slid under the pig's front legs and clamped his shiny white teeth onto the pig's throat. The dog then threw his weight at a right angle to the hog's body, jerked the hog off its feet, and climbed on top. The hog squealed for dear life, and the crowd roared. A team of five handlers jumped the fences and pried the dog's jaw open. They pulled the dog off the hog, and the hog got up with nothing hurt other than its feelings.

The handlers chased the hog out of the pen, and as they did, other handlers placed a new dog and a new hog in the cages.

"Nine seconds," the queen announced, and those in the crowd who had won bets went to the booth to collect their money.

Before the spectators had time to return to their seats, the queen announced that the name of the second dog was *Dolly*. Dolly was a brown bulldog, and she had a hairless spot on her side. She and the second hog entered the pen.

The hog attempted to side step the dog, but it was too slow. Dolly caught its throat, flipped it backward, and slammed it on its back in one sweeping plunge.

The crowd went wild with applause, and the Queen announced: "Five seconds!"

Only three spectators had dared to risk a bet on five seconds this early in the evening, and they went to collect their money as the handlers separated dog and hog.

"*What a dog*," Caleb thought, "*I wish I had a dog like that to protect my sheep.*"

The third dog was named Midnight, and he was so black that even the whites of his eyes were not perfectly white. They were bloodshot red. Unlike the first two dogs, Midnight did not twist about in the cage as he waited for the door to open. He stood perfectly motionless and stared at the hog.

Caleb supposed that he had never seen a dog that looked so purely evil.

The handlers opened the cages, and Midnight dashed under the hog, and sank his teeth into the hog's throat. The hog tried to squeal, but the sound that came out of its mouth was choked and incomplete. Midnight jerked the hog forward and threw it on its back, and the hog made no more sounds.

The handlers jumped in to remove Midnight, and he bit one of them on the knee. The handlers moved away from him, and he returned to the hog's throat. A man on the side of the pen tossed one of the handlers a pole with metal rings attached and a rope that ran through the rings and formed a loop at the end of the pole. A handler slipped the loop over the Midnight's head, and the team pulled the dog off the hog.

Midnight tried to reach the rod with his teeth, but he could not, and the handlers successfully removed him from the pen.

The hog did not move. A handler examined its body, made a hand motion to the queen, and she announced: "The hog is dead. You may place bids for the body at the booth, and if you're the winner, you and yours will eat pork for breakfast."

Caleb grimaced, not because the hog had been killed, but because the atmosphere of brutality unnerved him. The spectators seemed to enjoy the hog's death far too much.

The handlers placed the next dog and the next hog in the cages, and a loud mood of expectancy permeated the crowd.

Caleb suddenly got lost in his thoughts, so lost that the crowd sounded like a distant distraction instead of a mass of humanity that surrounded him on all sides.

He closed his eyes, and he saw himself at the age of four lying in his warm bed in his family's country cottage. His mother sat beside him on the bed and read him a story from a book with drawings.

The story was about a baby polar bear that got stuck on a drifting hunk of ice. The little bear drifted away from his mother and into the open sea. At sea, the little bear saw a bird fly overhead, but the bird would not speak to him. He saw a big fish leap into the air, but the fish would not speak to him either, and the little bear began to cry. On the page where the bear began to cry the drawing showed big tears dripping down his face and onto the ice.

Caleb saw himself (little Caleb) begin to cry, and then he saw his mother hurrying through the story to the part where a friendly porpoise befriended the baby polar bear and   pushed the hunk of ice back to land.

Caleb's mother tried to comfort him, but no matter what she said or did, he would not be comforted. Little Caleb would not accept the happy ending. He cried and cried, and he would not stop crying.

After awhile, his mother went for his father. He returned to the room with her and sat on one side of Caleb as she sat on the other. His mother ran her fingers through his hair, and his father placed a hand on his shoulder, and eventually little Caleb stopped crying.

Caleb's mind slowly returned to the hog-catch, and he noticed that tears had dripped down his cheeks. He looked around to see if anyone in the crowd had noticed. If anyone had, he could not tell, and if anyone had, he or she had probably assumed that Caleb was just another emotional drunk. He could not tell how long his mind had been lost in the memory, but it had to have been a long time because the hog-catch was drawing to a close.

Midnight threw an exceptionally fat hog half way across the

pen, bit its throat, and prevailed as the night's hog-catch champion. The hog died like the first hog that Midnight attacked, and Caleb heard someone say something about Midnight killing every hog he caught. The dogs were not supposed to kill the hogs, but Midnight's performances had been so spectacular that the officials had dismissed the deaths as "accidents."

"Open Dog Challenge!" the queen announced. "Bring on the accepted challengers, and place your bets."

The handlers led the third place dog, a tan colored half bulldog half mastiff named *Giant,* to the dog cage, and a short nervous looking man who looked vaguely familiar to Caleb led a donkey into the center of the pen.

The Queen yelled "Go," and Giant charged from the cage. He shot like an arrow toward the donkey and dived at its throat, but at the last possible moment, the donkey turned and kicked Giant in the ribs. Giant rolled, got up, circled the donkey once and plunged toward its throat for the second time. The donkey tried to avoid the dog, but it was not able to do so. Giant bit the donkey's throat and took it down.

The handlers raced into the pen and removed Giant, and the queen announced that the first challenger had failed.

Dolly, the evening's second place dog, returned to action against a bull. A different man led the bull into the pen, but Caleb thought he looked familiar too, but he could not say where he might have seen the man's face.

Though the bull was many times larger than Dolly, she dashed toward it, clamped its throat, swung herself in the air, swung back, and downed it with only the slightest effort, showing everyone present why bulldogs are called bulldogs.

The handlers rushed in to remove Dolly, but she relinquished her hold on the bull before they reached her.

Before the last challenger entered the pen, Caleb remembered where he had seen the faces of the men. He had seen the first man cleaning tables at *The Oaks,* and he had seen the second man brushing down a horse in the stable behind *The Oaks*.

A third man stepped to the side of the pen, and Caleb immediately recognized him. He was a stable keeper at *The Oaks*. Caleb had paid him to feed Big Head some corn.

Because the crowd was standing, Caleb could not see what kind of animal the man was leading to the pen, and a terrible thought entered his mind.

"Oh no!" he yelled.

He climbed down from the bleachers and all but ran toward the pen, but by the time he reached the place where the keeper had been standing, it was too late. His hunch was correct. The keeper stood in the center of the pen with Big Head.

"No!" Caleb shouted.

He tried to climb the fence, but two men in the crowd pulled him down.

"No!" Caleb screamed. "That's my goat."

"Shut up, old man," a man said.

At the same time, the police saw what was happening and began to work their way through the crowd to Caleb.

"You don't understand," Caleb protested to the man who had spoken and to anyone else who would listen. "I'm staying at *The Oaks*, and that man is a stable keeper there, and that's my goat."

"Congratulations," another man said, "Fine looking goat."

Caleb turned his head toward the pen and saw that Midnight stood still in the dog cage, waiting to attack Big Head. The dog looked vicious and hungry to kill.

"No!" Caleb screamed again, and as he did, two police officers grabbed his arms. He struggled to break free, but he could not.

The Queen announced that the impending catch would close the night, and many in the crowd pushed toward the booth to place bets.

Caleb pretended to settle down, and the policemen seemed to buy his act so he went a step further and pretended to pass out.

"Yep," one of the policemen said. "Just like I thought, a stoned old drunk."

"Let's lay him down on his back on the bleacher," the other policeman said.

They lowered Caleb's body onto the bleacher's bottom wooden plank, and as soon as they released his wrists, his hand moved faster than any eye could have seen into the folds of his garments.

Out came his knife. Its blade glinted in the light of the lamps that surrounded the pen, and the policemen backed away. Caleb stood up straight and swung the blade through the air to establish his space.

"Drop it, old man," one of the policemen said. "We don't want to have to hurt you."

"And I don't want to have to hurt you," Caleb said. "Now stay back!"

He swung the knife around two more times, and the policemen kept their distance.

Caleb reached for the fence to climb over, but just as he was about to pull his weight onto the edge of the top board, the cages swung open, and Midnight exploded into the pen like a bolt of lightning.

All four of the policemen who had been patrolling the hog-catch moved toward Caleb's back now.

He turned, swiped the knife through the air in a great semicircle, and shouted: "I said stay back!"

He attempted to climb over the fence, which at his age was no easy task, and one of the policemen grabbed his boot.

Caleb fell on his side, and the policemen jumped on top of him, but through the pen's board slats he watched what was sure to be the end of his beloved old friend.

Midnight bit at Big Head's throat. He tossed the old goat, and down Big Head fell.

Caleb cried out: "Noooo!" but no one heard.

Then Caleb saw that Midnight did not have Big Head by the throat, and he released a sigh of relief.

Midnight's teeth had caught in Big Head's beard, and that was all. Big Head rolled, kicked the dog aside, and stood. The dog had taken him by surprise at first, but now Big Head seemed to understand the situation.

Big Head backed up against the fence, and Caleb thought that the goat might be able to defend himself for a few seconds but that he certainly would not last much longer than that. Caleb had to find a way to break free from the police and get into the pen. He struggled but to no avail.

Midnight lunged a second time, and the goat rose on his hind paws, lowered his head, and charged the dog with all the strength and the weight of his body.

Midnight showed no fear. He opened wide his mouth to bite the goats face, but his timing was off.

Big Head rammed into the dog's snout and knocked the dog out as cold as the ice upon which the little polar bear had been stranded. The noise of the blow sounded like a gun going off, and the crowd roared.

"Guess I was wrong," Caleb thought.

The crowd cheered for the goat, especially those who had bet on him against the odds.

The handlers led Big Head back to the stable keeper. They poured water on Midnight, and he came to, but he did not seem so vicious. The dog glimpsed Big Head as the keeper led the goat onto the stage, and he whimpered like a spanked puppy.

Big Head's troubles in Loaden seemed to be over now, but Caleb's were just beginning. He had swung a knife at four policemen, and now they were on top of him, holding him down.

THIRTEEN

"We got us a real fighter here, Sheriff," one of the policemen said as the sheriff opened the door to the Loaden jail.

"He's drunker than a jellyfish in a water spout. He keeps talking nonsense about how he was trying to rescue a goat at the hog-catch," another policeman added. "Maybe the alcohol made his heart too soft."

"And of course he says he only had one drink," a third officer added. "They all say they've only had one drink."

The sheriff tossed the fourth officer a ring of keys and said, "Lock him up for the night. We'll take him before the judge in the morning. Anything else interesting happen?"

"No," one of the policemen said, "pretty calm evening, really."

"Good," the sheriff said. "It's time for me to go home and go to bed now. Dan, you stay here with the old drunk, and the rest of you can go watch Sailor Street."

Two of the policemen pushed Caleb into a cell, and the officer with the key ring locked him in. The fourth officer locked Caleb's knife in a desk drawer.

Caleb paced the floor of the cell and scratched his head. He could not stop thinking of what might have been happening to Big Head. He wanted to believe that the keeper had taken the goat back to the stable, but he could not be sure. He stepped to the back of the cell and looked through the bars of its single window. The stars twinkled, and the wind blew.

Caleb ran his hand through his hair. He could do nothing tonight, and that was certain, so he thought he might best occupy his time by lying down, trying to relax, and planning what he would say to the judge the next morning.

He tried to fall asleep, but he could not so much as close his eyes for more than a few seconds at a time. The more he thought, the more his stomach filled with nervousness. One way or the other, he had intended to visit the Court of Loaden the following day. Visiting the court had been his main purpose for coming here, but he did not want to visit it under these circumstances.

After an hour or more of lying in the dark, he heard what sounded like a cannon blast. The noise of the explosion filled the air. He sat up on his cot.

"What was that?" he asked.

"I don't know," the officer in attendance said, "but it's nothing that concerns you. Go back to sleep."

Holding a candle, the officer stepped to the jail's door and peered out into the night. He rubbed and scratched his chin, stood on his toes, and stretched his neck. Caleb could tell that curiosity was eating the policeman alive, but he did not say anything to him for fear of being rebuked.

Caleb then heard heavy footsteps of a man running in the street.

"Big emergency," said the man, who was obviously out of breath, "big explosion on Sailor Street." The man panted and spoke as he tried to catch his wind: "Officers say they need help."

The policeman needed no more encouragement than that so even without asking the man his name, he said, "Thanks, pal."

He turned to Caleb.

"Don't you try anything funny while I'm gone."

Caleb did not have time to say *yes* or *no* to the policeman's order because the officer ran out the door as soon as he spoke.

Within seconds, through his window Caleb heard the voice of the man in the street.

"Go to the far side of your cell," the voice said, "I'm about to blow out this window."

"Who's there?" Caleb asked.

"It's me, Andrew."

"Yes, of course," Caleb said, "you were disguising your voice, but now I recognize it. What is this nonsense about blowing out the window? Do you want to get me in worse trouble?"

"No, I'm here to get you out of trouble, and you'd better do what I tell you. I've put enough gunpowder around the window's bars to blow them to bits. Go to the far side of your cell."

"Andrew, this is wrong. I'll go before the judge in the morning and straighten all this out."

"This city is corrupt from top to bottom, Caleb, and unless you've got a large sum of money, you can forget about getting a fair hearing. I did my army training in the town south of here. I learned more about this place than I ever wanted to know, but we can discuss all that later. We don't have all night. The officer will be back in a few minutes. Hurry up and do what I say. Turn your cot on its side and use it as a shield."

Caleb thought that breaking out was a bad, bad idea, but Andrew's voice exuded so much sincerity that he could not refuse to do what the young man said. He stepped to the front of his cell, squatted, and shielded his back with his cot.

He heard the hissing of the gunpowder trail, and he covered his ears with his hands. Then he heard and felt the breaking of the bars by the explosion of the gunpowder. Debris showered the cell, and Caleb felt dust and smoke cover his body. He held his breath.

When he could hold his breath no more, he stood. He stepped to the window, and there he saw Andrew motioning for him to climb out.

"Come on, let's get away from here. The officer will be back any second when he realizes what happened, and he'll probably have others with him," Andrew said.

151

"Not so fast," Caleb said, "I've got to get my knife."

"You can buy another knife tomorrow," Andrew said. "Come on."

Caleb did not obey this time. He walked around to the front of the jail, entered the door which the officer had left open, lighted a candle, and searched for the key to the drawer where his knife had been placed.

"Please come on," Andrew said.

"Give me a second," Caleb said. "They put it in one of these drawers. I'm trying to find the key."

"They're coming," Andrew said, "I just saw the first one pass under a street lamp."

"One more second," Caleb said.

"Hurry," Andrew said.

"Here it is," Caleb said as he opened the drawer where his knife was stored.

"Good, but climb out the window again, they're running toward the front of the jail."

Caleb moved as fast as he could, but just before he was able to get himself through the window, the jail's front door burst open, and three officers ran inside. They stopped to light candles, saw what Caleb was trying to do, and grabbed his legs.

Andrew tried to pull Caleb through, but it was no use. He released his hold on Caleb's arms, grabbed the knife out of Caleb's hand, and ran. Caleb did not know where the young man was going, but he knew that he was now in the worst trouble of his life.

The officers pulled Caleb back into the jail and held him face down on the floor. They shouted at him and drove their kneecaps into his back. They threw punches, and they kicked.

"Please stop," Caleb begged, but they did not listen.

Caleb covered his head with his hands to ward off the heavy blows, but something suddenly changed. He felt one of the officer's fall on him. Then another fell. Then the third officer fell.

Caleb uncovered his head and looked up.

Holding his gun, Andrew Scar Chest stood over him.

"They were too busy hitting *you* to see that I was about to hit *them*," he said, "got'em with the butt of my gun. They'll be all right in the morning, but you won't if you don't come on now. Here's your knife."

Caleb took his knife and followed Andrew. They exited through the jail's front door, but they walked around to the back of it as fast as they could.

"We'll have to take the back streets," Andrew said. "Where are you camping?"

"I'm not camping," Caleb said. "I'm staying at *The Oaks*."

"*The Oaks?*" Andrew said, "Moving up in the world, are we? Or did you have no choice after the bandits stole your goat and your belongings?"

"They weren't bandits, they didn't steal my belongings, and they didn't exactly steal Big Head. They borrowed him," Caleb said. "They're keepers from *The Oaks*. This really is a corrupt city, isn't it? By the way, how did you know I was in here? How did you know about Big Head?"

"Yes, this place is corrupt. There's a darkness darker than night in this town," Andrew said, "but we can discuss everything later, and I'll tell you how I found you. Let's go to *The Oaks*. That's the last place they'll look for us."

As Caleb and Andrew walked, they kept to the shadows as much as possible, and they avoided Sailor Street except for the one time they had to cross it.

When they reached *The Oaks*, they went to the stable first. In the stall where he had been placed earlier in the evening Big Head nibbled on corn. He looked as if nothing at all had happened.

The keeper lay sleeping on a cot in the back of the stable. Caleb put his finger to his lips, and neither he nor Andrew said anything.

They did not speak until they reached Caleb's room. The room was furnished with two beds so they each took one.

"All right," Caleb said, "start explaining."

"I think you should start," Andrew said. "What happened at my grandmother's house?"

"I felt afraid that Big Head would get eaten by a bear or a wolf so I brought him in to sleep on the floor beside me. Sometime in the

153

night he got up and ate every piece of cloth or paper he could reach. I felt so ashamed that I left. Don't worry; I'll make it up to your grandmother. In fact, Big Head's own earnings, so to speak, are going to make it up to her. Tomorrow morning that stable keeper is going to give all the prize money to me, you can believe that, and then I'll give it to your grandmother."

"Caleb, did my grandmother not come across to you as a Christian woman? Could you not tell, even from the short amount of time that you spent with her, that she has a kind heart? I would think that anyone would be able to sense my grandmother's good nature and good humor. Why did you assume that she would treat you cruelly for a thing as small as a goat chewing up some of her stuff? Are you one of those people who think that everyone has a cruel heart? Is that why you're a shepherd? On some deep level, are you afraid of people?"

Caleb had not been addressed so personally and so directly in a long time, and he did not like having to think about the inclinations and attitudes that made up the core of his being, and he felt that Andrew had hit a sore spot in his soul.

"Andrew Scar Chest," he said, "I will not answer your questions in detail tonight, but I will say that your questions are justified. I will answer them over time and in my own way. More strange things have happened to me in the past couple of weeks than had happened in the past fifty years. If an old man can change, then I think I am changing. I pray that the changes will be for the best."

"Speaking of changes," Andrew said, "what happened to your beard? I was searching for a man with a white beard, not a man with a clean shaven face. Otherwise I might have found you before tonight."

"I shaved it," Caleb said, "but we'll come to that later. What did your grandmother say when she woke up and saw her stuff chewed to pieces and me gone?"

"She wasn't happy of course," Andrew said, "but she thought your running away was silly. We got her house into the best shape we could, and the next day she sent me after you. She said you would need me to look out for you, and she was right. She told me to tell you that her house needed new hangings and coverings anyway and that she looked forward to getting the ones you were going to buy for her. Simple and to the point– that's her style."

"So she's not angry at me?"

"Of course not."

Caleb and Andrew told each other the details of their journeys down the coast. Andrew finished by telling Caleb how he had spotted him at last only after Caleb had tried to rescue Big Head from the bulldog. Afterward, he had followed at a safe distance behind the officers as they had led Caleb to the jail, and he had set off a gunpowder explosion in an alley near Sailor Street to create the diversion that got the policeman away from the jail.

When they finished catching cach other up on what had happened, they planned what they would do the next morning. Andrew believed that none of the policemen had seen his face clearly. He believed that he would place himselt in no jeopardy by going to the Loaden Courthouse. No one would suspect that a guilty man would go to the courthouse anyway so that was exactly what he decided to do. He would obtain the legal documents to complete Caleb's mission.

Caleb would stay at *The Oaks* where he would be safe from police searchcs, and he would take care of the business with the stable keeper.

Caleb and Andrew woke early in the morning. They had breakfast in the dining room and set off on their tasks.

Caleb walked to the back of *The Oaks,* opened the stable door as quietly as he could, and tip-toed over to where the keeper lay snoring. He leaned down and brought his face so close to the keeper's face that their noses almost touched. He hesitated a moment, and all was silent in the stable except for the keeper's snoring and the breathing of the animals.

"Boo!" Caleb shouted.

"Arrgghhh!" the keeper yelled.

The keeper's eyes popped open. He tried to sit up, but Caleb pushed him back down with one hand, which required little effort since the keeper was a bone-skinny man. Caleb used both hands to pin the keeper's shoulders down on the cot.

"Good morning," Caleb said with a polite smile. "Sorry to wake you this early, but we have urgent business to attend."

"I ain't got no business. I ain't got no business. I ain't got no business with you," the keeper stammered.

"Oh, but I think you do, you do, you do," Caleb said. "You are going to give me all the money you won last night using my goat."

"I don't know what you're talking about," the keeper said.

"I didn't expect that you would, but that's all right, I will refresh your memory. The black dog Midnight clamped his teeth into my goat Big Head's beard. It probably felt something like this," Caleb said as he reached toward the keeper's face and pulled hard on a handful of the keeper's beard. "Are you starting to remember? If not I can keep pulling until you do."

The keeper kicked and squirmed beneath Caleb's strength, but he could not push Caleb aside.

"All right, I remember, I remember," the keeper said through howls of pain. "Just stop pulling my beard."

"Good, I thought a little reminding would help you remember," Caleb said. "Now about the money…"

"I spent it," the keeper said.

"All of it?" Caleb asked.

"Yeah, sure, all of it."

"You spent all of two-hundred pieces of silver in one night? That's too bad because I made up my mind last night that if I didn't get all of it, I would have to tell the owner of *The Oaks* about our little mix up. You don't think he would fire you over something ever so insignificant as stealing a guest's goat and entering it in a match against a vicious dog, do you?"

"Well, I did save some of it, but not very much."

Caleb coughed and chuckled at the same time.

"And what is more," he said, "the stealing of livestock, while it might not seem such a big deal in Loaden, is a violation of national law. I could send word to the regional marshal. There were about a thousand witnesses at the hog-catch."

"Oh, all right, all right. I spent twelve silvers for drinks at an ale house, bought two rounds for all my friends. I had five silvers in my bag before the hog-catch so now I've got a hundred and ninety-three silvers, and that's the honest truth."

"Where is your bag?" Caleb asked.

"Behind the jars on the top shelf of the stable's storage room," the keeper answered.

"We'll go get it then, but in case you were thinking of running off, I'd better do this."

Caleb turned the keeper over, pinned the center of his back with one knee, untied the keeper's boots, and took them off his feet.

"Even *I* could catch a bare-foot man on the streets of this filthy city, what with all the broken glass everywhere. And if you were thinking of picking up a pitch fork or a shovel to start a fight, then have a look at this."

Caleb showed the keeper his knife.

"Sharp and shiny, isn't it? And you know what? I can hit a bull's eye with it from thirty paces." he said.

The keeper led Caleb to the silver, and Caleb counted it out one coin at a time.

"There are one-hundred and nincty-three silvers here. You're an honest man after all," Caleb said as he gave the keeper a slap on the back, "You should try to stay that way. I'll be going back to my room now. You may brush down my goat while I'm gone."

"Hey, that's not fair; I gave you all the money."

"Yes, it is fair. You gave me all you had, which is seven silvers less than what you won, but I will take your work in consideration of the seven coins."

The keeper huffed, but he did not reply.

"And I think I'll take your boots to my room. You can have them back when I'm ready to leave," Caleb continued, "and that should-n't be a long time from now."

He went inside *The Oaks*, climbed the stairs, reached his room, and waited for Andrew.

Andrew returned before lunchtime, and he held the court documents.

"The Loaden registrar will contact the Pranville and the

Merrydale registrars," Andrew said. "He'll also contact Bruker's wife here in Loaden. He said he knew where she lived."

"Good work," Caleb said. "I've got the silver coins right here, one-hundred and ninety-three of them. Are the police looking for me?"

"Yes," Andrew said. "The city is swarming with them. They're searching all the sailors' inns even as we speak. *The Oaks* is a rich man's inn so they probably won't search here or even think they need to search here, but once the stable keeper learns that the man who took his prize money is the same man the police are looking for, we won't be safe. We'd better leave now."

"How do you propose we do that?" Caleb asked.

"I've got a plan," Andrew said. "I'll tell you about it as we walk."

When they reached the stable, Caleb gave the keeper his boots back and told him to go have lunch.

"I don't have any money for lunch," the keeper said.

Caleb shook his head, reached into his pouch, produced five silver coins, and said, "You really are trouble, but I can't leave you to starve. Here, go have lunch. Now you're no richer or poorer than you were before you borrowed my goat."

The stable keeper took the coins and hurried out of the stable.

"We'll have to move fast," Andrew said. "It won't take long for the keeper to figure out who you are. The policemen are asking passers-by if they have seen the old man who caused the commotion over the goat at the hog catch."

"And you're convinced this plan will work?" Caleb asked.

"No, but can you think of a better one?"

Caleb could not answer. To complete the first step of Andrew's plan, Caleb squeezed himself onto Big Head's goat cart. He pulled his knees up to his chest, and his back, which was already sore from the blows administered by the policeman, ached anew.

Andrew covered Caleb with a blanket, and he stacked and tied Caleb's stuff on top of him.

"Stay put," he said to Caleb with a snicker.

"As if I had any choice," Caleb groaned from somewhere

beneath the load.

Caleb felt the cart jolt when Andrew hitched it to Big Head.

"I'm going to take the long way out of town," Andrew said. "I don't want to get close enough to anyone for the goat to be seen. If he's recognized as the goat from the hog-catch, we'll be caught."

FOURTEEN

Without incident, Andrew led Big Head to Loaden's south side, and before he turned onto one of the paths that bypassed Loaden to the west, he whispered to Caleb that he might want to lift the edge of the blanket and have a peep at the high cliffs that jutted out of the sea.

"Is anyone near?" Caleb asked.

"No," Andrew answered.

Caleb lifted a corner of the blanket and strained his neck to catch a glimpse of the cliffs. Their massive white faces stood at angles that suggested they had been shaped by great landslides instead of slow erosion. Caleb tried not to think of the fact that if Big Head got stung by a bee or frightened by a dog and dashed out of Andrew's control, he might go flying off a cliff in a goat cart.

He smelled the salt on the wind from the sea and took a deep breath. He listened to the noise of the waves splashing against the base of the cliffs and let his mind relax.

"You don't think we could stop and I could get out for a stretch, do you?" Caleb asked.

"It would not be safe. Wait until we are a few miles north of Loaden. We'll be out of the Loaden police jurisdiction then, and only a marshal could arrest you if you were spotted."

The goat cart rattled along the trail, and Caleb groaned as loud as he thought he could without being heard by anyone but Andrew.

An hour or so later Andrew stopped Big Head and told Caleb that the path was clear for him to get out of the cart. He removed Caleb's stuff and uncovered him.

Caleb climbed out, and he and Andrew restacked the stuff.

"How do you feel?" Andrew asked.

Caleb's eyes drooped.

"After a long ride bundled in the bottom of a goat's cart, I feel merrier than Christmas, sure, just merry," Caleb said.

"Speaking of Christmas," Andrew said, "this is the month, and I can hardly wait. This will be my first Christmas home since my service in the Army, and my grandmother bakes the finest Christmas sweets in the world."

"Yes, well, I *can* wait." Caleb said. "I've got much to get done before Christmas, and that means we've got to hurry back to Merrydale."

"We've got time to get back before Christmas with a few days to spare," Andrew said. "What do you have to get done?"

"Clara's going to sing in the Christmas concert at the Merrydale church, but I'm going to have to work to make sure she gets the opportunity. I'm going to do my best to ruin Bruker's life because a life like his deserves ruining. Who knows? Maybe it will make an honest man out of him, or at least teach him that sooner or later the truth always comes out. The hard part is: In the process of ruining Bruker, I will be hurting Susan. She's young enough that she still has a lot of dreaming hope in her heart, and though she truly knows that Bruker is just plain rotten, there are parts of herself that just will not allow her to believe it. Those parts are going to get bruised, and there's no telling how she'll react, but as we shepherds say, *must be done.*"

"Yes, must be done," Andrew agreed. "Maybe if we caught a ship in Pranville, it would shave a day or two off our travel time."

"Good idea," Caleb said.

They walked at a brisk, steady pace, stopping only to eat and sleep on their way to Pranville. There they boarded a vessel that sailed the Pranville-Merrydale route once a week.

Big Head stayed on the ship's lower level in a cargo area especially for livestock, and a steward assigned Caleb and Andrew hammocks in a room at deck level. On the first night and through half the first day of their voyage, they put their hammocks to extensive use, making up for rest lost on the journey from Loaden. The waking hours of the final part of their journey they spent swapping army stories, and they learned that they were alike in many ways.

Just after a foggy dawn on a cold morning the ship sailed into the port at Merrydale. Caleb led Big Head onto the deck and down the wooden gangplank to the pier where the ship had docked. Andrew followed holding the goat cart by the harness.

Caleb looked about him. Over the tops of the houses and shops he saw the Merrydale Church steeple. It felt good to be home.

"Andrew," Caleb said when they were out of the dock area and onto one of Merrydale's front streets, "from the bottom of my heart, I thank you for your help. You've helped me more than you understand. Here, take this sack of silver to your grandmother and give her my apologies and my greetings. I have business to attend here in town today, but I look forward to seeing you soon in the open fields where we shepherds are knights and kings."

Andrew shook Caleb's hand and thanked him for the silver, and he told him not to worry that his grandmother might harbor some resentment over the loss of her furnishings. She was not a woman who loved material things. He also told Caleb to stop by and see her sometime, and when he told him, he raised one of his eyebrows and one corner of his mouth as if to imply that the visit might give rise to more than friendly connections.

"Oh stop that," Caleb said. "I'm an old man, and she's an old woman."

"You look ten years younger without the beard," Andrew said, "and for an old dog, you seem to be learning new tricks every day."

Caleb felt he had so much to do that he could not get it all done

163

without having breakfast first so he stopped in one of the sailors' inns and ordered eggs, toast, coffee, and a slice of ham. He ate it all in haste, but he relished the flavor of every mouthful. He reflected that for a shepherd he might be getting a little too friendly with kitchen-cooked meals and that he might miss them too much when he returned to his regular life.

When he finished eating, he walked to the Merrydale parsonage and knocked on its door.

Parson Rivers' house keeper answered the door wearing a house coat.

"Caleb, what are you doing here at this time of the morning? Nobody's up yet. And where's your beard?" she said.

"Who's that at the door?" Caleb heard the parson ask in a sleepy voice.

"It's Caleb," the housekeeper said, "and he's lost his beard."

"Yes, it's Caleb," Caleb said, and I've got urgent business with you, parson. I need to see you now."

Wiping his eyes, the parson dragged his feet into the receiving room, and his house keeper went back to bed.

"What is it, Caleb? Is something wrong?" Parson Rivers asked.

"Many things are wrong," Caleb said, "but I'm going to try to make a few of them right, and in order to do that, I'm going to need to understand everything about Susan that I can, and I do mean everything. I need to know the secret you would not disclose to me the other day. Why does she get upset at the mere mention of your name?"

"Oh Caleb, it's probably not important."

"Yes it is important, and if you won't tell me, I'll start asking everybody in Merrydale, and whether I learn the truth or not, rumors will start flying around town. You know how people talk."

"All right, enough. If it comes down to blackmail, I will tell you. Better yet, I'll show you. Give me a few minutes to put my clothes on."

Caleb waited for the parson in the receiving room. The parson dressed for the day, returned from his room, and led Caleb to the orphanage.

When they arrived, the sisters were serving the children breakfast.

"Have they got plenty to eat?" Caleb asked.

"They've had plenty to eat for as long as I've been here, and they will have plenty for as long as I remain, but the food is better now than ever since the mayor wrote the orphanage into the town's annual budget. I only hope that the town's taxes going to help the orphans don't dampen the true generosity of the people," Parson Rivers said.

They walked past the dining hall and down a long corridor. They turned a corner and approached the entrance of a classroom, and Parson Rivers removed his key chain.

"You've got more keys than an organ," Caleb said.

"Yes," the parson said, "too many keys. I haven't used some of them in years, but I can never remember which keys go to which doors so I'm afraid to throw any of them away."

The parson opened the door, held it for Caleb, stepped in behind him, and closed it.

"It started in here," the parson said, "but before I tell you about it, I want to say that while it may explain a few things about Susan, it won't explain all of them."

"Go on," Caleb said.

"In a minute," the parson said, "I also want to tell you that we don't do this thing at the orphanage anymore, and we never should have done it in the first place. It seemed like a good idea at the time, a more humane way to discipline children according to the book we read, but in the long run I believe it did far more damage to the children than good."

"Just go on," Caleb said.

The parson ran the palm of his hand across his forehead, took a deep breath, and slowly released it.

"Well," he said, "Susan was nine or ten at the time, and Old Sister Fionna was her teacher. I remember that it was after she had stopped singing in the choir, and that means it was after she had stopped being obedient to her teachers and had started questioning every word they said. She had already become a difficult child, and she had a hard time relating to the other children. Maybe she was going through some kind of stage. Maybe all she wanted was attention. I don't know."

"So what happened?" Caleb said.

"I don't like talking about this, Caleb. Not even Sister Fionna knew what happened."

Parson Rivers paused, but Caleb did not tell him to continue. He could tell that the parson was gathering his thoughts and his courage.

After a minute or so, the parson said: "One day Susan started throwing a tantrum, but she would not tell Sister Fionna why. She ran away from the sister, which wasn't hard since Sister Fionna was ten years older then than either of us are now. Susan hid under the big oak table in the back of the class and would not come out for bribes or threats. Sister Fionna sent one of her students to my office in the church to tell me about the problem, and I followed the child to the classroom."

The parson paused, and Caleb saw that he was fighting back tears.

"I knelt beside the oak table, reached under it, and dragged Susan out by one arm. She kicked, screamed, and tried to bite me, but I pulled her out anyway. 'Come on,' I said, 'you're going to be punished. You haven't been behaving for nearly a year now, and it's time you learned your lesson. You're going to the lonely room.'"

"What's the *lonely room*?" Caleb asked.

"Come on, I'll show you," Parson Rivers said, "but I want to remind you that we don't use it anymore."

Caleb followed the parson out the classroom door, down the hall, and around the corner to another door.

The parson fumbled through his keys again.

"It's been years since I opened this door," he said. "I may have to try a few of these old keys to get the right one."

The parson found the right key, and opened the door. He and Caleb looked inside, but the room had no window so they could not see much.

"Do you have a match, Caleb?" the parson asked.

Caleb reached into his pack and found a match.

The parson took the match and lit a candle on a holder beside the door. Because the room was small, the one candle provided enough light. The room was not as small as a broom closet, but it was not much bigger.

A dust-covered, child-sized chair sat in the center of the room, and a brass framed plaque hung on the far wall. The plaque contained one verse of a poem:

> *To ponder the terrible things they have done,*
> *Disobedient children must sit alone.*
> *To punish them when their manners have gone,*
> *Disobedient children must sit alone.*

"Oh brother," Caleb said. "I'd hate to meet the witch that wrote that."

"The poem was written in the book that suggested this form of punishment," Parson Rivers said, "and one of the sisters made the plaque. Again, it was all a mistake."

Caleb and Parson Rivers stood for a few seconds looking into the room, and then the parson said, "Go inside and have a closer look. Look at the walls, especially near the floor."

Caleb did what the parson asked.

"That's not?" he asked.

"Yes, it is," the parson said, and he began to cry.

"Caleb," he said, "if there were one thing and only one thing in my entire life that I could take back, what I am about to tell you would be it. You are looking at claw marks and blood stains on the wall, and Susan left them. I led her into this room and locked her inside. As soon as the lock snapped tight, I heard her scream, and with a voice as rich and strong as hers, it sounded like the wail of death. I assumed that the scream was a furtherance of her tantrum so I ignored it and walked away, and I thought she would calm down once she realized that I was gone."

The parson stopped talking altogether now. Tears dripped down both his cheeks and onto his shirt. He turned his face away.

"Just a minute," he said through thick sobs. "Give me a chance to regain my composure."

"Take your time," Caleb said, feeling sorry for his old friend.

"I had intended to come back in half an hour or so," the parson said, "but when I returned to my office, Sister Kate said that a parishioner had been taken to the infirmary and was close to dying. Without thinking twice, I walked straight to the infirmary. The family had gathered around the bed of their dying grandmother, and I stood with them and prayed and said all the things a parson is supposed to say when a loved one's time of departure is near.

"While trying to help the family's feelings, I forgot about the little girl I had left in this room. Susan did not enter my mind again until the next morning. I must have seen her in a dream because at the crack of dawn I sat straight up in bed wide awake with the sickest feeling I had ever felt. I trembled as I dressed, and I got to the orphanage as fast as I could. As I walked I kept telling myself that surely Sister Fionna had heard that I had been delayed, had remembered Susan, and had let her out of the lonely room, but I knew as well as I knew my own name that Sister Fionna was too old to have remembered and that Susan was still here. I tried to tell myself that if she were here, she had fallen asleep on the floor and that all would be well when I found her, but somehow I knew that wasn't true either.

"I opened the orphanage and sprinted down the halls. I opened the lonely room's door, and there she lay in the corner, and…"

The parson looked down at the corner, and he contorted his face in a cringe of pain. His hands trembled, and beads of sweat stood out on his face and neck. He crossed his arms in front of him and gripped himself around his upper torso.

"She lay trembling and crying, and she didn't even know I had opened the door. Her red hair was wet and stuck to her face. Her body flinched and shook, and the sound of her crying was like… it was like… *agony*, maybe that's the word, but that's not quite it. Caleb, it was the most heart-breaking sound I've ever heard. She had spent something like sixteen hours in the room, but she was still terrified, absolutely terrified."

168

The parson stopped for a moment to cry some more, and Caleb said nothing.

In a few minutes the parson continued: "I picked her up and carried her to the orphanage's sick room. Sister Kate had been with me longer than any of the other sisters, her disposition had always been naturally sweet, and I trusted her more than anyone so I went to find her. I made taking care of Susan her exclusive responsibility, and over the course of a few days, she brought the child back to normal, or at least I thought she brought her back to normal. Maybe Susan never came all the way back to normal. I don't know Caleb. I think there's more to Susan than what any of us understand. Like I told you, she started to change even before the lonely room incident. She started showing problems, but the incident made her problems ten times worse, I think. Her problems didn't seem any worse because she held her feelings inside, and that's the worst thing anyone can do, not that she knew any better.

"You know, Caleb, I never even told her I was sorry. I always meant to tell her, but after awhile I felt that bringing it up would have caused more embarrassment for both of us than what it would have been worth. Anyway, now you know all. I hope it'll help with whatever you're planning to do, but please don't tell anyone you don't have to."

"I won't," Caleb said, "but one more question: You really don't know why she stopped singing? That seems important somehow."

"I don't have the faintest idea," the parson said, "unless it was just a general sadness. I think everyone gets that sooner or later. It's one of the side effects of living. You feel sad for a time but for no particular reason. When children feel sad that way we say it is a growth stage. When grown ups feel sad that way we say they need help, but maybe they don't need help. Maybe it's just another growth stage, a search for something missing from the soul."

"Yes," Caleb agreed, "sadness has taken me to some places that happiness never has. Parson, I thank you for your honesty. I must be going now. I'm in the process of ruining Bruker's life."

"Oh, quite nice, quite nice," Parson Rivers said as he showed Caleb out the orphanage's front door. "And by the way, you look ten years younger without the beard."

Caleb thanked the parson for the compliment and walked to where he had tied Big Head. He searched through one of the boxes on Big Head's cart, found some cheese, cut himself a nibble, popped it into his mouth, and led Big Head to Farmer Quigley's to gather all his sheep and goats, each of which he fervently missed.

"They'll be overjoyed to hear about how you knocked out Midnight," Caleb said. "I think I'll tell them about it myself. Come on, old boy, let's walk faster."

Caleb hurried along the familiar path to Quigley's farm, but as he ventured through the fields, he saw unfamiliar faces.

FIFTEEN

"Who is that man walking toward us on the path, Big Head? I don't recognize him. Another man is walking on top of the hill to our left. Is that a shovel he's carrying? I've never seen him either. And look to your right, Big Head, a third man is standing beside an oak tree. Who are these men?"

Caleb dismissed his curiosity about the men for a few minutes because he felt that three strangers were not much to worry about, but the more he walked, the more strangers he saw. Many of them carried shovels. All of them behaved in odd ways, scratching their heads and ambling about in no particular direction as if they were trying to solve some mental puzzle.

"This is my territory, Big Head, so I must find out what is happening."

Caleb approached one of the men and attempted to make polite conversation. The man paced and studied the ground, and he did not look up when Caleb spoke.

"Cool weather, isn't it?" Caleb said.

"Yes, cool," the man said.

"Can I help you with anything?" Caleb asked.

"Not unless you've got a treasure map," the man said.

"A treasure map?" Caleb asked.

"Of course, everybody's looking for the treasure. It's around here somewhere. It has to be." the man said.

"I've been living in these parts my whole life, and no one has ever said anything to me about a treasure," Caleb said.

"Of course they haven't, all the facts have only just now come to light since that fellow Barker found out about the old man."

"Who is Barker?"

"He's a sailor that's married to the woman who met the man who stole the king's treasure."

Caleb began to feel uncomfortable.

"Do you mean *Bruker* instead of Barker?"

"I don't know. Maybe it's Barker, or maybe it's Bruker. Doesn't matter, does it?"

"Are you a sailor?" Caleb asked.

"Aye, you could say that," the man said.

"Very well, I will say it," Caleb said. "Under what flag does your ship sail?"

"Not every ship sails under a flag," the man said.

"Ah, so you're a pirate?"

"I prefer to be called a free trader." The man said.

He had still not looked up at Caleb.

"This man who stole the king's treasure, what does he look like?"

The man looked up at Caleb for the first time now.

"His hair was the same color as yours, but he had a thick, curly beard. He was a shepherd, and he died a couple weeks ago. It's a good thing Barker found out who the old man was," the man said. "Barker must have been a very good friend of his. It was probably one of those deathbed confessions."

"You say the old man with hair like mine has died?"

"That's what Barker said, or at least that's what my friend told me that Barker said. I believe my friend heard it from our captain, who heard it from Barker's captain, who heard it from Barker's best friend. It's the truth on good authority. You can believe that."

"Oh sure, I believe it," Caleb said. "You don't have to convince me. Thanks for telling me about the excitement."

The man looked up again for a moment, but he did not say anything. He lowered his head and continued to search the ground.

Caleb walked away, and as he walked he spoke to Big Head: "Old fellow, it would not be safe for us to return to the cottage just now. Come to think of it, it's not safe for us to be on this path. If these men knew who I was, they would capture me and torture me for knowledge I don't have. Well, at least I don't have very much of it. There is the one thing I buried beneath the cottage's chimney of course, but that is beside the point. I've got to get out of sight and stay out of sight until I can summon the brotherhood. Where shall we go? Yes, we'll go to the mountains, good idea, but we must leave your cart somewhere. Yes, another good idea, we'll take it back to Merrydale and leave it behind the parsonage with a note asking Parson Rivers's housekeeper to keep an eye on it."

Caleb hurried back to town, unharnessed Big Head, and left the cart propped against the parson's house. He knew that it would be safe there. Even many of the town's greediest thieves feared to steal from church property.

Without the cart, Caleb and Big Head could move at a faster pace. They went north along the coast before they turned northeast to enter the mountain passes.

Being a goat, Big Head felt very much at home climbing through narrow passages and slowing himself with all four hoofs as he descended steep slopes. Being an old man, Caleb did not.

Caleb turned and hiked south. Sometime around the middle of the day, he stood on a high ledge that overlooked all of Merrydale and the surrounding region. He removed his horn from his pack, and blew the notes that signaled the brotherhood to meet. He heard horns blowing in response in many directions, and he heard the horns repeat the signal several times. Then Caleb blew another signal to indicate the place where the shepherds would meet, and the shepherds repeated it on their horns.

Caleb circled around and down the mountain to the mouth of a secluded cave, the shepherds' most secret meeting place and Orfel Little Mountain's Christmas residence. Christmas was Orfel's favorite time of year for singing, and he chose the cave because he liked the way his voice echoed among the stalactites, stalagmites, and rock walls.

Orfel had never known how often the other shepherds had gathered outside the cave to listen to the beautiful sounds that came from within. Orfel had never even known how great a gift he possessed.

Caleb found Orfel sitting at the cave's mouth, waiting for the gathering.

"Were you here when I sounded the signal?" Caleb asked.

"Yes," Orfel answered.

"Sorry to drop in on your place like this, but we're facing an emergency," Caleb said.

"I know," Orfel said, "and we've been facing it for two weeks. Where you been? We've all been looking for you. We were afraid something terrible had happened. The bear maybe, you know."

"I've been down the coast on personal business. I would tell you about it now, but if I did, I wouldn't feel like repeating it when the brotherhood gathered. I'll wait and tell all of you at once."

Orfel Little Mountain, who was one of the most agreeable people Caleb had ever known, said: "Fair enough." And that was that.

Because of the remote location, several hours passed before all the shepherds reached the cave. None of them had to take the same route that Caleb took, but the hike was not easy for any of them.

The fellowship began a little after dark.

Caleb stood and said, "Shepherd brothers, we now face a danger greater than that of bears and wolves."

"Speaking of bears," Nick the Sick interrupted, "I found a giant bear track yesterday. The old devil must still be alive. Unless the track is old, the gunshot wound didn't kill him."

"Of course he's still alive," Caleb said. "He didn't get to be as big as he is by dying easily."

Caleb paused, not sure that what he had said sounded logical, but then he thought it must have made sense because the shepherds

174

nodded their heads in unselfconscious agreement and mumbled things like: "That's the truth."

He continued, "Yes, the great bear and the wolves remain a danger, but the danger upon our hills is now multiplied a hundred times. I assume you all know about the pirates."

"I just found out today of course," Andrew Scar Chest said. "They've been digging up my grandmother's pecan orchard."

Caleb did not think the brotherhood knew what Andrew meant so he explained: "Andrew and I have been down the coast on business that is indirectly related to the danger at hand. It all revolves around this fellow Bruker, the husband of the woman Susan. She lives in my Christmas cottage.

"I've been spying on him," Loak the Fat said, "and..."

Before Loak could finish, Old Timothy Peg Leg said, "You? Spying? I didn't know there were trees near the cottage big enough for you to hide behind. I didn't know there were trees on earth big enough for you to hide behind."

The brotherhood laughed, and Loak turned red in the face. He did not like jokes about his weight, but he knew better than to show irritation. Making light of each other's personal faults and frailties helped bind the brotherhood together somehow. The good-natured jokes spoke of unconditional acceptance, an odd phenomenon, but a real one.

Loak continued: "I didn't have to hide behind anything. I just tended my sheep near the cottage. Bruker's got a gang of rough characters lying around your cottage all the time now, Caleb. They do nothing but drink, but unlike our friend John here, they don't keep quiet when they drink. They fight and yell obscenities at each other and tell dirty stories. They stay up all hours of the night, and I think they're beginning to run the red head woman crazy. When she walks to work, she drags her feet and keeps her head down, and she's too tired to carry the little girl on her back. She makes her walk beside her. And speaking of the little girl, at night Bruker makes her work around the cottage's campsite like a slave. He says things like: 'Clara, get Joe another glass of beer. Clara, throw a piece of wood on the fire. No, you're not too small. Go on, get the wood. Clara. Clara, you know better than to spill the beer. I should slap you down for that…"

Caleb interrupted, "Have you actually seen him slap her, or does he just talk?"

"I saw him raise a hand to slap her day before yesterday, but the red head woman…"

"Susan?"

"Yes, Susan. Susan stepped in and wouldn't let him. She took the little girl inside."

"I'm glad to hear it," Caleb said, "because if he hurt Clara, I would…"

"Don't say what you would do, Caleb," Marsel Long Legs interrupted, "I wouldn't want to have to repeat it in court at your trial. Besides, if I saw him slap her, I would do the same thing. How much do you know about what these pirates are up to? They believe that it relates to you."

"First, I need to know everything you've all heard," Caleb said. "There are some wild rumors flying about the countryside, and we're going to have to sift through to the truth."

"We heard you were dead," Mud Face Richard said.

"I flatly deny that," Caleb said.

The brotherhood laughed.

Marsel Long Legs spoke again: "The pirates are telling a story that they heard a few years ago, and they believe you are the subject of it. At the end of the Big War, the King of Nishfidor died while sitting on his own throne. Somebody chopped his head off. Everybody knows that of course. It's world history. It is told that no one ever knew who killed the king, but according to the pirates, someone did know.

"The king of Nishfidor held a prisoner in the dungeon across the courtyard from his chambers, an important political prisoner of some kind. The dungeon had a window at ground level. The prisoner was standing on his toes watching the battle in the courtyard when he saw a young soldier step out of the king's chamber carrying something in a bag. The young soldier looked both ways and thought no one had seen him. After a minute or two had passed, the prisoner heard someone call the name *Caleb*, and the young soldier turned and walked out of the courtyard. Our soldiers released the prisoner an hour later, but the prisoner told no one what he had seen. Instead he set out to find the soldier because he was convinced that the soldier had taken the encoded map to the king's treasure, surely the last thing the king would have offered as a ransom for his life. The prisoner searched until he died, absolutely convinced that the soldier and the treasure would turn up someday and even more convinced that he would be able to blackmail the soldier and take all the treasure for himself. The prisoner recorded the details of his search in a diary that eventually fell into the possession of one of the pirate captains. According to the diary, the prisoner visited Merrydale once as everything he heard pointed him here, but by chance he never learned the soldier's whereabouts. He met three men named Caleb, but none of them had been soldiers in the Big War. Some believe the diary is a forgery and that the story of the prisoner is all made up, but the captain of one of the pirate ships is convinced that it is genuine because of what he calls its *internal unity*. He won't let anyone see the diary of course, but he has shared some of the important details to recruit men to help him find the treasure.

"So tell us, Caleb, are you the man who killed the king, and do you know where the royal treasures of Nishfidor are buried?"

"Marsel, if you had asked me that question two weeks ago, I would have lied to you, and for that I am ashamed, but I tell you one and all; I am the man who killed the king of Nishfidor."

The shepherds gasped, but Caleb continued.

"However, the part about the treasure map is bogus, and I do not know where the royal treasure of Nishfidor is buried. Do you think that I would have spent the past fifty years following a herd of sheep and goats if I knew that?"

The shepherds laughed, but they did not sound entirely convinced.

"Come on fellows, I spend every Christmas camping in a crumbling cottage. Really, I don't know where the treasure is buried. Come on. Lighten up. I'm a shepherd for crying out loud."

The shepherds relaxed a little and laughed somewhat naturally.

"Why did you never tell anyone that you killed the king of Nishfidor?" Old Timothy Peg Leg asked.

"At the time, I was afraid I would be hanged or sent to prison. Our commander had ordered us to spare the king's life, but when I saw him, I remembered the thousands of our countrymen who had died at his command. My sword had tasted much blood that day, and I did not restrain myself from killing him. And as for being punished, according to the Pranville Registrar, the statute of limitations has run out on the crime. I cannot stand trial for it."

"What was in the bag?" Willy asked.

"Personal things," Caleb answered and quickly changed the subject. "A couple of weeks ago I set out to obtain the church or court documents that would prove Bruker is a polygamist. I located the first set of documents in Pranville, and Andrew located the second set in Loaden. Bruker is married to two other women, and Susan will learn about them as soon as I can tell her. On the day I left the region, I saw three pirate ships sailing toward Merrydale. What has happened around here since then, and why hasn't the sheriff organized the men of Merrydale to drive the pirates out?"

"He almost did," Mud Face Richard said. "The pirates had been here for about a week, and they were starting to tear up the town. The sheriff sent one of his officers out here to tell us he was gathering the able-bodied men and to ask for our help. We intended to help of course, but then everything changed. What the pirates were saying about a former soldier named *Caleb*, what some of the old townsfolk said back to them about a shepherd named *Caleb*, and what Bruker told them about the white bearded man named *Caleb* all ran together in the pirates' minds, and they left Merrydale to come out here to treasure hunt. The sheriff called off his plan to get rid of the pirates, but I think he was wrong not to follow through They're doing damage out here in the countryside the same as they were doing damage in town."

"Well," Caleb said. "What are we going to do about them?"

"I shay we fight them," Jerubabel said.

"We do have knowledge of the landscape to our advantage, and

178

that is of immense importance to the success of a battle plan. We know every trail, cave, and hill in the region. Still, there are so few of us and so many of them," Caleb said. "Even with our knowledge, success would not be guaranteed, and fighting them would be more dangerous than fighting wild animals."

"I say we divide them against themselves. It wouldn't be hard. We tell the pirates stories about how the crew of one ship plans to betray the crews of the other two ships and take all the treasure away in the night. With a little shrewdness, we could have them fighting each other." Charley Bat Ears said.

"A wise idea," Caleb said. "Better to have your enemies fighting among themselves than to fight them yourself."

"I have an idea," Andrew Scar Chest said. "Why don't we forge a diary for Caleb and include treasure maps inside it? The maps would have to be cryptic of course, and so would many of the entries in the diary, just ambiguous enough to keep the pirates hunting for the treasure for the rest of their lives. A couple of us would offer to sell the diary to the pirate captain who owns the prisoner's diary, saying that Caleb was a friend of ours, but that we couldn't make heads or tails of the symbols he had drawn. The captain would be suspicious of course. He would want to read a page or two, and we would allow him to do so. He would search for the dated pages relating the battle in the courtyard and the execution of the King of Nishfidor to see if they matched the prisoner's account of course, and when he found the pages, he would be overjoyed because the Caleb's diary's account would mirror the prisoner's account: same story, different perspective. Caleb remembers it all, I'm sure, and his memory of the events would seem to validate the genuineness of the diaries. These memories, which Caleb alone possesses, could not be forged. The captain would be convinced, and the pirates would sail away without conflict."

"In short, throw them off the scent, eh Scar Chest?" Old Timothy Peg Leg asked.

"Yes," Andrew said.

"Sounds like a fine plan," Old Timothy said.

The shepherds voiced their approval of Andrew's plan, but they questioned him about the difficulty of making a false diary.

"Oh that's easy," John the Beer Drinker said. "You just cook the pages in an oven for a short time. They'll turn yellow and brown like last year's leaves."

"You speak as if you had experience with forgery," Mud Face Richard observed.

"We've all got our secrets," John the Beer Drinker replied. "Even Caleb, the most respectable man any of us have ever known had a secret."

Caleb shook his head.

"John," he said, "apart from the grace of God, there's not a respectable human being on the face of the earth. I'm not respectable. You're not respectable. Nobody's respectable. If I've learned one lesson in life, that has to be it."

The shepherds heartily agreed.

"Now," Caleb said, "which of you has good handwriting?"

"Believe it or not," Billy said, "Jerubabel has the most beautiful handwriting you've ever seen."

"Yes, it is true," Willy said. "We've had him do Christmas cards for us."

"Is that so?" Caleb asked Jerubabel.

"Yesh, I guessh it'sh sho. When I wash jusht a shchool boy, I couln't talk sho good sho I made myshelf learn to write good." Jerubabel said.

"Makes sense to me," Caleb said. "I nominate you to inscribe the diary, but don't use your very best handwriting. Make it look nice but not too fancy. We'll send Andrew to Merrydale in the morning to buy a diary and we'll get started when he brings it to us."

"I know just the perfect oven for baking it," Andrew said. "My grandmother's! You should take the diary by yourself, Caleb. This morning my grandmother said she missed you."

"What's this?!" Charlie Bat Ears said.

"What?!" Billy and Willy said at the same time.

"Who's your grandmother?" Mud Face Richard asked.

"Has Caleb got himself a girlfriend now? Is that where he's

really been for the past couple of weeks? That would explain the clean shaven face. Do tell, young man, do tell," Old Timothy Peg Leg said.

All the shepherds laughed their loudest, and ribbed and teased Caleb, and Caleb knew that Andrew had gotten his revenge for the teasing on the night they met.

After supper and a warm drink, Caleb fell asleep earlier than usual, feeling very glad to be back in the presence of friends. When the sun rose the next morning, the shepherds began their tasks, one of which was the retrieval of Caleb's sheep and goats from Farmer Quigley's. Caleb remained at the cave with Orfel Little Mountain and waited. Feelings of impatience filled him as he thought about the potential danger to Clara. He would rescue her, yes, all his plans would revolve around the single purpose of rescuing the little girl.

SIXTEEN

Early in the afternoon Andrew returned with a leather bound diary and a few sheets of parchment, and Jerubabel and Marsel Long Legs returned with Caleb's sheep at about the same time.

Caleb dictated the contents that should fill the diary, and Jerubabel wrote.

Since diary entries are seldom more than a few sentences long and since for the sake of time Caleb and Jerubabel decided the diary should be of the sort that spoke of major life events instead of daily happenings, they finished filling out the book just before sunset.

Andrew's army service had carried him to some out of the way places so the shepherds thought it best for him to forge the treasure maps on the parchment. The first map directed the would-be treasure hunter away from Merrydale and across the sea to the other continent. The second map directed the would-be treasure hunter to the barren high plain that separated east from west, a desert place with no human inhabitants. The third map pictured the sun, the moon, a stream, a rock, and a tree with X's and dotted lines pointing the would-be treasure hunter to several locations that didn't even exist.

After sunset, most of the shepherds at Orfel's cave settled around the campfire to get some rest, but Caleb felt too anxious to relax.

"Andrew," he said, "There's no time to waste. You must take the notebook and the parchments to your grandmother's now. Have them ready to sell to the captain by morning time."

"You should come too," Andrew said in a low tone of voice that the other shepherds would not be able to hear, "My grandmother really would like to see you again. She enjoyed speaking with you."

"It would be dangerous for me to leave the fellowship," Caleb said. "If those pirates knew who I was, they would capture me like a bear. You can believe that."

"The fellowship isn't large enough to protect you, Caleb," Andrew said, "and you endanger them by remaining here. Why don't you go with me to town tomorrow and help with the sale of the diary? Call yourself by another name and say that Old Caleb the Shepherd was a friend of yours. That way if the captain gets suspicious and starts asking questions you will be there to give the right answers."

"Ah, you're right. I must play the part of the deceased's friend. I have no choice since we don't know how much the prisoner managed to record in his diary," Caleb said. "Let's go now."

Caleb whispered the plans to Billy and Willy and told them to tell the brotherhood in the morning. He instructed Andrew to load his gun in case of bad surprises, and the two of them began their trek in the darkness, relying more on Caleb's memory of the trails than on the light of the moon.

When they reached Beatrice's, Andrew knocked, and she said, "If that's a treasure hunter out there, you can leave now or I'll shoot, and don't think I won't do it."

"Grandmother, it's me," Andrew said.

"Oh I'm sorry, Andy, just being careful. Crazy things are happening in these parts lately."

She opened the door.

"We know all about it," Caleb said, "and that's why we're here.

We've got a plan to put an end to it, and we need to use your oven."

"My oven?" Beatrice asked.

"Yes, your oven. We need to bake a diary," Caleb said as if baking diaries were nothing unusual.

"You say you need to bake a diary? Any particular flavor?"

"What are you talking about?" Caleb asked.

"What are you talking about?" Beatrice asked.

"I'm talking about baking a diary," Caleb said.

"Why on earth would you want to bake a diary?" Beatrice asked.

"Shhhh, we'd better not tell you out here. May we come in?"

"Yes, but you can't bring any goats with you this time."

As they entered the house, Caleb apologized profusely for the damage that Big Head did. He assured Beatrice that nothing of the sort would happen again because he would be camping in the outdoors with his sheep that night.

Andrew explained the plan to divert the pirates from Merrydale, and Beatrice warned him to be careful.

"We'll be careful," Andrew said. "In Merrydale, I have a couple of old friends who I'll ask to back us up. We'll meet the captain in an inn or an ale house, and we won't allow ourselves to be cornered."

After Caleb spent some time talking with Beatrice about the specific damage done to her house and after she thanked him for the money to restore her furnishings, Caleb and Andrew spent the night behind Beatrice's house, and Andrew told Caleb that the first thing he intended to do with any left over money was to build a sheepfold. His grandmother, he explained, would be glad to have the extra accommodation for his visits.

At sunrise, Andrew built a fire in his grandmother's oven, and she baked biscuits. After she baked the biscuits, he placed the forged diary in a pan and placed it in the oven to bake for a few minutes. He removed it, flipped through the pages, and concluded that it was not quite done. Caleb agreed that it needed to cook a little longer so Andrew put the diary back into the oven.

"Just don't overcook it," Caleb said, "We can always cook it a little longer, but we won't be able to un-cook it if it gets too brown."

When the diary looked just the right shade of brown, Caleb flipped through it, tore out a few sheets, wrinkled a few, and broke the edges off a few more.

"This was supposed to have been a shepherd's diary," he said. "It needs to look like it's been through rough treatment. As a final touch, why don't you tear one of the maps into two pieces?"

"Good idea," Andrew said.

He ripped one of the parchments then folded the sheets so that anyone could have seen how they pieced together.

"Caleb, what name are you going to use?" Beatrice asked.

"I haven't thought about it," Caleb said. "Any suggestions?"

Beatrice said: "Why don't you use the name *Robert*? I always liked that name."

"Very well," Caleb said, "When I leave this house, my name will be Robert. Will you remember that, Andrew?"

"Yes I will, Robert," Andrew said.

When Caleb and Andrew were preparing to leave the house, Beatrice gave Andrew a hug and a kiss on the cheek.

Caleb saw the kiss and imagined how it must have felt. He imagined the warmth of Beatrice's lips against his cheeks, and he envied Andrew before he had a chance to remind himself that women caused more trouble in his life than what they were worth.

Though Beatrice could not see his thoughts, Caleb blushed anyway, and when he and Andrew left the house, all he could manage to say was a very weak *goodbye*. Beatrice laughed at his shyness, but he did not laugh. He could not remove from his mind the imagination of the warmth of her lips pressed against his cheek, and he had to admit to himself that it was an enjoyable thing to imagine.

Once Caleb and Andrew arrived in Merrydale, they decided that a large inn's dining room would serve their purposes best so they herded their sheep into the town sheepfold and took a table at *The Open Arms*.

Caleb sat at a table beside a window, and Andrew went to make arrangements for backup protection with some of his old army buddies who now worked in the shops in town. After he arranged the extra protection, he went to the pier where the pirate ships were docked to send word to the captain.

The captain, a tall man with a gray beard, met Andrew and Caleb in the inn, and they told him the story of their "dead friend's diary."

The captain wanted to know why they wanted to sell it, and they told him that they could not decipher the maps. In order to make their ploy seem real, they asked the captain for one-thousand pieces of silver, which seemed an outrageously high price for the diary, and he made a counter-offer of eight hundred pieces on the condition that first he be allowed to thumb through the diary.

Caleb and Andrew agreed to his request, and as predicted, the captain turned directly to the account of the battle in the courtyard. When he read it, he began to struggle not to smile and not to act too overjoyed, but Caleb saw the man's feelings and he knew that the captain had taken the bait. Caleb also struggled not to smile.

The captain sent one of his crewmen for the money, and when he returned, the captain handed the money over saying: "I've got my doubts about this, Robert. If this here diary leads us to nothin', I will return to this miserable town, find ya, and take my money back. And, I might take more than money, understand?"

A little burst of fear ran up Caleb's spine, but then he remembered that false hope never dies, especially in the heart of a pirate, and he realized that he would never see the captain again.

The captain would believe the diary to be genuine. He would not stop believing it even if someone proved otherwise, and he would spend the rest of his days on the barren high plain looking for a treasure that did not lie beneath any of its rocks, trees, or streams. Caleb knew it as well as he knew his own name.

When the captain rose to leave the restaurant, Caleb and Andrew kept their seats.

When the captain stepped out of the inn, Caleb leaned over and said: "We wouldn't want to risk going outside just now. If one of my town friends saw me and called me by my name, we'd have a hard time explaining it to the captain. Where are your friends?"

"Two of them are here in the inn sitting at the corner table, and two are walking the street in front of the inn. They've all got knives. Come what may, I think we're safe."

"Just give the captain time before we make another move," Caleb said, "and be sure to give your friends some of the money."

"Speaking of the money, Andrew said, what are we going to do with it?"

"We're not going to do anything with it. Susan has endured much trouble because of the pirates, and the pirates would not have been here had it not been for something I did wrong when I was a young man. When and if I can get Bruker out of Merrydale, I'm going to put a new roof on the cottage, and Susan's going to get the rest of the money."

"How do you plan to get Bruker out of Merrydale?" Andrew asked.

"I'm not sure, but I know I will have to be delicate about some matters for Susan's sake. I'm not sure how she'll take the news that her husband is a polygamist. Any suggestions about how I should tell her?"

"I suggest *you* don't tell her the news. When it comes to the delivery of bad news, a person's best friend is always the one who should do it because it's easy to hate the messenger if you don't know he's got your best interest in mind. Who's her best friend?"

"I don't know," Caleb said, "but Sister Kate would know."

"Let's go ask her," Andrew said.

After they waited long enough for the captain to walk back to his ship and dig into the contents of the diary, Andrew paid his friends for secretly standing guard, and he and Caleb stepped over to the Merrydale Church.

Sister Kate told them that Susan's best friend was a young woman named Darla and that Darla was married to one of Merrydale's barbers.

"This is what we'll do," Andrew said. "We'll have Darla break the bad news to Susan here in town during the work day. Meanwhile, we'll rid the cottage of Bruker and company."

"Anything we can do to help?" Sister Kate asked.

"There will be soon," Caleb said. "I'm hoping for reconciliation

188

between Parson Rivers and Susan."

"Ha! They're both as hard-headed as mountain goats," Sister Kate said.

"Well I'm going to try anyway. The parson is a good man, and I'm convinced that Susan's mostly just scared: scared of people, scared of the future, scared for her daughter." Caleb said.

"How do the two of you plan to get rid of Bruker?" Sister Kate asked.

"I say we get the sheriff and call the brotherhood together." Caleb said.

"I agree," Andrew said, "but first we'll have to give the pirates enough time to leave, and then we'll have to spy on Bruker to know what we're up against. It could be several days."

"We don't have several days," Caleb said. "Christmas is only six days away, and I would like Clara to sing in the Christmas concert on Christmas Eve. We've got to move fast."

Caleb and Andrew left the church, and as they did, they noticed a commotion in the direction of the docks. Caleb stayed behind a building, and Andrew went to investigate.

"Well, maybe we *will* get everything done before Christmas," he said when he returned. "The pirates are already leaving."

"Already?" Caleb asked.

"Yes, they're already leaving. The captain got so excited after he bought the diary that he sent word to his men to board immediately. They sail at sunset."

"Right now we should go talk with Susan's friend Darla, and right after that we should talk with the Sheriff. This afternoon we'll speak with the shepherds, and tonight, we'll spy on the cottage."

"Sounds like a good plan," Andrew said.

Finding Darla posed no challenge. They found her husband's barber shop and asked for directions. He was reluctant to tell two shepherds where to find his wife until they told them all the details relating to why they wanted to speak with her.

"I'm glad to hear what you're planning," the barber said. "That Bruker is an evil man, and we've known it for a long time. Darla tried to tell Susan how bad he was once, and that led to the biggest fight the two of them ever had. Susan wouldn't believe Darla, and she wouldn't have her husband insulted. Darla never tried again after that. Now that you've got proof, she'll have to listen. If there's anything I can do to help, just let me know."

Caleb and Andrew left the barber shop and went to see Darla.

Darla, a brown haired, brown eyed young woman who walked with a slight limp, welcomed Caleb and Andrew's news.

"I know I shouldn't say such a thing, but I hate Bruker," she said. "I hate the sight of that man like I hate the sight of rotten guts. He's done nothing but hurt Susan for as long as she's been married to him. The only good thing about him is that he comes around just once a year. Too bad it has to be Christmas time. Clara hasn't had a happy Christmas yet. Sure, I'll be glad to help get rid of him."

When Caleb and Andrew left Darla's they paid a visit to the Merrydale jail and told the sheriff their plan. At once the sheriff said he would send three of his best officers to arrest Bruker for polygamy, but Caleb insisted that the sheriff not do so.

"Polygamy is a crime but it doesn't carry a strong penalty," Caleb said. "The court would send him to jail for a month or two, and after that, he would be able to sweet talk his way back into Susan's life by telling her that he still wished to be a father to Clara or some other nonsense, and life would go on as usual. But the *threat* of arrest: That would keep Bruker away from Merrydale for the rest of his life. Besides, it would probably take more than three men to arrest him. Several men are staying at the cottage. We don't know how many men, but we'll try to find out after all the pirates have sailed, and that should be tonight. We'll signal for you tomorrow. Just sleep on the plan tonight."

The sheriff agreed to Caleb's request for help, and Caleb and Andrew started out of Merrydale on the north side of town and sent word of their plan to the brotherhood.

Word traveled fast, and the shepherds agreed to help.

Caleb and Andrew then went to spy on the cottage.

SEVENTEEN

"Do you have a hat?" Andrew asked.

"Why, is your head cold?" Caleb asked.

"No," Andrew said. "If my head were cold, I would wear my own hat. I was thinking that since you shaved off your beard, Bruker won't recognize you so long as we stay a fair distance away from the cottage. The one thing that could give you away now is the color of your hair, but if you wear a hat, he won't see your hair. He'll just think we're two shepherds passing through from one pasture to another."

"Another good idea," Caleb said. "Yes, I've got a hat in one of the boxes on Big Head's cart."

Caleb and Andrew halted their flocks, and Caleb pilfered about in Big Head's cart until he found a crumpled black hat that looked older than dirt. Caleb slapped it on his knee, and dust flew. He picked a few cob webs out of the hat, shaped it as best he could, and placed it on his head.

The hat was round with a wide brim. The right side of the rim stood out like it was supposed to do, but the left side of the rim

191

flopped down beside Caleb's head like an elephant ear and rested on Caleb's shoulder.

"How do I look?" Caleb asked.

After a very long pause, Andrew said: "Unique, you look absolutely unique."

"Thank you," Caleb said.

They snapped their fingers and clucked, and their animals followed them as they continued down the trail to Caleb's old Christmas abode.

"We're ahead of schedule," Caleb said when they were half a mile of the cottage. "I wouldn't want to risk getting too near before sunset. Why don't we eat supper?"

"Gladly," Andrew said, "I'm so hungry I could eat my own hand."

From Big Head's goat cart, Caleb gathered a loaf of bread, a small tub of butter, two strips of dried beef, and a jar of apple preserves. Half way up a grassy hill, he and Andrew sat, leaned their backs against a tree, and ate their supper. Because they were hungry, the food tasted and smelled good, but as they dined, the smell of food much more delicious than theirs came to them on the wind.

"Do you smell that?" Andrew asked.

"Ahhh, yes, I do," Caleb said, "Smells like meat roasting, and with that much aroma, Bruker and his friends must be roasting a bull."

"The cottage has an oven big enough to roast an entire bull?" Andrew asked.

"No," Caleb said, "The cottage doesn't have an oven. I would venture to say they've dug themselves a roasting pit."

As they sat nibbling their supper, their mouths watered for the taste of the meat.

"I wish I had some of what they're having," Andrew said.

"And so does every living creature within three miles of the cottage," Caleb said.

They finished eating around the time the sun went down, and they walked the distance necessary to get a clear view of Bruker and his gang. They stood in the long shadows of late evening and studied the scene in the valley.

"How many men are down there?" Andrew asked.

"I would say no less than fifteen," Caleb answered, "Maybe as many as twenty."

"There's the roasting pit," Andrew said.

A few yards away from the cottage, Caleb saw the orange-red glow of a wood fire. Above the fire, a slab of meat was suspended on a long horizontal pole.

In the distance, something howled.

"Was that a wolf or a dog?" Andrew asked.

"That was a wolf," Caleb answered. "It smells the meat."

"I thought we got rid of the wolves," Andrew said.

"For the most part, we did," Caleb said. "The one that just howled is probably a stray now. With its pack gone, it hasn't had any hunting partners, and it hasn't been able get much food. That's why it's interested in the meat."

As the sky darkened, Caleb and Andrew moved closer to the cottage, and they saw Bruker walking around and talking big to all who had gathered there.

"Are they pirates?" Andrew asked.

"No," Caleb said, "They're Bruker's shipmates. I saw most of them at a fake fight that Bruker rigged in Merrydale. I feel sure the pirates have all gone by now."

After a short while, four of Bruker's friends removed the pole with the roasting beef from over the glowing pit. Two others cut the meat from the pole and placed it in a pot. They covered the pot with a towel and announced supper time.

The sailors gathered around the pot and reached in with forks. Caleb's and Andrew's mouths watered as they watched the sailors begin to eat.

"Is that bread ready yet?" Bruker shouted.

"I'm coming with it," Susan answered from inside the cottage. "You don't have to shout at me."

All of Bruker's friends laughed.

Susan stepped outside.

Clara held Susan's dress and walked close beside her mother.

Caleb noticed immediately that the child's demeanor had changed. She looked nervous.

Susan served the bread and said: "Come on, Clara, let's go back inside."

"No," Bruker said, "Leave her out here."

"Bruker, I'd rather not," Susan said, "You know how you all get when you start drinking."

"Well, we haven't started yet," Bruker said. "Go on now, leave her outside. I'll make her sing for my friends. You just go back to getting our dessert ready. She'll be fine."

Susan sighed and went back inside without Clara, and as soon as she stepped through the doorway, Bruker opened a wooden chest and pulled out a bottle of rum.

"Strongest rum you can buy," he announced. "I bought it from a distiller on the Island Cirem. Who wants a shot?"

Shouts of "I do!" went up all around.

Bruker drank a long, hard slug, passed the rum, and pulled a bottle of whiskey from the chest.

"Strongest whiskey you can buy," he announced. "I bought it from a shop in Loaden. Who wants a shot?"

Shouts of "I do!" went up again.

Bruker drank a shot, passed the whiskey, and pulled out a bottle of brandy.

"I bet that's the strongest brandy you can buy, huh?" one of the sailors asked.

"That it is," Bruker answered with a loud laugh. "How did you know?"

He drank down a gulp, hiccupped, patted his chest, and passed the brandy. Then he removed an unmarked bottle from the chest. He held it up but said nothing.

"Well, what is it?" one of the sailors asked.

"None of your business," Bruker said. "This one's all mine."

The sailors snickered with Bruker, and he continued: "But we've got as much ale and beer as you could want. Gentlemen, we've sold many trinkets. We've made much money, and it's time we have some fun."

"Yeah!" one of the sailors said.

Bruker took Clara by the hand and led her into the center of the circle, and as he walked, he drank hard from the unmarked bottle.

"I've been teaching my daughter a song, and we're going to sing it for you."

Bruker started, but Clara did not follow:

In Loaden I once met a lass.
Who liked to talk back and sass.
"Shut up," I told her,
But she got bolder,
And so I spanked her...

Before Bruker finished the first verse, Susan stepped out of the cottage and said, "I told you I don't want my daughter singing those kinds of songs."

"*Our* daughter," Bruker reminded her as he winked at the sailors, "And there's nothing wrong with my songs. I've been singing them since I was her age, and look at *me*."

Susan did look at him. She looked at him long and hard, and her bottom lip trembled.

"Anyway," she said, "your dessert's ready now. Come along, Clara, and help me serve it."

Clara went inside with her mother, but Susan returned without her. She carried bowls of pudding and served them without saying a word. She stepped back inside, and the sailors ate their pudding and continued to drink.

Bruker drank harder than the others, and when the feeling overtook him, he got up and danced.

"Somebody, play me some music," he screamed.

A sailor opened a case from his knapsack and produced a fiddle. The sailor tuned the fiddle, but not too finely, and began to play it.

Bruker kicked up his feet and jumped around like a frog in a snake pit. The sailors clapped time between sips of strong drink, and the more they clapped, the harder and faster Bruker danced.

When his dancing reached a feverish pitch, he shouted and ran inside the cottage. He returned a few seconds later holding Clara in his arms, and he began to dance around with her.

Susan tried to stop Bruker and take Clara back, but he put one hand against Susan's face and pushed her down.

She struggled to get back onto her feet, but two of Bruker's friends put their hands on her shoulders.

"Relax, lady," one of them said. "He ain't hurtin' nothin'."

"Yeah, lady, he's just trying to show us all a good time," the other said.

Susan squirmed and tried to tear herself from their grip, but the men were big and muscular, and she could do nothing against their strength.

"Should I go do something?" Andrew whispered to Caleb.

"No, just wait. Tomorrow it'll all be over. Be patient." Caleb said.

Bruker laughed like a hyena as he danced. He held Clara under her arms and swung her round and round, sometimes high and sometimes low.

Clara's face turned bright red, and she cried for help.

"Come on, Caleb, I've got to do something," Andrew said.

"I don't think he's hurting her," Caleb said. "I think she's just afraid. There's too many of them. They'd beat you to death."

"Yes, but they're drunk, and I've got a gun," Andrew said.

"Just be patient," Caleb said.

Bruker danced and swung Clara in broader and broader circles until he reached the edge of the roasting pit. Through her tears, Clara screamed when he swung her over it.

"Don't like that, do you?" Bruker asked.

In reply, Clara screamed and cried out louder.

Bruker stopped swinging her.

"See, I knew he'd stop," Caleb said.

Bruker then turned Clara upside down and hoisted her by one leg.

"Wait. What is he…" Caleb started.

Bruker held Clara over the roasting pit, and heat, smoke, and fumes surrounded her body.

"How do you like that?" Bruker yelled as he twisted Clara's leg around in his hand.

Without saying anything, Caleb dropped his pack, and walked straight toward Bruker.

"What are you doing?" Andrew asked as Caleb stepped away, but Caleb did not answer.

Since his childhood, Andrew Scar Chest had heard stories of Caleb's battlefield exploits. Only children repeated the stories because no reasonable adult could believe the stories were factual. The stories sounded too big. They sounded exaggerated and grandiose beyond all sensible proportions, and some people suspected that the shepherd had planted the stories, himself, but the stories contained more truth than the adults suspected, splinters of a far greater actuality.

The Caleb that Andrew saw walking down the side of the hill toward Bruker *was* that actuality, though dormant for more than fifty years, returned to life.

To understand the actuality of the young soldier, a glance into his commander's journal serves the purpose best. During the Big War, Caleb's commander wrote not only his official daily reports; he also wrote his personal thoughts in a journal. Though the commander did not mention Caleb by name in his journal, he wrote of him on three occasions:

April 8. During the past thirty years, I have served in two wars, and I have ordered three companies. I have trained and commanded some of the most fierce and skilled soldiers of my generation, but only now have I seen the greatest. He is a berserker of the severest intensity. A berserker is a valuable though not uncommon weapon, but he is no ordinary berserker. He does not forget his skills in the midst of his savagery. Today I saw him rush six enemy soldiers at once. No companion fought with him, but his sword found success, drinking the blood of all six, striking with an outrageous speed and force. If I had not seen it I would not believe it. The young man glories in the shedding of blood, and he sheds much of it.

197

As of today, the company calls the young man's sword The Iron Thunderbolt. *I suspect that the young man suffers from uncontrollable anger or a kind of insanity, but be that as it may, he is an asset, and may his* Iron Thunderbolt *strike many of our foes.*

October 29. Today a great battle drew to a successful conclusion with the young berserker marching at the head of our company. He is more skilled but also more savage than ever. He is a whirling circle of strength and death. Since I last wrote of him, I have changed my mind about the source of his valor. I do not believe it comes from anger or insanity. I am convinced the young man is possessed by a strong hatred. No soldier could fight so mindlessly and so intelligently at the same time. He is thirsty to kill. He must be full of a most bitter hatred, and the battlefield is where he expresses it.

March 16. This war now draws to its close, and it appears that we have prevailed. After today's battle, all that is left for us is the taking of the castle where the King of Nishfidor and a few of his soldiers have taken refuge. Though the king is a proud and evil man, I am certain he will surrender with little or no conflict. As for today's battle, we won it chiefly because of the bone grinding wrath of the young berserker. He is a man of war unmatched by any of his generation, but surely the comparison must extend much further. In a hundred generations, I would not expect to see more than one soldier of his kind. He drinks violence like water, and he allows our enemy no respite. I hereby discard my prior assessment of his internal composition, and I hold forth yet a third explanation of his warrior genius. I cannot imagine how the explanation that I am about to offer is true of his life, but I am convinced it must be. Hatred, no matter how venomous, cannot account for the young man's tireless and vicious labor with the sword. I am convinced that in some way the young man fights for love. Surely, it has to be love. No other force ever has or ever will embolden, intensify, and drive a man like love.

The warrior heart of Young Caleb began to beat in the body of old Caleb. As Old Caleb walked down the hill toward Bruker and Clara, he felt less of the soreness in his joints and more of the strength that had made him the subject of legend.

Two sailors saw Caleb approach. They saw the expression on his face and knew that he came not to join their party but to break it up. They stood to resist him.

One sailor took a swing at Caleb, and Caleb caught the man's fist in mid-flight, stopping it as suddenly as if the man had struck a brick wall. Caleb pulled the man close to him and struck him down with one blow.

The other sailor tried to tackle Caleb, but as he dived at Caleb's legs, Caleb kicked him like a mangy dog.

The kick cracked something inside the man's rib cage and left him rolling on the ground in pain.

Caleb incapacitated both the sailors without taking his eyes off Bruker. He breathed in deep, and his nostrils flared as he slowed and stopped in front of the wild eyed, drunken party host.

"Hand her to me," Caleb said.

Bruker laughed as he dangled Clara over the roasting pit.

"Nobody tells me what to do, old man," Bruker said. "You want her? Catch her."

Bruker let go of Clara's leg.

Caleb did not think. His warrior reflexes moved his hands. He tossed his staff aside, and he reached out to catch Clara.

She fell into his hands, but he stumbled forward.

Bruker tripped him.

Caleb's body's momentum carried him down toward the glowing embers. He landed on his right foot but fell backward onto the ground. He set Clara down, pulled his right foot up from the pit, and snatched his shoe off.

Bruker picked up Clara, and the rest of the sailors stood to attack Caleb, but before any of them moved toward him, Andrew stepped in front of them with his gun and said, "I've got one shot for whoever moves first."

The sailors stood down.

Caleb stood up.

"Hand her to me," he said.

Bruker attempted to say something, but the words came out of his mouth in an incomprehensible slur of filth and profanity, and when he stopped making noise he spat at Caleb.

"Try to take her from me," he said after he spat, and Caleb barely understood him.

As Caleb stared into Bruker's eyes, his nostrils flared, and his lips curled.

"Bruker, give me the child now!" Caleb said.

Bruker stuck out his bottom lip like a pouting child, and he pulled a long knife from a scabbard on his hip.

He placed the knife to Clara's throat and said: "Back away, old man."

Caleb studied Bruker's blood shot, wild eyes, and he realized that Bruker was not bluffing.

"All right," Caleb said. "Sure. I'm sorry. Just don't hurt her."

He turned as if he intended to walk away, but when his back was to Bruker, he reached under the tip of his staff with the toes of his bare foot, and kicked it up. He caught the staff in air, whirled back, swung it low, and struck Bruker on the knee.

Bruker's knee snapped like a twig. He dropped Clara and his knife, and fell down screaming.

Caleb swung his staff again and cracked Bruker's rib cage.

Caleb had gone berserk, and would have beaten Bruker to death, but he looked down and saw Clara, and he could not continue.

At the same time, Andrew felt someone jerk the gun from his hand.

Thinking that one of the sailors had taken his gun, Andrew shouted: "No!"

Andrew turned.

Caleb looked around.

Susan stood over Bruker with the end of the gun's barrel shoved against Bruker's forehead.

"Let's get'em," one of the sailors yelled.

Three of them jumped Andrew Scar Chest and took him down with little effort.

A group of five charged at Caleb, but before they reached him, he removed his knife, and swung it in a great circle.

They removed their knives, but they did not proceed.

"Gentlemen," Caleb said, "We are here with the permission and cooperation of the Sheriff of Merrydale. Take heed to your actions and all may go well with you."

The sailors saw by the expression in his eyes that Caleb spoke truthfully, and the three that held Andrew released him.

"Go back to your ship!" Caleb said.

He turned his attention back to Susan.

Tears of rage dripped down Susan's cheeks as she glowered down at Bruker.

"*I'm going to kill you,*" she repeated several times.

"Susan," Caleb said, "Don't do this. You, Andrew, and I saw Bruker attempt to kill your daughter. Three witnesses settle a matter in this town. Let the court handle this."

Susan did not indicate that she heard Caleb.

"Susan?" Caleb asked.

She did not answer. Her tears gushed.

Bruker squirmed and groaned.

"Susan!" Caleb said.

She said nothing.

She squeezed the trigger.

Nothing happened.

"I didn't have time to load it," Andrew said.

Caleb sighed.

Bruker crawled into the darkness and shouted obscenities as he dragged his injured leg.

"Don't go out there," Caleb said. "It's dangerous. Come back. You can cast yourself on the mercy of the court."

Bruker continued to crawl away and shout obscenities.

"There are wolves out there," Andrew said. "Come back, Bruker, come back."

Bruker shouted louder and crawled faster.

Suddenly, a great dark shape rose from the shadows to which Bruker crawled.

Andrew snatched his gun from Susan's hands, reached into his pack, and began to load it, but there was not enough time.

A somber growl issued from the dark shape, and Caleb knew that the giant bear had come to eat.

Clara was crying so she did not perceive or understand what followed.

Caleb, Andrew, and Susan heard a crunching noise.

The sailors who were walking away turned toward the noise.

Everyone heard Bruker shout one last obscenity, and then they heard nothing more.

The dark shape slunk back into the shadows and disappeared.

Susan took Clara in her arms and went back inside the cottage.

"Go on," Caleb shouted at the sailors, "And tell your captain to sail tonight, or his entire crew will be arrested in the morning."

The sailors continued to walk.

"We still have much to do," Caleb said to Andrew.

EIGHTEEN

"Go to Merrydale," Caleb continued, "and speak to the Sheriff about what happened. Find Darla, and tell her our plans have changed. Ask her to come to the cottage in the morning. Speak to Parson Rivers too, but don't ask him to come to the cottage. Tell him he *must* come. I'll stay here tonight."

Andrew lighted his torch and departed for Merrydale.

Caleb removed his horn and signaled the brotherhood to gather. He called his sheep and goats, paused, wiped his brow with his shirt sleeve, and approached the cottage. He knocked on its front door, but Susan did not answer. He knocked two more times, but she did not answer.

"Susan," he said, "I know you can hear me, and I know that you want to be left alone, but please don't shut me out. If for no other reason, open the door because I have a rather large sum of money for you, nearly eight-hundred pieces of silver."

"You're lying. All men are liars. Go away." Susan said.

Her voice sounded weak and broken.

"I'm not lying. Here, I'll show you." Caleb said.

He removed money bags from Big Head's goat cart. He opened one and slid a coin beneath the door. Susan did not come to the door so he pushed through another and then another until coins began to make a pile on the front room's floor.

Susan was sitting on the bed beside Clara, but the door to the bedroom was open, and she could not help seeing the glint of the silver. She lifted her candle from beside the bed, and went to collect the coins. She set her candle on the table, and picked up as many coins as her hands could hold, but more and more came from the other side.

Caleb heard her set her handfuls of coins on the table, and he said: "Please, Susan, just open the door, and I will hand you the rest of the money."

"Why are you giving me this money?" Susan asked.

"Because you are living in my cottage," Caleb said, "and it needs some work, would you not agree?"

Susan opened the door.

"Come in," she said, "and say whatever it is you want to say."

"First of all," Caleb said as he stepped through the doorway, "I don't blame you for trying to kill Bruker. After what he did to your daughter, nobody's going to blame you for what you did, and you don't have to feel bad."

"Do you see me crying about it?" Susan said.

"Well, no," Caleb said.

"Then don't assume that I feel bad." Susan said, and as soon as she said it, a tear dripped out of her left eye, and she turned her head.

Caleb just let her cry until she said: "Who am I kidding? I knew he was bad all along, Caleb, but I wouldn't admit it to myself. I kept hopin' he would change, but more than anything else, I wanted him to be a father to Clara. I never had one of those, ya know."

"I know," Caleb said, "and I know it's going to take a long time for you to work out your feelings. For now, I want you to know you're safe. The pirates have sailed, and they won't be coming here again. I have summoned the brotherhood of the shepherds to gather here at the cottage tonight. They will protect you and Clara from anything that might threaten, not that I believe there is anything left in the region that poses much of a threat."

"Is Bruker dead?" Susan asked.

"Yes," Caleb said, "you may be sure of it."

"Well, sit down," Susan said. "You may as well have something to eat, and we've got more than enough."

"Thank you," Caleb said, and Susan served him some bread and cheese.

"You didn't actually kill him, you know," Caleb said.

"What's the difference? I tried to." Susan said.

"As for what was in your heart, there is no difference, but as for the final result, there is a big difference. I've killed many men. Trust me, I know," Caleb said.

"So I've heard," Susan said, "but you were in the war."

"And you've been in a war too," Caleb said. "Every woman's got the right to protect her offspring."

Before the conversation progressed any further, Caleb heard the approach of the first shepherd.

"Go and spend the night with Clara," he said. "Things are going to get better starting in the morning. You'll see."

Susan returned to the bedroom where Clara was already asleep. She kissed Clara's cheek and lay beside her on the bed.

Caleb placed the remaining coins on the table and stepped outside. He greeted Loak the Fat, and told him why the brotherhood had been called together, but he put off explaining the details until all the shepherds, except for Andrew Scar Chest who was away in town, had gathered.

When Caleb concluded, Nick the Sick said: "So what you're saying is that the giant bear is alive and probably not far from here?"

"Yes, but he won't be hunting tonight. He's had a big supper already." Caleb said.

"We let the bear go without a chase the last time because we didn't think he'd be much of a threat with his hurt paw," Mud Face Richard said, "but in the morning we need to speak with the farmers that own dogs about putting a hunting party together."

"I agree," Billy said.

"So do I," Willy agreed.

"You can all take care of the bear problem," Caleb said, "but I have work to do around here. Will you forgive me if I don't join you?"

"Of course we'll forgive you," Old Timothy Peg Leg said, "As old as you are, we'd forgive you if you didn't so much as wake up in the morning."

The brotherhood laughed, and so did Caleb. He felt glad that his shepherd responsibilities would not interfere with his plans to set right Susan's situation.

Andrew joined the brotherhood later in the evening when the shepherds were winding down to sleep. Caleb called him aside, and he and Andrew walked to the rear of the cottage.

"Did you speak with the sheriff?" Caleb asked.

"Yes," Andrew said, "He'll be here with his officers first thing in the morning."

"And Darla?"

"Yes, Darla's husband is going to take tomorrow off and bring her out here in their wagon."

"Good," Caleb said, "And the parson?"

"Parson Rivers said he would meet you in front of the cottage but he would not go inside unless he was invited by Susan."

"We'll see about that," Caleb said.

He and Andrew returned to the fellowship and slept.

The next morning, the sheriff arrived first. He rode a tall, spotted horse, and he sat high in the saddle. He asked Caleb a few questions, studied the place where Bruker's tracks intersected with the bear's tracks, and went inside the cottage and asked Susan a few questions.

"There's no crime to investigate here," he concluded, "but my officers and I will help you any way we can."

"Thank you," Caleb said. "We can use all the help we can get, and we'll let you know."

Caleb and Susan followed the sheriff outside and thanked him for coming.

The sheriff galloped his horse back toward Merrydale, and Darla arrived next. She rode beside her husband on the wooden seat of a wagon.

When Darla climbed down, she and Susan embraced, wept, and without speaking a word, felt what each other felt as only women can.

Susan and Darla went inside the cottage, and Caleb remained outside.

"I know you took a day off work to bring Darla out here, and I know that's a sacrifice, and I thank you for it." Caleb said.

"It's no trouble," Darla's husband, who was known simply as *the barber*, said, "I like to get out here and view the countryside from time to time. It's lovely really. I don't care if I do miss the few silvers I might have made today."

"Wait," Caleb said, "You don't have to miss those silvers. There's plenty of work for you to do here."

He turned to the shepherds. Most of them were sipping coffee and sitting around a freshly rekindled fire.

"Look at their hair," Caleb said. "See what I mean? You can wash my sheep shears with some soap and some water from the well, and you should have enough work to keep you busy until this afternoon."

Caleb turned back to the shepherds.

"Listen up," he said. "The barber has been kind enough to ride out here this morning, and by the looks of things, it's good for us he did. Take a look at your hair."

The shepherds looked around.

"The barber will be cutting hair for his standard price. Christmas is only two days away, and we all need haircuts, except for Jerubabel of course because he doesn't have any hair."

Caleb handed the barber his soap and his shears, fetched a chair from inside the cottage, and volunteered to have his hair cut first.

Parson Rivers arrived a little while after the Barber finished his work on Caleb's head. When Caleb saw the Parson approach, he signaled for him to walk with him to the back of the cottage.

When the two of them reached the cottage's back side, Caleb

leaned against a tree and said: "You're going to have to embarrass yourself today. It's the right thing."

"What do you mean?" The parson asked.

"You're going to have tell Susan just how stupid you were to try that ridiculous lonely-room nonsense when she was a child. What is more, you're going to have to tell her that by leaving her there overnight, you went far beyond the point of stupidity. You're going to have to beg her for forgiveness if that's what it takes to get it. If she will agree to talk with you at all, you're going to have to humble yourself down lower than dirt. If you will do that, then you will get rid of most of the guilt that you've been carrying, and if she'll confront what happened, she will get over some of her anger."

"I'll try, Caleb" Parson Rivers said.

"Good," Caleb said. "Wait here until I call you."

Caleb walked around to the front of the cottage, knocked, waited for Susan's answer, and stepped inside.

"Susan," he said, "I know I'm about to ask you to do a hard thing, but it must be done. Will you allow Parson Rivers to talk with you?"

"No," she said in a most matter of fact tone of voice.

"Darla," Caleb said, "Would you mind stepping outside for a moment?"

Darla heard the seriousness in Caleb's voice and stepped out the door without asking any questions.

"Please listen," Caleb said, "I know the parson did a terrible thing to you. He showed me the lonely room a couple of days ago. I'm not going to ask you to excuse what he did, but I am going to ask you to forgive it. We've all done terrible things, and the parson deserves forgiveness the same as the rest of us. If you can't forgive him for his sake, at least you should forgive him for your own sake. Bitterness will eat a hole in you and keep you in chains for years. I wasted a lot of my life with bitterness, and I don't want you to make the same mistake. Talk to the parson. Try to work out your feelings. The worst you can do is fail."

Susan did not answer out loud, and her face seemed to hold back a tidal wave of emotion as she nodded her head *yes*.

Without giving her a chance to change her mind, Caleb opened the door, stepped out, and walked to the back of the cottage.

"I feel that she will not say anything to you," he said to the parson, "but she will hear you, and you had better not hold anything back. Tell her the story of the lonely room from your perspective the same as you told it to me two days ago. Let her hear the sorrow in your voice. Let her see it on your face."

"I'll try," the parson said.

Caleb walked the parson around to the front of the cottage, but he did not go inside with him. He waited outside and paced back and forth.

The cottage's door remained closed for more than an hour so Caleb had to find other ways to occupy his mind besides pacing. He tried to talk with the shepherds, but he could not concentrate long enough to get very far into any conversations. He tried to watch the barber cut hair, but he kept glancing back over his shoulder toward the cottage. He tried speaking with his sheep and goats, but too many people were around, and he could not open up to them in his usual manner.

When at last the cottage door opened, Caleb darted toward it.

With a somber expression on his face, Parson Rivers exited the cottage, and closed the door behind him.

"Well?" Caleb asked.

"Well, what?" The Parson asked.

"Did the two of you work things out?"

"I'm afraid we didn't move any mountains, but we might have moved a few mole hills."

"What do you mean?" Caleb asked.

"I mean that Susan does not wish to spend anymore time around me than she has to, and she doesn't know if that will ever change. I can't say that I blame her for that. Can you?"

"No," Caleb said.

"However," the parson said, "Susan wants Clara to sing in the Christmas concert. I'm going to give her the part she sang in the church on the morning you brought her to Merrydale."

Caleb wanted to jump for joy.

"Oh, this is wonderful," he said, "truly wonderful!"

"And you're responsible for getting Clara to the church this afternoon for rehearsal," the parson said.

"She'll be there," Caleb said.

The parson departed for Merrydale, and Caleb went back inside the cottage.

Susan was in the bedroom helping Clara get dressed.

Clara did not know what her mother meant by "singing in the choir," but she felt excited all the same, and it showed on her face.

"Good morning," Caleb said to Clara. "Are you looking forward to rehearsal?"

"I don't know what that is," Clara said.

"You'll be singing with other children," Caleb said.

"Is that the same as singin' in the choir?" Clara asked.

"Sure is," Caleb answered.

"Mama says it's going to be fun."

"It surely will be fun," Caleb said, "the most fun you've ever had."

Clara clapped her hands together and smiled.

As Susan finished tying Clara's shoes, she said, "I'm going to use part of the money you gave me to get Clara a new dress."

"Good," Caleb said, "Buy her some new stockings and shoes too, but don't stop there. Take her to one of the ladies' parlors and have her hair done."

"I will," Susan said.

"And get some new things for yourself," Caleb said, "and get your hair done."

"Are you trying to tell me my hair is a mess?" Susan asked.

"No," Caleb said, "I only want you to know that you can afford the best for yourself and your daughter for Christmas. The roof will cost less than a hundred and twenty five silver pieces to repair. You've got eight hundred, and if you run out of that, we've got furs to sell. Speaking of the furs, I think I'll go have a look at them."

Caleb stepped into the roofless room where the furs lay.

The furs were ready to be taken to town to trade so Caleb rolled them up and tied them with some twine from his pack. He walked outside and asked Jerubabel if he would look after his sheep.

Jerubabel said he would not mind at all, and Caleb asked Darla and the barber if he, Susan, and Clara could ride to town on the back of their wagon.

Darla and the barber said they would be delighted to give them a ride to Merrydale so after the barber cut the last shepherd's hair, Caleb helped Susan and Clara climb onto the back of the wagon. He sat behind them with his legs dangling off the back, and away they rode.

They arrived at Merrydale Church just before choir practice time, presented Clara to Sister Gertrude, the choir assistant and organ player, and rode to Darla's house.

When Susan left her, Clara felt frightened at first, but when she remembered how her voice had sounded in the church, she forgot her fear.

When Parson Rivers entered the church, he directed the choir to sit down. He told the children that the most important lesson to be learned in choir is that each person must sing the part that he or she is best suited to sing. He said he had recruited a new girl to sing the very difficult chorus of *Tender Child*, and he introduced Clara to the children.

The introduction did not last long. Sister Gertrude struck a chord on the organ, and the rehearsal began in earnest.

At Darla's house, Susan and Caleb waited impatiently. They kept exchanging glances, but neither said a word.

Susan wondered why Caleb had been so concerned about her and her daughter. She guessed the old man was just lonely, and that he got as much out of showing kindness to them as they did from receiving it.

Caleb wondered how Susan was dealing with the death of her husband. She did not appear to be in mourning, but maybe the grief had not yet set in. Had she been in love with Bruker? Was she crying inside her heart?

Caleb guessed that Susan had known the truth of what Bruker was, even if she had not heard all the details and that now she was simply accepting what she had long known instead of grieving the loss of what she never truly had.

Rehearsal time drew to a close, and Caleb and Susan thanked Darla and the barber and went for Clara. They met Clara in front of the Merrydale Church, and the three of them went shopping.

Susan bought a long, navy blue dress, white stockings, and a pair of shiny, black leather shoes with silver buckles for Clara, and she asked a store clerk to cut a strand of white silk ribbon for Clara to wear in her hair.

For herself Susan bought a pair of brown leather shoes, green stockings, and a green dress that complemented her red hair.

Caleb sold the hides for the going rate at the Merrydale sheep market, and he purchased a new suit for himself at the town haberdashery.

It was the first new suit he had ever bought, and though it was simple black and not fancy in the least, he felt awkward when he tried it on. He stood before a full length mirror, and looked at himself from head to toe. With fresh haircut, no beard, and a new suit, he felt like a new man. He even ventured so far as to think that he looked handsome.

Susan confirmed his venturesome thought a few seconds later when she said, "You look handsome."

He turned from the mirror.

"You really think so?"

"I know so," she said.

"We'll show these town people, won't we?" Caleb said.

"Yes we will," Susan said. "Yes we will."

NINETEEN

Caleb spent the night in his Christmas cottage, and Susan and Clara spent the night at Darla's.

Jerubabel stayed at the cottage as Caleb's guest, and he and Caleb spoke at length of the events of the previous evening.

"I shay that you and me go hunt that bear tomorrow," Jerubabel said.

"But tomorrow will be Christmas Eve," Caleb protested.

"That bear don't know that," Jerubabel said.

Caleb agreed to hunt the bear with Jerubabel, and they both agreed that Andrew Scar Chest should come along with his gun.

Early the next morning Jerubabel blew his horn to signal for Andrew. Andrew was camping on a hilltop not far from the cottage so he blew his horn in reply and went to the cottage.

Caleb, Jerubabel, and Andrew discussed their task in front of the cottage, and after they decided on a plan, Jerubabel signaled for any shepherd within hearing.

Charley Bat Ears blew his horn and came to the cottage. They offered him two days' wages to keep their sheep and goats, and he accepted their offer.

Andrew loaded his gun, and the party of three set out tracking the bear, which was not difficult since the bear had left a considerable trail as it had dragged Bruker.

They spotted the bear in an area of thick woods two or three miles west of the cottage. In a shaded, tree-lined hollow beside a bubbling brook, the great bear lay still.

"Do you think it's dead?" Andrew whispered.

"I believe it is," Caleb said, "But why don't you go down there and touch it just to make sure?"

Caleb kept a straight face, but Jerubabel could not keep himself from smiling at Caleb's suggestion to Andrew.

Andrew half grinned.

They waited, and the bear did not move. Still, they did not want to go near it.

"Here's an idea, Andrew," Caleb said, "why don't you shoot it just to make sure it's dead?"

Andrew shot the bear, and it did not move.

"It's dead," Caleb said.

The three hunters walked down to the giant body and stood beside it. As they rolled it over and started skinning it, they speculated about how the bear died, but they did not speculate long, for when they cut open its belly they found much of Bruker's jewelry. With many spikes, points, and pins, the jewelry had punctured the bear's entrails, and it had died of internal bleeding.

They took the bear's hide and climbed out of the hollow. They got onto a walking trail as soon as they could find one and hurried back to the cottage. There they scraped, cleaned, and salted the hide and left it in the same roofless room where the smaller hides had been kept.

"Tomorrow Clara will be singing in the Christmas concert," Caleb said to Jerubabel, Andrew, and Charley. "I hope you three will be there."

"We will," Charley said, "as will all the rest of the shepherds. Most of us attend the Christmas festivities each year, but this year we all want to hear the little girl."

Jerubabel, Andrew, and Charley bid Caleb *good day* and walked in different directions: Andrew toward Merrydale to buy a Christmas present for his grandmother, Jerubabel toward his hut to the north of the cottage, and Charley to his pappy's farm.

Caleb walked to the well, drew some water, drank it, and spoke to his sheep and goats. He told them that he felt good, and none of them argued with him about it.

He passed the day of Christmas Eve doing little more than grooming his animals. He picked tangled twigs from their wool, and he brushed them.

He spoke of the adventure that he and Big Head fell into in Loaden, and he spoke of his new friend Beatrice.

TWENTY

While Clara attended the final rehearsal for the Christmas concert, Susan had her hair styled in Merrydale's most expensive women's parlor. Under normal circumstances, she would not have allowed herself such a luxury, but her daughter singing the main part in a concert was no normal circumstance, and for Clara's sake, she wanted to look the part of a respectable lady.

The hairdresser did not attempt to remove the curl from Susan's hair. Instead she worked with Susan's hair's natural tendencies. She clipped out the dead, split ends, and washed, waxed, and swirled Susan's hair into a most fashionable and complimenting design. She powdered Susan's face, applied a touch of color to Susan's cheeks, and showed Susan herself in the mirror.

"Is that me?" Susan asked.

"Who else would it be?" The hairdresser asked.

Susan had never seen herself looking so pretty, and she felt like crying, but she had cried so much in the past couple of days that no tears came.

She exited the women's parlor at the same time that Andrew

Scar Chest, whose sheep rested in the town sheepfold, passed by on his way to a shop that sold, among other things, books of recipes.

When Andrew saw Susan he stopped walking.

Susan looked at him for a moment, but she could not think of anything to say.

"You're Caleb's friend, Susan, aren't you?" Andrew asked.

"I'm acquainted with him, yes." Susan said.

"Acquainted with him, eh? Well I know someone who would like to get better acquainted with him," Andrew said.

"Who's that?" Susan asked.

"My grandmother, *Beatrice*," Andrew said. "I think she likes him."

"Of course she likes him. He's a nice fellow. How could anyone not like Caleb?"

"No, I mean to say that I think she *likes* him."

"Oh." Susan said.

"And you know what?"

"What?"

"He hasn't admitted it, but I think he likes her too." Andrew said.

"You don't say." Susan said.

"I do say."

"Hmmm, are you coming to the concert tomorrow night?" Susan asked.

"I intend to," Andrew said.

"Then bring your grandmother along. Caleb will be wearing a new suit so tell her to dress up."

Andrew and Susan conspired and plotted until the end of the choir rehearsal.

"I've got to be going now," Susan said.

"See you later," Andrew said.

TWENTY ONE

Caleb woke up early on Christmas morning. He gulped some water, built a fire, nibbled on some buttered bread, drew several buckets of water from the well, heated it over the fire in the simmering pot, and scrubbed himself as best he could.

He shaved, combed his hair, and put on his ordinary clothes for the walk to Merrydale.

When he reached Merrydale, he left his sheep and goats in the town sheepfold. From there he walked to the Merrydale parsonage. Parson Rivers's housekeeper told Caleb that the parson had already gone to the church to prepare for the day's services and festivities, but Caleb said that he needed to come inside just the same. Once inside, he asked if he could use one of the rooms to change clothes, and the housekeeper offered Caleb the use of the parson's bedroom.

After Caleb changed out of his old clothes and into his new suit and returned to the main room, the housekeeper asked him who he was trying to impress.

"Why, I'm trying to impress everyone, thank you for asking," Caleb said. "By the way, I've got a present for you."

He gave her a jar of jam he had brought from Big Head's goat cart and thanked her for allowing him to use the parson's room to change. He walked outside, looked up at the cold, clear blue sky, and decided to spend a couple of hours strolling about Merrydale.

Some of Merrydale's shops were open on Christmas day, and Caleb ventured into a few of them. He bought a few presents but nothing so large that he could not carry it in his pockets or in one bag.

He ate lunch at a seamen's inn and spent the afternoon sitting on a bench near the sea. He fed seagulls and thought about Clara's singing.

Caleb entered Merrydale church long before the announced time of the concert. He sat on a pew near the back and looked around at the decorations. Christmas greenery hung suspended from the ceilings and the four walls. Red and gold candles stood along the ends of the pews.

A life-sized manger stood in one corner, and Caleb remembered that Orfel Little Mountain loaned the church two or three of his most docile sheep and goats each Christmas to give the manger scene realism during the concert.

As Caleb sat and gazed at the silent sanctuary, he dozed and fell asleep, and as he slept, he dreamed of the shepherds who first heard the announcement of Christ's birth. The dream brought neither new revelation nor clearer vision, and if Caleb had been asked to describe the dream after he woke, his description would have been as applicable to the painting in the church hall titled *The Shepherds and the Angels* as it would have been to what he had seen.

The dream served only to affect Caleb's mood. When he woke, he felt absolutely like it was Christmas day in its fullness and entirety, and he could not remember having had that feeling since his childhood.

After his nap, Caleb stood and walked outside the church for some fresh air. A harsh wind blew, and without his beard, he felt it cold against his face. He looked up at the sky and saw neither snow nor snow cloud, but that did not matter. To him it felt like Christmas just the same as if a foot of white powder had fallen and every tree, stone, and house had been dusted.

While Caleb stood breathing in the cold air, Orfel Little Mountain approached the church. Behind him, Orfel led two goats and three sheep.

"Hello, Caleb," he said.

"Hi, Orfel," Caleb said, "Are your animals ready for the concert?"

"I hope so," Orfel said. "I know I'm ready for it. The singing brings back many good memories."

"Parson Rivers says you're the best he ever trained," Caleb said. Orfel smiled.

They went inside the church together, and Caleb helped Orfel tie his sheep and goats to the sides of the manger.

Before they sat down, a few townsfolk filed in and sat near the front of the church, and Caleb greeted them with a nod.

He and Orfel sat in a pew behind them, and though Caleb was a big man, he looked small sitting beside Orfel. A full hour before concert time, the church began to buzz with activity. People walked in, found seats, talked to their friends, changed seats, and changed seats again. A feeling of excitement charged the atmosphere, and Caleb could not help turning his head and looking around the church.

At a quarter 'til time to begin Susan and Andrew entered the church at once. To Caleb, this did not seem unusual, coincidental, or planned.

Susan walked up the aisle, but Andrew stopped and waited. He held the church door and Beatrice stepped inside. She wore a long white dress, white shoes, and a white hat. Beneath the hat, her hair looked fancy and stylish. She seemed to glow as the evening sun shone behind her.

The moment he saw Beatrice, Caleb smiled without noticing he had done so.

As she walked down the aisle, Beatrice saw Caleb and waved, but before Caleb had time to realize what was happening, Susan and Andrew were shuffling into the pew where he and Orfel sat.

Susan started saying things like *"Slide down please,"* *"No, you stay there,*" and "*Pardon me.*"

When the commotion ended, Orfel sat on the outside end of the pew. Susan sat beside Orfel, and Caleb sat on Susan's other side. Beside Caleb sat Beatrice, and on Beatrice's other side sat Andrew Scar Chest.

To Caleb, the arrangement seemed random enough, but Caleb did not see Susan and Andrew wink at each other when everyone was in place.

They all made friendly conversation until the children marched into the church from its back doors. The boys marched in from the left side, and the girls marched in from the right, and the girls crossed in front of the boys as they went to their seats in the choir loft.

When Clara saw Susan, she waved, and Susan, Caleb, Orfel, Beatrice, and Andrew waved back at her.

The children sat down, and Parson Rivers stood in front of them.

"The theme of tonight's music," he said in his best preaching voice, "is the grace of God. The human race is fallen and the world is sinful, but as the Bible tells us: *where sin did abound, grace did much more abound.* We're all sinners in need of forgiveness and transformation. Because of God's love for us, which he expressed by the sending of His son Jesus, we know that we are forgiven when we *make his soul an offering for sin.* Because of the Holy Spirit's dwelling in our hearts, we know that we are being transformed into the likeness of Christ."

The parson turned away from the audience and faced the children's choir. He raised his hands, Sister Gertrude struck the first chord, and the children began to sing.

The parson had trained the children well because no child sounded louder than any other. The children's voices blended and harmonized, and their sound resonated so full and strong that the listeners could feel the music.

They began by singing songs about the justice of the Almighty, how His commandments are pure and how His judgments against sinners are fair and good.

They moved from the subject of God's justice to the subject of

God's mercy: In His heart, God chose to have mercy on sinners, and because this was the will of God, it was good, but it was not fair since justice demands that sin be punished.

At last they began to sing of how God found a way to express both His eternal justice and His everlasting mercy: He Himself would satisfy His own demands. He would live among us as a human being, and He would bear the punishment for our sin in His own body. He would die for us.

The children began to sing songs about the birth of Christ. They sang of God's tender love for the human race, expressed through the virgin birth of a *Tender Child*.

The poor, the foolish, the weak, the ashamed, and the broken hearted listeners felt the words of the songs in their souls, and they knew joys that the rich, the wise, the strong, the proud, and the tough hearted listeners could not know. Those who had done things they regretted never being able to undo felt forgiven, justified, washed and ready to start over, but the self-righteous hypocrites in attendance felt very little of anything, except the pleasure of hearing the music.

Throughout the concert Caleb smiled and tears dripped from his eyes. His emotions flowed like water even before Clara sang her solo, but when Parson Rivers motioned for the little girl who lived in Caleb's Christmas cottage to stand and sing her special part, Old Caleb the Shepherd broke down and cried like a baby.

Clara's voice rang out as clear as a bell but as gentle as falling snow:

> *"Tender child, Prince of Peace*
> *Born this night to release*
> *Our souls from sin and death,*
> *With mercy from above,*
> *To give new life and breath,*
> *And raise us up in love."*

As she sang, Caleb felt the grace of God falling like rain into his spirit, and he felt better than he had felt in his entire life. He felt that if getting Clara into the children's choir had been the only good thing he had ever done, then his life had not been in vain. He felt glad to be alive, truly and deeply glad to be alive.

He glanced sideways at Beatrice.

Her cheeks were moist with tears. She glanced back at Caleb and feelings passed between them. They both knew that the other had tasted a morsel of Heaven's sweetness.

The concert ended, and applause erupted. The uppity folk clapped because they had enjoyed the music, and the humble folk clapped because they had been blessed.

As the congregation began to stir and stand, Susan rushed from her seat to the front of the church.

As the children filed from the choir loft and dispersed to find their parents, Clara saw Susan and ran to embrace.

"Did I do good, Mama?" Clara asked.

Susan was too choked up to answer her, but she nodded her head *yes*.

Parson Rivers remained where he had stood during the concert. He did not say anything, but to Susan, who looked directly at the parson for the first time since she could not remember when, it was obvious that he was experiencing silent joy as he watched the people talking and laughing in the house of God.

She approached him from the side, and before he realized she had come near, she reached out, and took hold of his hand.

He turned and looked at her.

"Everything is all right now," she said.

She and the parson embraced.

"Yes, everything is all right now," the parson said.

When Susan returned to the pew, Beatrice announced to her pew mates: "Everyone is invited to my house tonight. I've got a small feast ready that needs only to be warmed, and I've got beds and pallets to be laid for any who wish to stay until morning."

"Did you say *small feast*?" Caleb said, "I guess that means poor Orfel here won't be able to come."

He gave Orfel a good ribbing, and Orfel turned red in the face but smiled anyway.

"Just you wait, Old Caleb, one of these days, one of these days..." Orfel said.

Caleb, Susan, Clara, Andrew, Beatrice, and Orfel left the church, walked to the outskirts of Merrydale, and started up the path to Beatrice's house. Caleb suggested a round of Christmas caroling, and the group agreed.

Orfel started the first carol, and Clara joined him. Their voices danced together and flew into the starry, winter night sky.

They sang out in sharp and beautiful notes that created a blissful mood for the group, and Caleb felt he was walking on air.

Susan suddenly joined their singing, harmonizing in a range between Orfel's and Clara's, and Andrew and Beatrice joined in as well as they could. Caleb joined the singing last. He attempted to sing the low notes and actually succeeded with a few of them.

With so much merriment, the walk to Beatrice's house seemed short, and even after they had arrived and gone inside, the members of the little party found themselves humming Christmas songs.

Beatrice invited the company to sit at her table, and she and Andrew served them a feast that was anything but small.

TWENTY TWO

Ham, beef, greens, rolls, mashed potatoes and gravy, cranberry sauce, chowder, cheese, peas, cabbage, baked beans, sweet potato pie, custard, and chocolate pudding made for a fine Christmas dinner.

After dinner, the men picked up the plates and raked out the scraps, and the women washed the dishes.

Caleb's, Orfel's, and Andrew's sheep were safe in the town sheepfold for the night so they decided to stay at Beatrice's. Andrew and Orfel slept on pallets in the sitting room, Caleb slept where he had slept before his journey down the coast. Susan and Clara slept in Andrew's room, and Beatrice slept in her own room.

For breakfast, they all ate leftovers, but much food remained.

After Susan thanked Beatrice and Andrew for the dinner and the hospitality, she departed for the cottage.

Orfel departed after Susan, and Andrew followed him, but Caleb did not depart until he had sipped much coffee and talked long with Beatrice.

As Caleb talked with her, he forgot about past failures. He forgot about past hurts and lost time. He forgot about himself, and he forgot about everything but Beatrice.

In time the talking turned into flirting, and then Caleb found himself in a moment of awkward silence wherein he and Beatrice looked into each other's eyes. Caleb turned away, but by the time he turned, everything that needed to be communicated had passed between them.

"I'll come back tonight," Caleb said, "and help you finish off that custard if you wouldn't mind."

"I wouldn't mind at all," Beatrice said. "I would like for you to come back."

So began Caleb's courtship of Beatrice.

Caleb walked back to Merrydale, located one of the town carpenters, and asked him when he could come and repair the roof on the cottage.

"I could come out on the day after tomorrow," the carpenter said. "Would that be soon enough?"

"That will be soon enough if it doesn't rain or snow before then," Caleb said.

After he retrieved his sheep and goats, Caleb lost his sense of time. He thought so hard about Beatrice that the hours of the day flew by unnoticed, and before he realized it, it was time to walk back to her house.

The next day flew by even faster, and though to Caleb it did not seem possible that the time had already come, on the following morning, he had to walk to the cottage to meet the carpenter.

"Can I go along with you to the cottage?" Andrew asked.

"Sure, of course you can," Caleb answered, and he made a mental note that something seemed slightly self-conscious and ill at ease about the way Andrew posed the question.

When they arrived at the cottage, Caleb opened the door without knocking, and from the bedroom, Susan shouted: "Hey! Who is that?"

"Oh, I'm terribly sorry," Caleb said, "I thought you'd be at work this morning."

"I don't have to go back to work until New Year's Eve," Susan said. "I've got the week off for the holidays."

"Good for you," Caleb said. "Who do you clean for?"

"I work for the mayor and his wife," Susan said.

Something about Susan's answer troubled Caleb, and he knew there should be a reason, but he could not think of it.

He changed the subject: "A carpenter is coming out to work on the roof today. Maybe we won't freeze to death this winter after all."

"I'm glad," Susan said. "I didn't know what I was going to do if a hard cold set in."

"Andrew and I will wait outside," Caleb said.

When Caleb closed the door, Susan got out of bed and dressed herself and Clara. She invited Caleb and Andrew to come back inside and have some coffee, and they each had a cup.

The carpenter and his two sons arrived sometime around mid-morning. They brought split wood shingles, and Caleb was glad for that since making the shingles was the most time consuming part of the job.

Caleb and Andrew helped the carpenter and his sons, and by the end of the day, the roof stood repaired. Caleb thanked and paid the carpenter, and went inside the cottage to see the rooms.

"Looks comfortable in here for a change," Caleb said.

"Too bad we don't own the place," Susan said.

"Yes, that is too bad, too bad, but maybe..." Caleb stopped abruptly.

"Maybe *what*?" Susan asked.

"I'm sorry, what?" Caleb asked.

"What were you about to say?" Susan asked.

"What was *I* about to say?" Caleb asked.

"Yes, you said *maybe*, but you didn't say anything after that."

"Oh, it was nothing." Caleb said.

"Are you sure?" Susan asked.

"I'm sure," Caleb said, but he did not sound too convinced.

TWENTY THREE

Though he did not own it and though Susan lived in it, Caleb regarded the cottage as a place that required his attention and supervision so he divided the next three days between it and Beatrice's house.

On the walks between the two places he spoke fast and vigorously to his animals.

"*But what do I do, what do I do, what do I do?*" he would ask along with many other such questions, but his animals would not answer him.

Around sunset on New Year's Eve, Caleb was grazing his sheep alongside the path to the cottage when he saw Susan walking toward him carrying Clara on her back.

She drew close to him, but she did not speak.

He looked at her face, and he saw defeat, doubt, and dismay.

"Are you all right?" Caleb asked.

"I'm fine," Susan said.

"Why do you look sad?"

"Because they fired me," Susan said, but she offered no explanation or extra words.

"Who is, er, who *was* your employer?" Caleb asked.

"The mayor was my employer," Susan said without any emotion.

Straight away Caleb knew why she had been fired. He remembered that Parson Rivers had to make a change for Clara to get to sing in the concert. The parson had given Clara the part that the mayor's daughter had been practicing to sing. Clara had bumped the mayor's daughter out of singing the most important music in the concert, and now her mother had been punished for this unpardonable crime.

"I'll help you out. I'll think of something," Caleb said.

"It was your thinking that got us into this mess," Susan said. "Sure, my daughter got to sing, but when our money runs out, what then? Once word gets around that the mayor fired me, no one else'll hire me. I know you meant well, and I don't hold anything against you, but…"

Susan stopped talking and continued walking up the path.

When she was well out of hearing, Caleb said: "What do you think, Lop Ear? What's that? You say I should dig it up? Pretty Girl? You think I should dig it up too, eh? What do you think, Big Head? You think enough time has passed that no one will care? You're right. I know I can't be punished for the crime, but I will still have to give it back, won't I? What's that Half Hoof? You say that we need it more than the king's treasury needs it? Yes, I agree, but should I not honor my king and country? What's that, Brown Tooth? You say that I *have* honored my king and country very much and that for all I know Susan could be the king's daughter since no one knows who brought or *sent* her to the orphanage? Oh, I doubt very much that she's the king's daughter, but it doesn't matter if she is or isn't. She's a human being, she's got problems, and I might be able to help solve some of them. I'm taking your advice, Lop Ear. I'm going to go through with it tonight. You animals have made up my mind. I'm going to dig it up. I'm going to dig it up!"

Caleb used his horn to signal for Andrew Scar Chest, and he heard Andrew return the signal. They walked toward one another and met half way.

"I've got a favor to ask of you," Caleb said.

"What's that?" Andrew asked.

"Get Susan to stay at your grandmother's tonight." Caleb said.

"How am I supposed to do that?" Andrew asked.

"I don't know. You're cleverer than I am. Figure something out."

"Why don't you ask her?"

"I can't. I don't think she'd listen to me at the moment."

"Why would she not listen to you? You got her daughter into the choir, and she sang so well the whole town is still talking about it."

"That's what I did wrong, it would seem," Caleb said. "Until today, Susan worked for the mayor's family. The mayor's daughter was supposed to have sung *Tender Child*, but Clara bumped her out of the part so the mayor fired Susan."

"So you want Susan to come over to my grandmother's so you can make up to her there?"

"I don't think there will be any making up. Susan's not really angry with me. She's just angry with life in general. No, I won't be there." Caleb said.

"Where will you be?"

"I'll be at the cottage."

"Now I'm confused," Andrew said, "why do you want Susan to come to my grandmother's tonight?"

"I can't explain it to you. Just believe that it's going to help Susan."

"I'll invite her over then," Andrew said, "but this is terribly strange."

"You don't know the half of it," Caleb said. "It's going to get stranger."

When Andrew went to speak to Susan, Caleb removed a shovel from the bottom of Big Head's goat cart. He placed the shovel on the top of his stuff and began to make broad circles around the cottage.

Because he kept his distance, he could not hear whatever Andrew said, but he knew that Andrew had succeeded because a few minutes after he spoke with her, Susan and Clara departed with him.

As soon as they were out of sight, Caleb charged down to the cottage. With his shovel, he dug into the earth on the outside of the chimney. Down went the shovel blade and up came dirt. He tossed the dirt aside and gashed the earth again. He dug until the hole was so deep he knew he would have to step inside it to reach bottom, but before he stepped down, he took a break.

As he rested he looked up at the evening sky and said he was thankful that his secret had never been discovered. When he caught his breath, he lit his torch, stepped down, and continued digging. He dug for half the night before he reached the object that he had buried beneath the chimney after his return from the war, and his legs and arms trembled with fatigue and excitement.

Just before he reached his secret, he said, "It's not like it's very old, Half Hoof. The King of Nishfidor was a usurper. It won't matter if I destroy it."

Caleb removed a few more shovels of dirt and saw the stained edge of a cloth sack.

"There it is," he said.

He reached down and removed the sack from the dirt.

"It's still heavy," he said, "still as heavy as ever."

He shook the sack, knocked most of the dirt off it, and opened it.

"I thought I would bring this back as proof of my greatness in the war, Big Head," Caleb said. "I thought that if I came home a great man, she would love me. I wish I had known then that love doesn't work that way."

From the sack, Caleb withdrew a golden crown covered with many precious jewels. There were rubies, emeralds, diamonds, pearls, and sapphires, but Caleb thought of them merely as red ones, green ones, clear ones, white ones, and blue ones.

"What did you think it was going to be, Brown Tooth? You didn't think it was going to be the king's head did you? I might have been crazy in battle, but I was never crazy enough to think a decaying head would impress a girl. "

Caleb searched Big Head's goat cart and found a hammer. He walked inside the cottage, lighted a few candles, and sat down to work at the table.

He used the hammer and his knife to remove each jewel from the golden crown. He had never cared much for jewels, and he had no idea how much each jewel might be worth, but he felt sure he could use them to raise enough money to help Susan for quite some time.

After Caleb removed all the jewels from the crown, he used the hammer to beat the gold into a flat, otherwise shapeless piece of metal. After he collected the jewels and stuffed them and the gold into his pack, he went outside.

"No one will ever know it was a crown, Dog Bit," Caleb said, "day break will be here in a few hours, and I'll go down to the docks to trade. For now I'm going to take a nap. We're making improvements, and I can't bring you inside the cottage anymore, but I believe you'll be safe out here without me."

Inside the cottage, he unrolled his blanket and slept on the floor. Day break came, and he got up and went for his sheep and goats. They had not wandered far, and he gathered them together with a quick snap and a whistle. He walked to Merrydale, left his animals in the town sheepfold, and continued to the docks.

The ship closest to the dock entrance was a long triple mast, narrow hulled vessel that flew four flags. To Caleb it was obvious that the ship belonged to the merchant class so he asked permission to board, and the sailor standing guard asked him why he wished to do so.

"I've got some merchandise to trade," Caleb said.

"What kind of merchandise?" the guard asked.

"Gems," Caleb said.

"I'll speak with the captain," the guard said.

While Caleb waited, he whistled, rocked back and forth from foot to foot, and planned his haggling strategy.

The guard returned and said: "The captain's interested only if you're selling rubies."

"Rubies are red, aren't they?" Caleb said.

The guard rolled his eyes.

"Yes, they're red, old man."

I think I might have one or two of them," Caleb said.

"Then come aboard," the guard said.

Caleb boarded, and the guard led him to the captain's quarters. The guard knocked on the door to the captain's cabin and said, "Sir, the old man says he's got rubies."

"Are they high quality?" a voice from the other side of the door asked.

"Yes, tell him they're high quality," Caleb said.

"I heard that, and I doubt it very much," the voice said in a tone that indicated he had just climbed out of his hammock, "but I'll meet you in the dining room in ten minutes."

The guard led Caleb to the dining room and asked him to remain there.

Caleb sat at the main table's bench, and twiddled his thumbs as he waited

Wearing a robe and slippers, the captain entered the room ten minutes later. He reached for a piece of fruit from a bowl on the table, and sat across from Caleb.

"I understand you have rubies," the captain said.

Caleb fumbled through his pack, removed the smallest red stone he saw, and held it up for the captain to view.

"I don't buy costume jewelry," the captain said. "Now if you'll excuse me."

The captain began to rise from his seat, but Caleb said: "Have a closer look."

"Old man, I don't know what you're game is, but I've got plenty of real work to do. Now if you'll excuse me," the captain said.

"If you think this is a game, humor me anyway," Caleb said.

The captain sighed, mumbled something about not having time, and reached out his hand.

Caleb placed the ruby on the captain's palm.

From a pocket on his robe, the captain removed a magnifying glass. He held up the stone, and looked at it through the glass.

This amused Caleb because the magnifying glass made the captain's right eyeball look five times larger than his left eyeball.

Caleb watched for the captain's reaction.

The captain placed the stone and the magnifying glass on the table, rubbed his eyes, and lifted the objects again. He studied the stone for several minutes, placed it on the table, and wiped sweat from his brow.

He stared at Caleb, and Caleb knew that the captain knew the ruby's worth. Caleb felt sure the ruby had to be worth many silver pieces—probably at least three hundred.

"Would you like to make an offer?" Caleb asked.

"First, I must ask you: Are you in some kind of trouble?" the captain said.

"No," Caleb said.

"Is this stolen?" the captain asked. "You don't look like the type to own something like this."

"Oh, come on," Caleb said. "It's just a rock. I never can understand why some people make a fuss about such things."

Caleb's nonchalance surprised and relaxed the captain.

"I have heard that the richest of men do not dress or act rich, that this is a matter of wisdom, and I suppose it's true. Very well, I'll make you an offer: Fifteen thousand silver pieces, and please forgive me for having no more to offer."

Caleb's eyes widened and his jaw fell open.

"I'm sorry," the captain blurted out, "I have insulted you, and I am sorry. My company has accounts with the Merrydale bank. The bank is not open on New Year's Day, but the head of the bank is a friend of mine, and for a transaction so large, I think he will see me. Come back this afternoon, and I will make you a more appropriate offer. Again, I am sorry I have insulted you, but a man such as yourself understands the process of negotiation."

When Caleb recovered from the initial shock, he said, "Yes, a man such as I understands the process of negotiation, but shame on you for trying to take advantage of an old man."

"I'm sorry," the captain said as Caleb rose to leave. "Please return."

"I'm going to visit every ship in port," Caleb said, "and I'll accept the highest offer."

Caleb spent the rest of the morning going from ship to ship showing the one "small" ruby and hearing offers.

He returned to the first ship just before lunch time, and asked for the captain. The captain welcomed him aboard and offered him bank notes for forty-five thousand silver pieces, and Caleb accepted on the spot.

Caleb walked away from the docks feeling light headed and slightly confused. He gathered his animals and led them out into the country.

"A man could live for three years on forty-five thousand silver pieces, and if the one little ruby sold for that much, I can't even imagine how much the big ones will sell for. Animals, I believe Susan's money problems are solved. Let's go to Beatrice's. Maybe Susan will still be there."

Caleb walked to Beatrice's house and knocked on the door.

"Who's there?" Beatrice asked.

"It's Caleb. Is Susan still here?"

Beatrice opened the door.

"Susan hasn't been here," she said. "What are you talking about?"

"She was supposed to have stayed here last night. Andrew was supposed to have brought her here," Caleb said.

"I haven't seen Andrew since yesterday morning," Beatrice said. "Neither of them have been here."

"Where could they have gone?" Caleb asked.

He did not have to wonder for long, for as he spoke, he saw Andrew and Susan walking up from the direction of the sea.

Clara rode on Andrews back, and she sang as they walked.

"Where have the three of you been?" Beatrice asked.

"Down by the sea," Andrew said.

"When Caleb didn't find you here, he got worried," Beatrice said. "Shame on you."

"Shame on you!" Clara repeated with a giggle.

"I'm sorry, Caleb," Andrew said, "but yesterday evening when we set out walking, we started talking, and we were having such a nice time that we decided to stay out for awhile. We walked down to the ocean and built a fire there with drift wood. We sat beside it and talked the whole night. After day break, I made Susan and Clara a pallet on top of a rock, and I slept on the pebbles by the shore."

Caleb studied Susan's and Andrew's posture and positions. Their feet were angled so that they pointed toward one another's, and their bodies leaned slightly toward each other's.

"Oh my," Caleb said, "Oh my, oh my."

"What?" Andrew and Susan said at the same time.

"Oh my, oh my, oh my," Clara said.

They all went inside and sat around Beatrice's table. There was a long silence until Caleb broke it.

"Beatrice," Caleb said, "I could court you for six months or I could court you for a year, but the fact is, neither one of us are ripe apples, and neither one of us knows how much time we've got left on this earth. I'm going to cut right to the point, and I hope you won't mind. Will you marry me?"

Beatrice's face turned red, and she seemed to get lost in thought for the most uncomfortable half minute of Caleb's life. Without saying a word and without breathing too hard, Susan and Andrew looked back and forth between Caleb and Beatrice.

At last Beatrice said: "Yes, of course I will marry you."

"Good," Caleb said as he started breathing again. "That settles that. This is New Year's Day. Why don't we get married later this afternoon?"

"Better sooner than later," Beatrice said. "Sure, let's go see the parson now."

"Good," Caleb said. "We'll leave shortly, but first I'll have a word with these two."

He turned to face Andrew and Susan.

"Andrew," he said, "I'm giving you all my animals and Big Head's goat cart. My shepherding days are over now."

"Thank you," Andrew said. "You really don't have to..."

"I *want* to," Caleb said. "Just promise that you will bring them around often."

"I will," Andrew said. "I certainly will."

"Good," Caleb said, "And Susan, I've got something for you."

He reached into his sack, removed bank notes for ten-thousand silver coins, and slid them across the table.

"I'm offering you a job, and this is your first payment if you will accept. Beatrice and I are going to need someone to look out for us from time to time. You won't have to work every day of the week, but I would like you to stop in and help us when we need it. Do you accept the job?"

Susan could not believe what she was hearing and seeing.

"Yes, I accept," she said.

"Good, then everything's settled," Caleb said, "Let's all go see the parson."

TWENTY FOUR

"You want to do *what?*" Parson Rivers said.

"You heard me," Caleb said. "We're getting married. The ladies are with Andrew. He's taking our flocks to the town sheepfold. Since the shops are closed today, I'm going down to the docks to buy rings off a merchant ship. Meet us in the church in half an hour and don't be late."

Caleb ran off before the parson had a chance to ask any more questions. At the docks, he requested permission to board the same ship where he had sold the ruby, and the guard granted him permission, no questions asked.

"Please take me to your captain," Caleb said. "I want to buy a pair of wedding bands."

"Is one of your grandchildren getting married?" the guard asked in an attempt to make polite conversation as they walked through the ship's decks.

"No," Caleb said. "I don't have any grandchildren. *I'm* getting married."

"First time?" the guard asked.

"Yes," Caleb said.

"So that's why you sold the ruby, eh? You're marrying a sweet young thing, right?"

"I'm not sure how old she is," Caleb said. "It's not polite to ask a lady her age, but she is sweet. I can promise you that."

The guard did not venture any more questions. At the door to the captain's chambers, he announced Caleb's business, and the captain said he would be out presently.

The captain showed Caleb a pair of gold bands with matching floral designs etched along their circumferences.

"I'll take 'em," Caleb said. "How much?"

"Seven-hundred and fifty silver pieces," the captain said.

"Here's a note for a thousand," Caleb said. "Keep the difference for your willingness to trouble yourself for me twice on New Year's Day. In Merrydale, some of the shop keepers stay open on Christmas, making money right up until Christmas night, but they all close on New Year's Day."

After bidding farewell to the captain, Caleb rushed back to the church. There the small wedding party waited for him. Wearing his best clothes, Parson Rivers sat in the tall back, elaborately carved chair behind the pulpit, and Beatrice, Susan, Clara, and Andrew sat on the front pew. At the organ, Sister Gertrude sat waiting to play, and Sister Kate stood just outside the left back door and peeped into the church as she pretended to dust the furnishings in the hall.

As Caleb entered the church, the parson stood. Sister Gertrude played the organ, and Caleb and Beatrice met at the altar. Caleb placed the large ring for his finger in the palm of her hand, and he held onto the small ring for her finger.

As Sister Gertrude finished the organ piece, Caleb said: "I didn't mean to spring this on you so suddenly. Are you sure you want to do this?"

"At our age, things have to happen suddenly, or they might not happen at all. Yes, I want to do this with all my heart."

The music stopped and the parson began to speak. He tailored his remarks to the occasion, adding how personally happy he was for Caleb, one of his oldest, truest, and best friends. The parson read the wedding vows, and Caleb and Beatrice repeated them in turn. They exchanged rings, sliding them ever so gently onto each others knotty fingers.

Without realizing what she was doing, Sister Kate leaned all the way through the door and sobbed as she listened to the service, but it bothered no one since Caleb and Beatrice had not requested a private wedding and since even if they had, Sister Kate would have been a welcomed guest.

At the conclusion of the service, Caleb shook hands with the parson, and as he did so, he reached into his pack, removed three diamonds as large as pecans, and gave them to the parson without allowing anyone else to see what he did.

"A gift for the orphanage," Caleb said under his breath.

Caleb turned to Andrew and Susan: "What about you two?"

Andrew and Susan blushed, but neither answered.

"They've got more time to think about it than we do," Beatrice teased.

"*What do you mean?*" Andrew tried to say, but he choked back the words so much that the tone of his voice proved he knew exactly what they meant.

TWENTY FIVE

Caleb moved into Beatrice's house, and the two of them lived out their remaining years in happy contentment.

The love that Caleb and Beatrice shared started in smallness and uncertainty, but in time it grew large and solid.

Caleb had never hoped or imagined such a change in life would be possible for him, but he was very thankful. He gave up shepherding, but he had a sheepfold built in the pecan orchard, and he saw the members of the brotherhood often.

When he got tired of shaving everyday, he re-grew his beard, and Beatrice did not mind.

Beatrice cooked delicious meals for them and anyone who wished to join them at the table for as long as she could do the work, and when she grew too old to do it, Susan took her place and made sure there was always plenty of good food.

Andrew proposed to Susan exactly six months after New Year's Day, and they married soon after the proposal. In this way, Caleb became Susan's step-grandfather-in-law and Clara's step-great-grandfather.

Caleb bought the Christmas cottage and the land surrounding it. He paid the best craftsmen to remodel the cottage from top to bottom, and he presented the cottage to Andrew and Susan as a wedding present. He bought Susan and Andrew two horses and a wagon so they would not have to walk back and forth between the cottage and Beatrice's house.

When Clara grew up, she became a famous singer, for not only did she have a voice of extraordinary quality, she had a soul of great passion because during her growing up years she was surrounded everyday by that which came from what Caleb brought up from a deep place - not the crown, oh no, something from a place much deeper. She was surrounded by that which for a long time lay buried in Caleb's heart: Love.

Secret Energy: The Soul at Rest in Christ by Bob Bew, edited by Rhett Ellis, is an excellent series of audio tapes that will lift your spirit. If you feel weak and washed out in the Christian faith, *Secret Energy* will inspire you to move to a deeper level of fulfillment in Christ.

Many Christians find themselves struggling through hills and valleys, highs and lows, and they do not experience consistent, steady growth in Christ. *Secret Energy* will help you move toward consistency.

Secret Energy: The Soul at Rest in Christ by Bob Bew is available wherever fine books are sold.

If you enjoyed *The Wisdom of Shepherds,* you may also enjoy Rhett Ellis's first book *Castle of Wisdom.*

Castle of Wisdom is the story of a young man who sets out to find a mysterious old ruin where the meaning of life is written in stone. Along the way he encounters danger, romance, adventure, mystery and deep love. He meets a strange array of characters including a dying tyrant, a beautiful but empty-hearted young woman, a murderous pirate captain, an old wise man who teaches him to think through hard issues, and the kind woman he will eventually marry. At the end of the story awaits a wonderful and unexpected ending.

Castle of Wisdom by Rhett Ellis is available wherever fine books are sold.